The Gods Among Us

To my hero, Chairman Brooks Coleman Dare to Dream! [signature] 2/22/2017

Book One

of

The Divine Masquerade

by D. C. Belton

Illustrated by Molly Lesnikowski

Edited by Michael Naples

ISBN: 0983919305
ISBN-13: 978-0983919308

...to My Love,
who puts up with me...

My special thanks to...

Victoria who started it,
Coleman who gave it life,
Rachel who gave it heart,
Gabriela who finished it,
my daughters for answering my millions of questions,
but most of all to Jessica, who longed for it more than anyone else...

A note to the reader,

Throughout the series, I sometimes change Point of View from the heroine's first person perspective to another character's third person perspective, usually the cat. I know this is unorthodox, but feel it lets the reader enjoy a much fuller experience while keeping the heroine in a very personal first person narrative. This shift in Point of View is always indicated by the π symbol. I use the ∞ symbol to indicate a passage of time.

DC

Lords and Ladies of the Zoo

House	Office	City	Children	Ships

WATER

House	Office	City	Children	Ships
Uncial	*Chancellor*	Greenstone	Uncial IV, Eunice	
Catagen	*Commodore*	Catagen City	William, Dewey, Tiberius	*The Three*
Duma	*W. Northern Sea*	McFarland		*Hood*
Med		Navarre	Mark, Maureen	
Cannes		Calabria	Anthony, Amelia	
Joculo		Kelly Tree	Joculo IV, Janice	

FIRE

House	Office	City	Children	Ships
Excelsior	*Defender of Titan*	Turner Hill	Alexander, Adriana	
Quid	*Treasurer*	Greenstone		
Corsair	*W. Southern Sea*	Arcadia		*Yamato*
Hyperius		Hadrianus		
Arien		Alicante		
Salamandro		Sunna	Corona	

AIR

House	Office	City	Children	Ships
Gemello	*Defender of Twins*	Geminus	Borelo	
Miser	*Judiciary*	Greenstone		
Tel	*W. Eastern Sea*	Coldwell	Telmar	*Argo*
Djincar		Misty Dale	Djincar IV	
Liberion		Astraea		
Ganyme		Ganymii		

EARTH

House	Office	City	Children	Ships
Gauntle	*Master of the Pass*	Quartz	Oliver, Genevieve	
Jingo	*Marshal*	Greenstone		
Rance	*W. Western Sea*	Harper		*Bismarck*
Zeliox		Pythe	Clovis	
Oxymid		Capro Bay	Ophelia	
Virgon		Anatolia	Vigo	

DEME

House	Office	City	Children	Ships
Tzu	*Master of the Lone One*	Shangri-La		

The Past is Prologue.

William Shakespeare
English Playwright
circa 1600: Earth Standard

Chapter One

A Dozen Disciples

*Lo, a girl-child hath been given unto us
Alone, among the fishes of the Sea.
And she shall summon a wondrous Age,
and loose the great Catastrophe...*

"Lay of the Deluge"

Proteus V

"There we are!" I laughed aloud, tossing the rat into my cage. Gnashing his vicious teeth, he brawled against his motley fellows. "Twelve of you! A dozen Disciples of Poseida."

"Awesome!" said Cindy, my best and only friend. The two of us were prowling the sewers, intent on another devious prank. "This'll be loads better than when we stole the tithe. You know that, don't you?"

"Let the Gods feed themselves!" I loftily opined. "Why do they steal from us slaves?"

"I bet the Gods never see that food," said Cindy. "I bet those fat Jesters gobble it up."

"As if there were any Gods," I said.

"But...you sure you want to get Poseida again? I mean, we did

1

her last time. Why not Vulcana, or Terra, or…"

"You know why," I growled.

"I know, but…I thought…maybe just this once…you know," she giggled. "Don't want the other Gods to feel left out…they might get jealous, and…"

"No! It *has* to be Poseida."

Cindy sighed. "Fine, Pallas. Don't have to bite my head off. Why do you have to make everything so…personal?"

I bit my sullen lip. "Sorry," I whispered. "I…I don't know why."

Cindy donned a naughty grin. "Come on. Gotta hurry if we're gonna catch that Festival!"

"You're terrible!" I said with glee. Though I adored my father, Cindy was the only one who could tease me from my moody grief.

We journeyed through the bowels of the tiny village, hauling our treasure through the grimy maze. The putrid air tasted of reek as we neared the center of Kelly Tree. Finally beneath the Water Temple we dropped the heavy cage, baptizing our captives in the river of filth.

"Gotta make sure they're good and smelly," I said.

"You should know," Cindy wickedly replied. "You're the queen of the rats…Goddess of the sewers!"

I guffawed, savoring her jibes. "Leads right to the Volumetric Flask!" I said, gesturing up to a drain. It was marked by a sliver of light; graced with a chorus of solemn music. "You know, where the Jesters bless the *ambrosia*…in the very middle of the sanctuary!"

"Excellent! But…how are we gonna get 'em up there?" The ceiling was quite high. "There's no way we're gonna lift this thing over our heads."

"Way ahead of ya." Producing a fistful of rope, I strung it from a pair of pulleys that were hanging from the rafters. "Remember the pulleys we stole last week?"

"Yeah."

"Rigged 'em yesterday. Been planning this for weeks."

"The effort you invest in your hobbies is admirable."

"You know me...always have time for extra-curriculars."

Together, we hoisted up the cage until it was firmly against the drain.

"That Jester's gonna need some serious therapy."

"Especially if he drops the Volumetric Flask!"

"I hate that thing. It's so...strange."

"Duh!" said Cindy. "A gift from Poseida. Whatdya expect?"

"Yeah," I halfheartedly agreed.

Yet there was something alien about the Holy Volumetric Flask. The *ambrosia* it contained – ecstasy of the Gods – was definitely magical. The bliss it bestowed was an escape from reality, a holiday from the misery of our tenuous lives. Yet the goblet itself was strangely unreal. Its rounded bottom was oddly triangular, narrowing to an impossibly slender stem. The glass itself was crystal clear, yet there were lines and numbers painted on its side. It certainly embodied a strange aura, yet it didn't seem...holy.

"Ready?" said Cindy, poised to release the rats.

"Not yet! Wait till he does the magic."

"Oh, right," she sniggered, listening to the canticle. The music died a grateful death, replaced by the voice of a wizened old Jester.

"We ask you Mighty Poseida, Queen of the Unquenchable Sea, to bless this Holy Water..."

"Unquenchable Sea!" I spat. "It's so stupid!"

"Shh!" chortled my faithful friend.

"We pour this life-giving Water, into this, your Holy and Volumetric Flask. Give us the gift of your sacred bounty, that we might sanctify your beloved Disciples…"

"I've got your beloved Disciples," I said, nodding to my friend.

Cindy squealed as she opened the door.

Twelve pilgrims scurried up the drain.

"Come and drink of the Water which she gives. Drink, drink, ye Disciples of Poseida…"

"Eeeek!" someone cried.

"Holy Poseida!"

"Save the Flask!"

But the Holy Volumetric Flask smashed upon the floor, sending its divine contents down the rusty pipe.

Cindy howled with raucous laughter, soaked by the sacred cascade. "Look!" she said. "It's a shower from heaven!"

But I couldn't enjoy her giddy triumph. Instead, I scoffed and scowled. "Take that, Poseida – you stupid old cow."

Chapter Two

The Raft

Stupidity is also a gift of God...but one mustn't misuse it.

John Paul II
Bishop of Rome
circa 1945: Earth Standard

I sloshed down the sloppy, muddy street, trapped by the wealth I was clothed in. Three long years since my triumph in the sewers...three hungry years of want and pain.

"Is that the one?" jeered a leering old woman, "the one Dotty was on about?"

"Of course it is," said her spiteful friend.

"How'd a blacksmith afford that dress?"

"Colors are expensive."

"And it's dyed in purple."

"Who died and made *her* Poseida?"

I fled from the angry whispers, ruing my many-colored dress. A birthday gift from my loving father, it was made from a fabulous fabric no one had ever seen before.

That morning I was thrilled with my shimmering prize.

Now it seemed to imprison me.

I'd spent my sixteenth birthday working in the fields, pelted by a constant, driving rain. Wet and miserable, I'd tried to be thankful for showers that meant good harvest. Good harvest meant plenty of rice. Enough for us slaves, that is.

There's always enough food for the Gods! I spat. *The Jesters make sure of that.* The tithe came first – Gods before the poor. It was a lesson I learned as a little girl. Hunger was a powerful teacher.

"I might murder you for that dress," said Cindy.

"Just make it quick."

Toiling all day in the dreary fields, I couldn't wait to run home and don my new dress. I thought that people would be impressed...even the popular girls who never spoke to me.

Instead, they called it pretentious and crass. Instead, they said I stole it...

"Thinks she's so special," mocked a jealous peer. Her hair was blond, her eyes were blue, her face; a portrait of resentment.

"Apparently, I am," I snarled.

"Especially dense. Where'd a slave get a garment of the Gods?"

"Stop drooling. And do something with that sack you're wearing."

She stuck out her tongue in a spiteful glare before retreating to her knot of friends.

Cindy giggled.

"Spare me," I growled. I'd gained no pleasure from my clever rebuke, just an overwhelming sense of loneliness.

A pair of old Jesters approached. One of them jabbed a finger in my face. "That one comes from a cursed family if ever there was one."

"You saw what happened to the mother," said the other, "for her lack of respect to the hallowed Gods."

I glared at my sage detractors. "How brave you are, blessed Disciples, to find such sport in heckling a slave."

The Jester wore a pious frown. "You'll burn in Hades, just like your mother."

"Not bad," I smiled. "Not bad at all. But have a care, old man. Once I'm there, I might give you a curse in return."

Shocked at my insolence, he burbled an incoherent reply.

Seizing on the moment, I fled from my tormentors, slipping and sliding on the slimy morass.

Cindy followed at a sprint. "You're in a good mood! Trying to get yourself banished, exiled, or both?"

"Hopelessly lost, for starters."

"It's not wise to insult the Gods, or their Jesters."

"You're one to talk."

"We were kids. We're sixteen now. It's time to grow up…"

"If growing up means bowing to those stupid Gods…"

"Nice dress," crowed Derrick IX.

I ignored the lame jibe, strolling passed the pudgy teen. Son of a wealthy merchant, Derrick was fond of pointing out how wealthy his family was.

"Your father steal that too?" he said.

In one blow, he was crouching with pain; in another, he was writhing on the ground.

Excited peasants circled around, thrilled by the spectacle of unexpected violence. But I disappointed my eager audience, bullying through the brainless throng.

Cindy followed. "Nice one, Pallas. Plan on beating up every guy in town?"

"He deserved it."

"He deserves to marry a shrew, have a dozen brats, and live a short and miserable life. But punching him in the nose..."

"Maybe I broke it. It'd be an improvement."

"He likes you! Can't you tell? And his father just bought a title. You could be the rich wife of a House minor...maybe even travel to Greenstone..."

"I'd rather die."

Cindy huffed. "Who *are* you going to marry?"

"I don't know." *Maybe I don't want to marry.* "I hate this place."

"Get used to it, girlfriend. Because you're never, ever gonna leave..."

A gaggle of young men sauntered by. The tallest wore a look of disdain.

"Did you see that?" Cindy simpered. "Did you see the 'DG' he just gave me?"

"DG?" I asked, having no idea what she meant.

"Definite Glance!"

"He's a sissy," I said, annoyed. I didn't think much of Charles after he lost the wrestling match in the Games last year.

"You're just saying that because he didn't notice you," said Cindy. "Stop being jealous. It isn't attractive."

I didn't answer. *He did notice me! He noticed me all too well.* He actually asked me to the Festival of the Catch. I, of course, refused. I had no use for men, and no patience for a jerk like Charles.

"So…anyone asked you to the Festival?"

"No," I lied. I didn't like to lie, and I wasn't good at it. But I didn't want to alienate my only friend over a stupid guy. "How 'bout you?"

"Only that nervous Tommy brat."

I breathed a melancholy sigh. Cindy used to be a rebel with a crazy zest for fun: impish and irreverent, sassy and bold. Yet now her life was an impossible mission: a vapid quest to *finally* get noticed. Squashing herself into a cookie-cutter pattern – she martyred her bountiful spirit; burying it alongside her aching soul.

Bewildered, I mourned the slow death of my only friend. Yet I refused to join her crowded path to stale mediocrity. I was too smart, too stubborn to let anyone mold me into something I wasn't.

"So," Cindy asked, "whatcha do last night?"

"Daddy and I went walking."

"Again?"

"Yeah! It was fun," I said, the fragrance of tall pines fresh in my mind. "We talked about a paradox."

"A what?"

"Well…he said something funny. If all the rivers run to the sea, why isn't it full?" He claimed he heard it from a man named Solomon, an ancient philosopher from a distant world.

9

"Why isn't what full?"

"The sea."

"How should I know?"

"That's what I said. So he told me that water from the ocean floats into the sky. He called it…evaporation. Part of the…hydrologic system."

Cindy snorted.

"Yeah. Then the water collects into clouds," I said, pointing towards Volcano, the towering Titan that dominated our world. Fluffy white cotton decorated her craggy features, like a delicate wedding gown on a horrible giantess of stone. "When the clouds get too full, it rains, there in the mountains. The rain becomes the streams and the streams become the rivers which run into the sea."

"That's ridiculous."

"No, it's not. Why else would water fall from the sky?"

"Who knows?" said Cindy. "Who cares?"

I cared. For my father had played a trick on me: he taught me how to think.

My teachers didn't want me to think. They admitted I was very bright. Yet they scolded me all the more, telling me to concentrate on useful things. Churning butter, planting rice, sewing garments; these were the lessons a slave girl needed to become a valued wife.

Daddy wanted more for his little girl. *"Humans differ from animals only by a little. And most people throw that away…"* It was a doctrine taught by ancient Taoists – or…so he'd said. I marveled at his silly stories, wondering where he came up with such dangerous tales.

"What did you do last night?" I asked.

"Washed my hair."

∞

Whenever I was sad, I sought the solace of the shore. Somehow, the ocean's roar made me feel closer to my dead mother...

Don't think about that!

The sun was setting and I was alone, haunting the beach that stole my childhood. An hour of twilight to spend with my thoughts, an hour apart from my meaningless life.

A sand crab darted out its tiny hole. It ran a few yards before freezing like a statue. A year ago I'd have had fun chasing the elusive creature. Today, however, the crustacean was quite safe.

Absentmindedly strolling through the surf, I peered at the rolling, infinite sea. The breakers raged in glory in their eternal march to the beach. I felt a voyeur amongst the endless eddies, lonely amongst the ripples that curled around my feet. I wondered at the power of their mindless devotion, jealous of the God to whom the waves obeyed.

"I hate you!" I shouted at Poseida. "Why did you take her? Why did you take *my* mother?"

A tender breeze whistled in my ear, answering in a penitent reply. But I was far too angry to listen. Instead, I watched the sand crab make its escape, scampering down another hole.

"I wish I could hide," I moaned, envious of the witless creature, "escape from all my troubles..."

But the ghostly crab ignored me, safe within its powdery cocoon.

The sacred beach was long and wide, stretching as far as the eye could see. I gazed along the turquoise horizon, bounded by an endless ribbon of sugar-white sand. The sea-foam was a careful seamstress, cutting a delicate border of lace. It reminded me of a burial shroud as I cried a tear…

…for it was on this beach that I lost my mother.

The solitary tear fell into the sea, joining its compatriots in the vastness of the deep. I sullenly turned to leave…when I saw the strangest thing I'd ever seen.

Far out to sea was a small orange boat. Only it didn't have sails, and one end was bulbous and round like a bizarre giant egg. It sported a tiny flag and a flickering light.

That's dumb, I snorted. *Why would anyone make an egg-shaped boat?*

I cocked my head and bit my lip, peevishly angry at the stupid thing.

Maybe Poseida laid an egg, I mocked, *a big, fat, ugly…*

But my spiteful ridicule turned to solemn wonder. The more I stared, the stranger it became.

A year ago I'd have been delighted. But my moody self was merely irked. Deciding to let it drift out of my life, I turned to walk away.

Yet the surf had a magic of its own, baiting my inquisitive spirit. All at once, without really knowing why, I decided to swim out and fetch it.

Doubt leavened my recklessness as I hid my multi-colored dress. *It's really far…farther than I've ever swum before.*

But the enchantment of the flashing tempted me, luring my naked body in amongst the frothy waves.

I changed strokes often, pacing myself for the grueling swim. I was nearly halfway when I realized the boat was heading towards the mouth of the river.

The current will force it back out to sea!

Prompted into renewed effort, I took large, aggressive strokes.

Yet the cold fingers of the mountain river pushed me towards the perilous deep.

Cursing evaporation and the entire hydrologic system, I turned around and gasped. The village seemed miles away.

Yet the mysterious egg beckoned me, rolling on the cresting waves.

"Curiosity killed the cat," I quoted my father. "Maybe," I flipped on my back, "maybe this time he was right."

The current flung my prize away, farther and farther from my wearied reach. Its largeness, I now saw, was quite deceiving, a mirage that made it look closer to the beach.

Completely exhausted, I stopped altogether, trying hard to think.

"Maybe a fisherman will pick me up," I said, turning hopefully towards the east.

But the sun was a fiery red, drowning itself in the lilac sea.

"Stupid!" All the fishermen were back in the harbor. "No one sails at night. No one except the Commodore of the Three..."

That was when I saw it: a mammoth, towering fin. Portent of a massive monster, it sliced towards me with a toothy grin...

Shark!

The jagged teeth climbed higher and higher – the murderous predator, mere yards away. Panic rippled through my entire body...yet I refused to let it claim me.

13

Stay completely still, and the shark might pass.

But the shark did not pass. It gaped its maw ravenously open, promising an end to my miserable life.

I whispered a prayer to Poseida…hoping she'd forget about the rats…when suddenly a maelstrom erupted from the sea! Massive jaws snapped at empty air, as the brute leapt up from his angry spree.

The water crashed and thrashed around me, giants swirling with vile intent. Another shark surfaced beneath me.

I'd rather be on its back than in its mouth! I thought as I screamed.

Only its hide wasn't slimy and scaly, but soft and warm and smooth.

"A dolphin!"

Too stunned to be happy, too jubilant to be afraid, I grasped my steed with frightened legs. Briny water boiled around me knees, as my gallant charger leapt toward the egg.

How?

Remembering my fear, I glanced back at the man-eater. A dozen dolphins were driving it away. I looked forward again and stared at the egg-shaped boat.

Except it wasn't a boat, and it wasn't an egg.

It's a raft! Made of some sort of…some sort of…cloth?

I squinted my eyes at the garish color. *I guess it's a raft?* The craft was short and stubby with impossibly rounded sides. Its ugly exterior looked more like a hide than a hull. It had no keel, or sail – just a little red flag. The sorcerer who cast the spellbinding flashing was a small rectangular mirror.

The dolphins raced my valiant mount, jumping playfully in the windborne air.

"Woohoo!" I laughed, absolutely thrilled…when my champion plunged beneath the frothy waves.

I choked on a mouthful of brine. "Thanks a lot! Can't give a girl a warning?"

But my noble steed cackled in triumph, oblivious to my ingratitude.

Wiping the salt sting from my eyes, I found myself floating next to the raft. A short ladder was sewn into its supple side.

I grabbed a rung, hauling myself out of the water. I couldn't believe it, but the raft, the ladder…even the roof was made from the same, unworldly cloth. There was no door, or window…only the strange, alien material.

I pressed my hand against the knobby fabric, hoping to find a way in. Fascinated, I traced my finger along a thin black line. Shaped like a crescent moon, it was made of hundreds of interlocking teeth.

"Maybe this will open it," I said as I pulled the clasp. It made a "zzzz" noise, revealing the insides of the mystic craft.

I stood there gawking, aghast with wonder, when a sudden wave tossed me forward. Uttering a shriek of surprise, I tumbled inside.

I bounced on a springy floor. Splayed on all fours, it felt like someone was watching.

But the only other occupant was a snow white cat. Starved, he raised his gaunt head to greet me.

Grateful that no one had seen my fall, I reached out to pet the pathetic creature. "Poor kitty," I soothed. "How long have you been here, all alone?"

"Thirteen days!" he tersely replied.

Chapter Three

The Naming of Cats

Mighty Poseida – Queen of the Sea – was immediately informed. For nothing escaped Her purview within the vastness of the Deep. Yet She was greatly disturbed by the dolphin's rescue. For they recognized the significance of the cursed child, while She did not.

"Compendium, Chronicles of the Pentathanon Gods"

Ovid XII

"You can talk?"

"Well, of course I can talk," said the cat. "And aren't *you* a splendid mess? And you're wet. Do you mind dripping somewhere else?"

"Sorry." Resting on my knees, I scooted a few feet back.

"Quite a comedic performance: falling like an imbecile, limbs absolutely everywhere. Splayed upon your back like a stupid, drooling dog. Don't you know how to land on your feet?"

"Uh…no?"

"Humph," smirked the cat. "What completely amazes me is that your species survived the Late Pleistocene." He raised his brows with

16

obvious conceit, as if gloating over a private joke. "But enough about you, lets talk about *me*. I've been afloat a fortnight, and I haven't had a thing to eat." He nodded towards a bag. "Be a good dear and open a can of tuna."

"A what?" I said, perplexed. The cat used such odd words.

"Jupiter's Moons, you are going to be difficult." He alighted on his paws and cantered to the bag, nuzzling it with greedy anticipation. "There are cans of tuna in this bag."

I nervously crawled to the bag. On its sides were hundreds of strange symbols. *They look like the markings on the Volumetric Flask. But...how could that be?* Like the door to the raft, the bag had a line of interlocking teeth. I pulled the tag, revealing a cornucopia of things I'd never seen before. I picked up a small black box, marveling at its sleek construction.

"What's this?" I asked, amazed.

"Well, its not tuna, I can tell you. Yes, and did I mention I haven't eaten in thirteen days?"

"Oh, sorry. Poor kitty, we'll get something for you."

"My name isn't Kitty." Pointing his paw at a metal cylinder, he said, "Here, this one."

The cylinder was as perfect as the box. "It's so smooth and round! My father's a blacksmith, and he could never make something like this."

"He didn't have to, now did he?"

"But...why would anyone put food in something so...so beautiful?"

"Just open it," he said, pacing the floor.

"How?" I asked, feeling stupid.

"My, but you are clever! See the little key? Put it in the hole. That's it. Now, turn it round and round…"

The lid tore off like magic, leaving a jagged perimeter. The can was filled with tuna.

"I'll take that. You can get your own."

But I was too enchanted to think about eating. Instead, I pulled out every single piece of gear. Some things I recognized: a long knife, childishly short paddles, and a tiny mirror. But I had no clue about most of the items.

"What's your name?"

The cat didn't answer, devouring his tuna. I picked up a tiny orange case. One end had a thin, glass-like cover. On the opposite end was a black protrusion. I pressed it.

The case erupted in a blinding light!

I squealed with surprise, dropping the horrid thing.

But the light kept flashing its wicked warning.

"Turn it off," drawled the cat. "You'll run the batteries down."

"I…I…I don't know how!"

"Jupiter's Moons, you are dense. The same way you turned it on."

"What's 'ON?'"

Walking lazily to the terrifying object, he pointed at the black protrusion. "Here, press this."

I didn't dare. The blinking brilliance yanked at my heart, piercing my soul with its caustic rapidity. "No," I mewled, "you push it."

The cat rolled his emerald eyes. "Let's see…how many thumbs do I have?"

"What?"

"Opposable thumbs. Do you see any of the ugly digits on my sleek, beautiful paws?"

"I don't know what you're talking about."

"Obviously."

"Make it stop. I beg you." The light terrified me.

"Afraid of a wee bit of magic?"

"I'm not afraid," I said as I hid my face. "I just…hate the Gods, and everything about them. And that, whatever that is, *must* belong to the Gods."

"You don't approve of your creators? A bit ungrateful, don't you think?"

"Not if you're a slave."

"Humph," he said, raising his brow into a demanding stare. "How foolish of me to expect anything but cowardice from an inconsequential drone…"

"I'm not a coward!"

"Then press the button."

Humiliated, I conquered my fear. Tentative and afraid, I stuck out my thumb and jabbed the button.

The horrible flashing stopped, much to my relief.

"That's OFF," he sarcastically explained. "Now, press it again."

I forced my hand to comply. The menacing light magically

returned.

"That's ON. ON and OFF. Now turn it off, and leave it off."

"Fine," I smarmed. I didn't think he liked me.

The cat returned to his tuna, waving his tail like an insolent snake. I looked away, bewildered by my strange surroundings. It was like being encased in a monstrous cocoon, bathed in a dull, orange light. The source of the light was attached to the ceiling, fixed at the peak of the egg-shaped bulge. Like the blinking case, it was sheathed with a thin transparent shell.

But what's causing the light? There was no fire in the case. *It's as if the Gods took a piece of the sun.*

Yet it wasn't like the sun, for the sun was bright and yellow, while the light was sober and orange. In fact, everything was orange, an alien glow that cowed me.

I rubbed my hand against the buoyant floor. *Why...it isn't cloth at all!* It had a soft, leathery feel, like the hide of the dolphin...

"The dolphins!" I cried, bolting out the door.

To my surprise, the entire pod was swimming dutifully along.

It was now quite dark, the two moons hanging low over the pencil-thin horizon. Selene was full, while Selena was just a sliver. The Jesters warned that if both moons were ever full at the same time, a catastrophe would occur that would cause the end of the world. I, of course, didn't believe such nonsense.

But...why are the dolphins following me? According to the Jesters, dolphins were minions of Poseida.

Yeah! I scoffed. *Like I believe that!*

Yet there they were, like a royal honor guard, causing my cynicism to quake.

They saved my life. I can't deny it. Almost like…a miracle?

"Why did you save me?" I beseeched my rescuers. "Who sent you? Was it…was it Poseida?"

But the only answers I received were my own confusing thoughts. *Come on! Just because a bunch of fish saved me from a shark, and are following me in this really weird raft, that doesn't mean…*

But how could I explain the light, or the can?

Or that cat?

"But Poseida isn't real!" I shouted. "And even if she was…why did she drown *my* mother?" For even if she rescued me a hundred times, with a thousand gallant dolphins, she could never repay that heinous crime…

"Because I hate you!" I spat at the mythic queen. "I hate you, and I always will!"

I was instantly angry at my peevish display…even a little ashamed. *I wonder what that cat would think?* For a bitter moment, I really didn't care.

Yet even if I couldn't forgive the waves, the ones that had drowned my mother, I did pay homage to my brave rescuers.

"I don't know how to thank you! I don't even know if you can understand me. But I want you to know, how beautiful you are." Indeed, the prancing dolphins – playing in the light of the twin moons – were the loveliest thing I'd ever seen.

To my surprise, the youngest swam close enough for me to touch her. There was a tiny notch on her dorsal fin.

I stroked her joyous face. "Can you talk too?"

The happy pup cackled with delight, tossing her head with an adorable grin.

Instantly, an older dolphin chirped a high-pitched squeal.

Admonished, the younger dolphin bowed her head. Whistling a wistful reply, she slipped beneath the gentle waves.

Did I imagine it?

For the next half hour I called to the dolphins, begging them to speak.

But they were as silent as monks, making me wonder if I was going crazy.

After a long while, I climbed back into the raft to find the cat asleep. As much as I wanted to wake him, ask him all sorts of questions, I didn't want to make him angry. Besides, I was tired after my grueling swim.

Instead, I thought about my father.

What will he think when I don't come home? I should start paddling to shore this very minute...

But exhaustion hit me like a sudden wave. I laid down my head, just for a minute...just a minute...to rest, just for a minute...

I fell asleep to the rocking waves, drifting me farther and farther away...

∞

She was alone on the beach, thinking about her mother, when four proud dolphins rose beneath the surf. Harnessed with silver too delicate to be believed, they pulled an elaborate chariot crafted from a single, enormous shell. Surrounding the chariot was a score of mermen, with rugged good looks that gave her heart a lurch.

But if the mermen were delicious, the driver was absolutely divine. The sea breeze tossed her stunning hair, as if destined to that sacred purpose. The woman had a proud, beautiful face, with dreamy eyes of green. She opened her mouth to speak…

"Meow!"

I woke with a violent jolt. My heart pounded violently against my heaving chest.

"I'm hungry!"

I winced at my alien surroundings. The air was hot, pungent with the smell of fish. The guilty culprit was the empty can.

"Yes, and you should throw that out, mind you, as you've made quite a mess. How untidy you disfigured creatures are! But first, open another can of tuna."

Nervous, I retrieved a cylinder from the magic bag.

"Not that one! I hate corned beef."

"How do you tell the difference?" The cylinder looked exactly like the other.

"Look on the side. Can't you read?"

"What's…read?"

It wasn't a stupid question.

I'd learned in school how to add and subtract; how to mend nets and plant rice. I'd learned how to tithe. This was important, as it was a slave's duty to feed the heavens. But no one on my world could read. No one but the Gods.

"I can't believe it!" he loudly complained. "I'm a pet, and *I* know how to read!" But then he sported an evil smile. "Ah…but I forget.

Sub-standard breeding. Of course. I can't expect much from a creature of your exceedingly limited intelligence…"

I felt angry and confused. *Is he insulting me?* His words were so exotic I couldn't even tell.

Rummaging through the bag, the cat found a cylinder more to his liking. A sneer commanded me to open it. I picked it up, staring at the markings on its side.

"I'm waiting!"

I nervously put the key in the hole, when I came upon a thought – a thought that changed my life forever…

"Wait a minute. I saved your life last night, didn't I?"

He squinted his emerald eyes, annoyed.

"You've had all these provisions, and…and you couldn't open any of it. You were surrounded by food, and yet you were hungry," I added, stumbling on the paradox of our strange first meeting. "You would have starved to death if I hadn't come along."

"What exactly is your point?"

"Well…you owe me. As a matter of fact, you *need* me. There's no telling how long it'll take to get to shore. And even when we do, I bet you don't know how to hunt or fend for yourself. Even if I can't…read…I can do a lot of things you can't." I was proud of myself for getting that out. I normally didn't think that clearly in the morning.

The cat tilted his head, scrutinizing me as if surveying a famous painting.

I watched in silent dread. *What if I offended him?* Part of me wanted to gush out an apology. But something stronger made me hold my ground.

"Excellent, most excellent!" purred the cat. "Yes, I do believe there's a brain inside that misshapen head of yours. One can't be sure with drones, you know. Your species does have its geniuses of course, but you also have your…" But the cat didn't say.

"Well, I'm not a genius. But I'm not an air-head either. And I'm not going to be bossed around by anyone, not even a cat."

This drew a smarmy chuckle. "Behold! The tongue is a little member, yet it boasteth many great things."

I scowled in reply.

"You have been of some use," he admitted, churlishly rolling his eyes, "And I'm rather fond of people who feed me…" With this, he twittered his feathery tail. "Very well," he said to great effect, "my name is…Othello!"

"I'm Pallas." I thought to shake his paw, but didn't know if that was proper when being introduced to a cat.

"Pallas?" he leered with surprising envy. "What an interesting name. Not one of the *standard* names, I dare say."

"No."

Long ago, the Gods decreed that children of slaves should be named after their parents. Thus my father, Gerard VII, was the seventh generation of Gerards, and my mother, Nancy VI, was the sixth in her line. But my parents ignored this tradition, much to the Jesters' displeasure. They warned my parents that such blatant sacrilege would incur the wrath of the Gods.

Inwardly, I felt the Jesters had been right. Though I adored my name – loved its individuality – deep down, I knew it had doomed my mother.

"Very interesting," he said, "very interesting indeed."

"What's so interesting about a name?" For though I was certain my name had doomed my mother, I had fistfights with anyone who drew the same conclusion.

"My dear child. Your name is written in the heavens. It's the vessel by which creatures know you. A creature *grows* into his name, *becomes* his name. Cats have three different names, of course, and all the important Gods have two." He paused, studying me with interest. "But you, my dear, have a very interesting name…very interesting indeed."

"Thanks," I sulked, deciding to change the subject. My name wasn't something I liked to talk about. Opening the correct cylinder, I set it before the cat. "You call this a can?"

"Precisely," he said with his mouth full. "It says fish on the side. F-I-S-H."

I examined the markings, which I supposed must say F-I-S-H. "Can you teach me how to read?"

"Why?"

I picked up the strangest item from the bag. Thousands of incomprehensible markings were plastered over its many leaves. "I want to know what these say. I want to know how to use these things."

Othello interrupted his ravenous meal. "My, but you *are* clever. Yes, of course, that is a survival manual, and it does indeed tell you how to use everything in that bag. How did you know?"

I shrugged my shoulders, glad the cat was no longer insulting me, though still uncomfortable with his probing stare. "I dunno. It just makes sense."

"The Gods don't teach mortals how to read, do they? Do you know why?"

I tried a blind guess. "They don't want us to know what they know?"

His snake-like pupils exploded with surprise. He didn't expect *that* answer, I was sure. Now *he* wanted to change the subject. "How far are we from shore?"

I cursed as I scrambled out the crescent door. The sea breeze cooled my glistening brow, welcome relief from the sweltering raft. The dolphins still surrounded the raft, but there was no land in sight.

I swore aloud, sure that the entire hydrologic cycle had once again conspired against me. *I knew the river would be strong, but had no idea it would push us out this far!*

"Well?" he said.

"I can't see the shore, so we're at least a few miles out."

"That's bad, isn't it?"

"Well...it's bad, but it's not terrible. The wind blows to the west, and we're on the eastern shore. So eventually, it'll blow us back..."

But deep down, I was quite worried. The village of Kelly Tree was very isolated. There were a few merchants who sailed from distant towns. And Lord Joculo visited Greenstone once a year. But most folk never left her quiet shores. "Did you see the dolphins?" I asked, wishing to change the subject yet again.

"Dolphins," he sneered, "they're so cute! For the life of me, I can't understand why everyone is so enraptured with the slimy beasts. Just a rabble of overgrown fish if you ask me."

I thought it funny that a cat would be jealous of a fish. "But why are they following us? And why did they save me from that shark?"

"Did they?"

"Yeah, like, couldn't you hear?"

"I heard someone squeal like a stuck pig."

"That shark was huge!"

"Really!" he said, disbelief written on his furry face. "How huge was he?"

"Big enough to swallow me with a single bite."

"And wouldn't *that* have been a shame. But please, dazzle me with your torrid account. I'm sure it will prove quite amusing."

I frowned, annoyed. "Where do I begin?"

"Begin at the beginning and go on until you come to the end; then stop."

I let out an involuntary giggle. *That's exactly what Daddy would've said!* But I kept that to myself as I told the cat my miraculous tale.

Though he listened with wide-eyed interest, he dismissed it as some sort of fluke. "I haven't the faintest idea why the mindless creatures took any notice of you."

But I could always pick out a lie, and was sure about this one. But I didn't press the issue. I didn't want to make him angry again. "How did *you* get here?"

"Well…it's a rather confusing story. Not at all what you might expect."

"Yeah, like I *expected* to find a talking cat, floating adrift in a magic raft."

He narrowed his emerald eyes. "Yes, well. The whole thing's a bit hard to fathom, even for someone as learned as I am. I seriously doubt that you, with your very limited intelligence and sub-standard breeding could begin to understand."

"Try me."

"Very well!" he announced with great importance. "I am the companion of Mulciber's daughter."

My jaw dropped. "Mulciber? Like…like the God?"

"Mulciber…yes. I live with his daughter, deep within the bowels of Volcano." He tilted his head to the heavens and said, "I will

28

ransom thee from the power of Hell. Oh Sheol, I shall be your destruction!"

I snorted. "I don't believe you. You're very clever, but you'll have to do better than that."

"Look around you, man-cub, and tell me what you see? Who made the raft, the cans, the compass?"

I didn't know what to say. My father was the best blacksmith in Kelly Tree. He could craft a knife as fine as the one in the bag, but could never make anything as perfectly round as one of those cans. As to the raft, I ran my hands against the knobby surface. *A cloth that floats?* I'd never seen anything like it.

"We were in a hover-plane," he said.

"A hover-plane?"

"We left Vulcana's fortress inside Volcano and were flying to Aeolia when we were ambushed by Cypris. When I heard the order to evacuate, I rushed to the nearest escape pod, certain my mistress was right behind me. But as soon as I got in, the pod jettisoned of its own accord. The pod had a parachute, of course, so it floated to the ocean where it automatically inflated into this raft."

I understood almost nothing of this story which, I thought, the cat must have counted on. But one thing I did understand. "The Gods fight each other?" *I don't remember any of the Jesters mentioning that!*

"Well...yes. It's quite rare, of course...but...it does happen."

"But...the Gods are immortal, infallible. How could one of them crash into the sea?"

"When the heavens war upon each other, who shall stand?"

"But...surely Mulciber didn't die?" Even though I didn't believe in the Gods, I had a hard time accepting that one of them just perished.

"Mulciber's daughter. And I'm sure she wasn't hurt. She was probably rescued by Poseida and taken to Atlantis for ransom."

"Why didn't she rescue you?"

"Poseida never liked me," he grumbled, clearly insulted by the queen's neglect.

"Well that's just fine, because I don't like Poseida either."

"And why is that?"

"Because...she...she killed my mother."

"Drowned, did she?"

"I guess," I sighed, allowing my sadness to swell. "They never...you know...found her body."

"Typical," he smirked. "What is shocking to me is how your entire species hasn't become extinct; what with all the interesting ways you've found to murder yourselves..."

I furrowed my brow. "What do you mean?"

"Never mind," he glibly replied. "And just when did this...unfortunate event occur?"

"Thirteen years ago."

"Thirteen? Are you quite sure?"

"Yeah, I'm sure."

"On the beach, near the village of Kelly Tree?"

"Duh...like, where else would she be?"

"Indeed. That's just...very sad."

But I found no compassion in his emerald eyes, only a mask of distracted curiosity.

"Tell me, dear child. Tell me about your mother."

"Well, she was very smart. She seemed to be an expert at everything. She knew how to fish and weave and build houses and bridges. She even helped Lord Joculo design the sewers."

"Did she have gray eyes?"

"Yeah. Why?"

"Because," he mused, "gray eyes are a very recessive trait."

"What does that mean?" I said, defensive. The blue-eyed girls use to tease me about my gray eyes all the time.

"It means they aren't very common. Most humans have dark eyes."

"Lots of people have blue eyes."

"Yes, well," he chuckled, "they got a bit carried away with the blond-haired, blue-eyed children. But I assure you in a few generations the dominant genes will weed them down to more nominal levels."

"Who got carried away?"

"The Gods, of course."

"What about them?"

But Othello only smiled. Not a pleasant smile intended for a friend, but a conniving, selfish smirk.

"You said the raft…inflated?" I said, steering the conversation away from my mother.

"That's right. Carbon dioxide cartridges fill the rubber with air, causing it to float."

"This…rubber…it's full of air?"

"Precisely."

"What if a hole got punched in it?" The idea that we were floating on something as insubstantial as air was unnerving.

"Well, let's see. According to the survival manual, the raft is self-sealing with any puncture less than three inches long; though I would not advise your trying it, as I do *not* like to swim. There also appears to be two levers attached to the carbon dioxide cartridges that deflate the raft."

"Carbon dioxide?" I said with pride. "I know all about that."

"How could you?" said the cat.

"Father told me. He uses it for pneumatics. It pushes things…I think. And it's photosynthesis. I know that for a fact."

"Do you?" he laughed.

"Yeah, I do."

"Well!" said the cat. "According to the manual, the cartridges act as an emergency propulsion device. They're located on the outside, near the sea anchor."

I scrambled out the door. "Anchor? No wonder we're not getting any closer to the shore!"

Othello lazily followed, taking a moment to hiss at the dolphins.

In answer, the young dolphin with the notch on its fin launched a well-aimed splash. The fur-ball shrieked with surprise before bolting inside the raft.

I doubled up with laughter. I laughed so hard, I actually fell off the raft. The water felt wonderful, so I swam a few strokes.

The dolphins seemed intrigued, yet they kept their watchful distance.

At the rear of the raft I found two cylinders and a rope attached to something dragging in the sea. I climbed back onto the raft, pulling the anchor in. It was made of the same cloth-like rubber, shaped into a cup. I secured the anchor to a loop before inspecting the deflation levers. One handle was just above the surface and another just below, both surrounded by more of the arcane markings. But these markings were bold and red, as if a warning not to touch them.

Climbing back inside, I found Othello ferociously cleaning his fur.

I giggled. "You should mind your manners around those overgrown fish."

"If I never see another dolphin!"

I spent the rest of the day rummaging through the magic bag. Othello kept saying things like, "Don't touch that," or, "I wouldn't do that if I were you." After a great deal of begging he explained some of the objects, but refused to describe the others.

I studied the items, taking particular interest in the backpack. The manual had a picture showing where each piece of gear should be placed. I was delighted. Even if I couldn't read, I could follow these simple instructions.

I put the backpack on. Its stretchy material hugged my body, supporting a feather-light frame. The manual described the frame as an AERO-FOIL, though the cat wouldn't tell me what that meant.

"The manual says the legs are cantilevered to your arms for greater pumping action," he yawned.

"What's a cantilever?"

"Does it have to be so inquisitive? Can't it mind its betters?"

I continued to pepper him with questions. But his mood was too foul to be polite. "It's not a backpack, oh ye of little knowledge, it's a survival harness. Now let me get some sleep."

"Fine," I huffed.

I took off the harness and climbed outside. The sea breeze played wonderfully upon my long blond hair as I tasted the tang of the salty air. I stared at the blue horizon, quieted my anger, and tried hard to think. The rocking of the waves stirred me into a comforting reverie. I seemed to *belong* to the sea, as if I *came* from the sea, as if...that's where my mother had gone...

Stop it! I rued, cursing my stupidity. *She's dead, and no one can ever bring her back.*

A single tear misted my eye. But before it could trickle down my cheek, it blew away with the summer wind. I said good-bye to my dolphin friends and climbed inside the raft.

Othello was, of course, asleep.

Chapter Four

Capro Bay

...for Fire hated the Water, far greater than Earth hated the Air; a burning loathing that was the engine of the world's calamities. For Mulciber, the indomitable Prince of Fire, would not rest until He snuffed out Poseida and all Her Watery kin...

The war ravaged the very Heavens, yet it was the slaves who burdened its pain. For who among the Gods shall die – who among mortals shall live – when the Divine brandish their pitiless Fury?

"Theocracy and Divine Right"

Virgil VII

It was a wet, wintry night. The toddler lay safe in her father's arms, giggling at his funny faces. Her mother sang a sad and lilting lullaby, a song she hadn't heard before.

But her singing was cut short by a blow to the door. Merciless soldiers, cold and cruel, roughly seized her father. The toddler cried, torn from his embrace, as they dragged him out into the freezing rain...

I woke with a start, dripping with sweat. A stab of ice jolted my frame as I remembered that haunted memory.

Sweltering, I scanned my alien surroundings. No. I wasn't in my cot in Kelly Tree. My father wasn't asleep in the next room. My mother...

"She's not here either," I whispered. "She's been dead for years."

The orb on the ceiling was weak and dying, changed from orange to a crimson hue. But there was just enough light to reveal Othello pacing outside the door.

I shuddered. There was something evil about that cat, splashed in the surrealistic blood-red glow. His demonic eyes glinted in the crescent, like an eerie phantom from some half-closed crypt. He sounded angry, muttering about something I couldn't hear.

I almost spoke. But I stopped myself, afraid to arouse his ire. Instead, I turned away, feeling safer somehow.

Of course, I'm being silly. What could the fur-ball possibly do to me? 'Meow' or something?

Still, Othello frightened me – deep within my soul.

A wave of loneliness overcame me, a familiar companion of my miserable childhood. My life had always been painful. Still, at the end of the day, I'd always had my father – to talk to me, to comfort me, to wash away my cares.

Now, I had no one.

I felt a sudden yearning to share my feelings with someone – anyone – even if it had to be a cat. But as much as I wanted to, I didn't look back at Othello, nor even speak. Instead, I closed my eyes, forcing myself to sleep, willing myself not to dream.

Not that dream. Not tonight.

π

Othello stretched his feline form, taking a moment to rest from his labors. He'd spent five days teaching the man-cub, and it was making him very irritable.

What that smelly thing learned in that "school" of hers would hardly impress a mouse! In fact, he'd hunted more intelligent mice, when he was a kitten and his life was still a joy.

Now my days are endless toil…

A few days ago, he could care less if the mindless dolt could read. Now, he was a rather insistent tutor. Nor was he concerned that they weren't getting any closer to the shore.

"The shore will come," he told the cub, "as to your understanding of King James' English…"

He didn't mean to be sarcastic. It's just – he had little patience for the stupid breed. *Moronic creatures, groveling in their filth and grime, warring upon each other like ruthless savages.*

But he had to admit, this one was different. He'd only been teaching her a few short days, and she could already recognize every word in the survival manual.

She literally pours over the pages, like a toddler with a favorite book. So inquisitive, so keenly aware. He couldn't help but be impressed by her curiosity. *A very admirable trait.*

Of course, what she doesn't know could fill an encyclopedia! It's amazing how ignorant the creature is of her true surroundings.

The man-cub pulled the flare gun out of the bag. "You sure you don't know what this is?"

The cub had a knack for dangerous questions. Besides, he hated guns. "I don't want you to ever touch that, as it could get you killed in an instant."

"What are these words?" she asked, pointing at the placard on the barrel.

He read the words written on the weapon. "WARNING. EXTREME HAZARD. FIRING END."

"Wow. What does it do?"

"It fires a pyrotechnic flare."

"A what?"

"It shoots a bolt of fire. Only I don't want you to touch it. Ever."

Her eyes were wide with wonder. "A bolt of fire? Out of this little thing?"

He amused himself for a moment, toying with her pre-historic fears. "Think of the sorcery endowed within its cold, steel barrel! Fire from the hands of a petulant God!"

She rewarded his theatrics with a frightened gasp. "Really!"

"Really," he pouted, already tired of his cruel little game. "Now put it away."

"Why?"

"Because I'm bored with your Neolithic questions. Put it away, and we'll continue at a more civilized hour."

"Like when?"

"Like two in the morning, when proper creatures are awake."

π

Six days later I spotted the shore.

38

"Land ho!" I yelled, delighted at first.

But then I looked closer. The shore wasn't west like it should have been, it was north. And it wasn't lined with a beach, but with dark, jagged rocks.

Othello joined me, careful to hide from the dolphins. "Where precisely are we, my dear lady?"

"Pallas will do. And I'm not exactly sure. The shore is north, when it should be west."

"Are you quite certain?"

"I think so." I looked at the sun, then back to the shore. "That should be north."

"One way to find out." Retreating inside the raft, he reappeared with something in his mouth.

"What's that?"

"A compass. It tells what direction you're facing."

"That's impossible."

"Oh, ye of little faith," he said. "Look. The arrow points north. You line north up with the arrow, and…"

I did what I was told, except I wasn't sure which letter "north" began with.

"It's the 'N'," he jeered. "And you call yourself an intelligent species?"

I'm going to read if it's the last thing I do! I murmured hotly to myself. But when I lined up the 'N' with the arrow, I saw that the shore was indeed north, and not west.

"So…where are we?" he asked, though not as politely.

I frowned. "I can't believe it, but we must be near Capro Bay."

"You don't seem very happy about that."

"Well, I'm not. We've drifted farther than I thought. Capro Bay is on an island, apart from the mainland, so we won't be able to walk back to Kelly Tree. We'll have to book passage on a ship, and I haven't got any money. I haven't got any clothes, either."

"You haven't any clothes? Why, I hadn't even noticed!"

"Shut up."

"Suit yourself," he said with disdain. "In the meantime, I suggest you navigate us to a more desirable locale."

"You don't understand. We're in the Misty Straights. If we don't get to shore, we'll miss land all together. We'd just float out into the Western Sea and get eaten by a sea-monster or...or fall off the side of the world..."

He rewarded me with an idiotic smile. "They're so cute at this age. They say the most adorable things."

"What are you talking about?"

"Nothing," he said with a lilt of his tail. "But it's really just as well, because I'm not walking anywhere. Get us ashore while I clean my beautiful coat." He disappeared inside the raft. "Hang on. I haven't had my breakfast yet!"

Back to that, are we? Deciding it would be easier to feed the cat than devise a way to get to shore, I descended inside the raft. Sorting through the cans, I found one with the letters F-I-S-H.

"Is this the one?"

"Precisely," purred the cat. "Well done, well done, indeed." He paused for effect, then bellowed, "She *can* be taught!"

Ignoring his sarcasm, I opened the can before climbing back

outside. The rocks were miles away. I thought the wind would push us to shore, but couldn't be sure of it.

If we miss this island, we'll die. No one, not even the warships, venture out into the Western Sea.

Remembering that the magic bag had a few paddles, I fetched one. Though they looked ridiculously short, the manual described how to expand the retractable handle to a reasonable length. Admiring its lightness, I started to paddle.

It was hot, grueling work. The raft was huge, as it was designed to hold over twenty people. I was quite athletic, but I doubted if four strong men could make much headway with the monstrosity. I wished Othello would help, then laughed at myself. A dog will work for its master; but getting a cat to do anything, *especially this one,* was impossible.

"Whoever built this thing," I panted between strokes, "doesn't know a thing about boats."

Laboring for an hour, shoulders burning like fire, I finally stopped. I felt a pang of desperation as I realized I had to reach the shore, but was powerless to do so.

"This is your fault!" I shouted at Poseida, petulantly spitting at the salty brine.

That was mature, I thought as I stretched my arms, hoping the cat hadn't heard me. Then I tried paddling again.

But my weary muscles betrayed me, heedless of my danger.

Think, Pallas, think!

Deciding that paddling was useless, I rummaged again through the magic bag. I came upon a shiny silver blanket. It was amazingly thin, like a leaf from a tree.

Maybe I should pray to Zephyr. Maybe he can move this monstrosity.

I gathered the blanket, two paddles, and some rope. Living in a fishing village, I was very good with rope. In no time I fashioned a crude sail.

Othello stared at my make-shift contraption. "What, pray tell, are you doing?"

"It's a sail!" I said with delight. "It's how we mortals get around."

"Humph!" he scowled. "Why don't you get those dolphins to push us?"

"What?"

"Have the dolphins push us. I'm sure they won't mind."

"Like that's gonna work."

"It won't if you don't try. Humans!" he swore. "Always have to do things the hard way."

"Maybe I like the wind. Maybe I prefer Zephyr. Maybe I hate Poseida."

Othello narrowed his emerald eyes. "I know the King of the Air. He's a flighty, egotistical womanizer, completely bereft of constancy. Trust me; you'd do much better to trust the creatures of the deep."

"Uh...OK." *That was weird.*

"Not only that, but he cheats at cards," he said. "No. It won't do sailing into Capro Bay using the power of the wind. You'll make a much better entrance driving a team of dolphins."

I curled my lips, wondering if this was another one of his cruel jokes. *Of course it won't work.* But I was too curious not to try.

"Oh, my beautiful friends!" I didn't know how to address a dolphin, but thought it wouldn't hurt to throw in a compliment. "Could you...uh...please do me a favor?"

To my surprise, the largest dolphin approached. I stared enamored at his gleaming eyes, quite forgetting what I was going to say.

"Tell him to give us a push!" hissed Othello.

The dolphin glared at the cat, cackling something that didn't sound friendly. Othello raised his hackles in turn. I smiled; delighted with the inferiority complex he had with the overgrown fish.

"Please," I said with my sweetest voice, "we'll die if we stay out any longer."

But the dolphin ignored me, retreating to his pod of friends.

"I hate you!" I spat at the cat. "You are so mean, pretending..."

When the raft gave a sudden jolt...

"Uh!" I gasped, nearly falling off the raft. To my astonishment, twelve dolphins were pushing us towards shore.

Othello looked smug. "What did I tell you? Nasty brutes. They knew better than to fool with me! Let that be a lesson, young mancub. You have to be forceful with dumb animals, let them know who's in charge."

Mesmerized by the churning fins, I barely heard his callous words. With a heart so full it might break – with a touch of forgotten longing – I considered for the first time, the ocean might be a friend.

I don't believe in Poseida. And even if I did, I'll always hate her for taking my mother. But in this magical moment – the sea breeze whistling its hollowed hymn – I said a timid prayer, thanking the Queen of the Sea.

"Get some clothes on," said the cat. "You can't arrive naked."

"I haven't got any!"

He stretched his regal head. "Wear that sail. You'll look quite the part." With that, he disappeared inside the raft. "And do something with that mane of yours!"

I ran my hands through my long blond hair, wincing at the tangled mop. *He is such a jerk!* "What am I supposed to do, wash it in salt water?"

"Use your tongue. Oh, I forgot…you can't," he chuckled. "They're such rum little creatures. Can't even keep themselves clean."

"Uh!" I grunted. I wanted to ask him why he hadn't suggested the dolphins before – when I suddenly realized there was a great deal the cat wouldn't share until it was quite convenient.

I guess I could wear the sail. But it'd look really weird. Slaves in my world wore plain, drab clothes. To show up in a strange town draped in a shiny silver dress…

…just like the multi-colored dress father gave me!

A pang of loneliness stilled my heart. *I have to get back home! He needs me so much!* Or was it I that needed him? I didn't know.

What I did know is that I couldn't arrive naked. So I folded the sail into a makeshift dress.

Then I remembered the harness. *I'd be sorry if I lost that.* The harness held most everything in the bag of tricks except for the survival manual. I donned the harness, and then folded the dress around me.

But what am I going to do about my hair?

There's nothing to do, but let it fly in the breeze! I turned to face the glorious wind, shaking my strands at the gathering storm.

Soon, we entered a narrow bay. We passed a motley boat, and then another. I waved at fishermen struggling with their nets.

"Look! It's a silver girl!"

"Riding upon a golden egg."

"She's got...she's got dolphins! Thar's dolphins driving 'er!"

"How could that be?"

I blushed, feeling sheepish, donning a merry grin. Then I spotted a warship anchored in the bay. She flew a pale brown flag, indicating she belonged to a House that was loyal to Terra, the Earth God.

"How scrumptious," snarled the cat. "Lord Rance."

"Best day ever!" I laughed. For the first time in a long time, I was actually having fun. "I mean, like...who cares? It's not like we're going to meet him or anything."

"How very little you understand."

Throngs of slaves flocked to the docks, desperate to get a better view. I managed a timid wave.

Othello paced in a neurotic trance.

"What's wrong?" I said, feeling like a conquering hero.

"Don't talk to me!" he hissed, quickening his pace to an agitated march. "Do you know what they'd do to a talking cat?"

My smile vanished. My stomach lurched. *How does this look? Here I am...a strange girl wearing an impossibly silver dress, floating into a foreign port on something that clearly belongs to the Gods.*

As if to confirm my worst fears, a group of Jesters gathered on the wharf. Angry and dismayed, their colorful robes were easy to spot amongst the crowd of peasant gray. Most of the Jesters wore dark brown, each carrying a polished stone. But others held flames in their hands, wearing a bright and bloody red.

The dolphins cackled a chaotic chorus as the raft bumped

against the wooden dock. Suddenly, I felt a mad desire to dive into the water and join them. But they disappeared beneath the foam and the brine.

"Come," said a Jester above clamor of the eager throng. The man was dressed in scarlet, a disciple of the Goddess of Fire.

The crowd immediately hushed itself. Triumphant a minute ago, I couldn't help but think my parade just turned into a funeral march.

Chapter Five

Lady Oxymid

Then Terra wed Poseida,
and in this holy union
the Good Earth and the Unquenchable Sea
formed the world from the chaos that shrouded them.

"Theocracy and Divine Right"

Virgil VII

The multitude seemed to like me. Or perhaps, they liked my dramatic entrance.

But the dourness of the Jesters cowed the eager crowd.

I looked for a friendly face among their many-colored robes. But all I found were scowls of displeasure.

Othello jumped into my arms, whispering, "Tell them nothing, except your name. The less you say, the better."

"Gotcha," I hushed.

The cat displayed a maniacal grin. "Here we go! Down the rabbit hole…"

I had no idea what he meant.

"Come with us," repeated the scarlet Jester.

"Why is he so angry?" I whispered.

But Othello kept his nervous silence.

Brown mailed knights bullied through the throng. They surrounded me, then escorted me to a mahogany carriage drawn by chestnut mares. The Jesters followed us on carriages of their own, painted in the garish colors of two Pentathanon Gods – scarlet for Vulcana and brown for Terra.

I'd have loved the ride if I wasn't so worried. Handsome young knights flanked my surrey as I rode through thousands of flattering stares.

"Wave," Othello hissed, "and smile."

I did, much to the delight of the crowd.

They like me! They really do! The surprise I felt was palpable. *No one's ever liked me before.* Women and children threw flowers and kisses; dogs barked happily along.

"Filthy beasts!" heckled the cat, with the air of imperious divinity.

"Jealous?" I giggled.

"Don't be ridiculous."

The streets grew wider and the throngs yelled louder as they sang my glorious praise. Merry cheers of "Child of Poseida" and "Daughter of Triton" reached my nervous ears.

"They think I came from the sea! Like I'm sort of a…a Water princess."

"Say nothing to the contrary. Say nothing at all," spat the cat. "It's those foul fishes' fault! Dolphins' revenge!"

I laughed. "They only did what you asked them."

"You asked them," he sneered. "They were probably planning this all along…ever since I ate that tuna. I might have known…another fine mess you've gotten me into!"

"You are so neurotic!"

But before I could say another word, the carriage veered left into the courtyard of a castle. On either side were stone monoliths carved in markings of Terra the Earth God. This worried me just a little, as the crowd was shouting praises to Poseida, the Water Goddess.

Well, Terra and Poseida always got along in the stories…don't they?

Evil gargoyles guarded the walls, sticking out their lurid tongues to mock me. The manor was made of rough-hewn rock, not at all like Lord Joculo's gorgeous keep of white limestone. I wished I could remember the name of the ruler of Capro Bay as the footman helped me from the carriage.

"Welcome to Capro Bay, Most Blest by the Gods," a thin man said, his silky voice lilting like a song. "Behold the hospitality of Lady Oxymid! Allow us to satisfy your every need."

Now that's what I'm talking about!

The dainty man led me to a splendid chamber. A bath was drawn, full of deliciously hot water perfumed with scented oil.

I thought I was in heaven. I hate to admit it, but I'd never had a hot bath in my entire life. A servant scrubbed my calloused feet while another washed my salty hair. After the bath, a muscular woman massaged my body as another painted my nails. I thought the paint was queer, but kind of fun. And I thoroughly enjoyed the kneading hands.

So this is what princesses do all day! My morning as a galley slave – struggling to paddle to the unforgiving shore – seemed eons ago.

The women idly talked to themselves, remarking how beautiful I was. They talked about my long blond hair, my shapely legs, the color of my eyes. At first this pleased me very much, as I'd never been

49

pampered before. But soon their flattery became tedious. I also noted they weren't talking *to* me, but *about* me. I didn't know that this was proper etiquette for servants of a great House.

I hoped they'd offer me a new set of clothes, but they didn't. I insisted on wearing the harness, and the slaves dared not refuse. They did, however, fold and tuck the silver blanket so it looked like a proper dress. They also fastened a platinum belt around my waist, revealing earrings to match. But as I didn't have pierced ears, I had to go without.

They offered me a draft of *ambrosia* which I tactfully declined. Father always hated the stuff – hated its unnatural hold on people. Besides, I needed my wits about me.

Sitting me in front of a mirror, the slaves finished my hair while applying paint to my face. I hardly believed my eyes. The silver dress, the paint, and the elaborate hair made me look like a princess.

My happiness died a sudden death, however, when a girl about my age entered the room. She wore expensive robes and a nasty expression.

The slaves quickly left the room, lowering their humbled eyes.

"I wanted a good look at the girl who thinks herself a Goddess," said the princess, "before she's sacrificed to the flame."

Who...me? I gasped. *But...I'm not...not even... Why would they wanna do that?* Unable to think of anything to say, I kept my frightened silence.

"Well!" she said, promenading across the room as if she were on a stage, "You'll make a lovely little lamb. I'll be seeing *you* in Mulciber's Temple." With that, she glided out the door, cherishing a wicked sneer.

I kept a straight face. But inside, my mind was screaming. *A princess indeed! More like a turkey for the oven!* Finding myself alone, I threw myself against the only door.

It was locked.

My heart was racing, my mind was crazed. *I have to get out of here!* I'd never heard of someone being sacrificed to a God, *but I don't want to be a trend setter!*

"What are we going to do?"

"Shut up!" spat the cat, nervously pacing the floor.

"That's nice!"

"Shut up!" He was deep in thought, frolicking his tail like a leaf on the wind. "I'm trying to think."

"They're going to kill us!"

"They're going to kill *you*."

I caught my frightened breath.

The beast adorned a scornful glare. "*I'm* the pet of Mulciber's daughter. *I* know a little girl who would be quite delighted to see me home again. *I* am perfectly capable of saving *my* skin. It's *your* skin they fancy, unless I'm very much mistaken."

I gaped in strangled silence. *Could he be so horrible, so utterly ruthless?*

The cat continued his fretful pacing. He looked angry and troubled; puzzled and confused.

"Please," I pleaded with puppy-dog eyes.

"That's *not* going to work with me."

Stupid! I scolded myself. I wasn't good at begging. *Besides, how thick can I be, trying a puppy-dog face on a cat?* "I did save your life."

"So?" he scoffed. "Survival of the fittest, isn't that what your species is always talking about?"

For the thousandth time, I wished I knew what a *species* was, as it was one of his very favorite words. Frantic and afraid, I forced myself to focus. "You…you said I had a special name. The dolphins think so too. Why…why else would they rescue me? There's something…special…about me. Why else would Mulciber…"

I stopped myself and cringed. Asking the selfish cat, whose only goal seemed to be self-preservation, to save me from an angry God was asking a great deal indeed.

Othello stopped his frantic pacing to look at me with skeptical contempt. "Still, you have gray eyes. I've never seen eyes that gray, except for…"

I desperately wanted to ask, *Except for whom?* But instead, I waited…and prayed.

"Oooooooh! I know I'm going to regret this."

"Thank-you, thank-you! I'll make it up to you, I swear…"

"Shut up," he shrilled, "and listen! There are a few things you must understand if you're going to see another morn."

I put my hands on my mouth. *Don't make him angry; don't interrupt!*

"You know, of course, that Fire is the enemy of Water, and Earth is the enemy of Air…"

"Really? Why's that?"

"Jupiter's Moons!" he complained. "You don't know anything, do you?"

I shamefully shook my head, vowing not to interrupt again. *I don't want him to change his mind.*

"Fire is the enemy of Water," he repeated, the bustle of his tail making me nervous and pale. "You just arrived, from the Sea, on an egg, with a train of dolphins at your command."

I wanted to point out that the raft was not an egg, *and it was your idea, you stupid beast!* But instead I kept my frightened silence.

"While I'm not certain why Mulciber wants you dead, it's entirely logical that it forms the very same reason the dolphins find you so very important."

"Oh, no!" I whispered, hopelessness shrinking my stricken soul. "But...if a God wants to kill me, what good is it trying to hide? I mean...can't he just pluck me away and be done with it?"

"How many people have you seen plucked away by a God?"

"Uh...none?"

"Of course not. It wouldn't be proper. No, not at all. The *Forms* must be obeyed."

"OK," I panted, having no idea what he meant.

"Now...Water is allied with Earth, and Air with Fire. They balance each other out...no side is stronger than the other. But Mulciber is scheming. He wishes to isolate the Water by forging a triple entente: Fire, Air, and Earth...all against the Sea."

"Uh...right."

"Never mind!" he scolded. "You're far too stupid to think anything out. Here, can you remember lines?"

I trembled like a leaf, terrified by his scorn. "I guess?"

"Recite after me."

For the next half hour he made me practice lines he wanted me to say; answers to questions the lady might ask.

I found I was surprisingly good at this. Even the cat seemed impressed, though he refused to give me a compliment.

"Even a parrot can repeat what he's heard."

Next, Othello devised a system of "Yes's" and No's." A meow meant "Yes"; a claw meant "No."

Let's hope there aren't too many "No" answers!

Finally, he told me a smidgen of his plan. "I don't know where the Water Jesters are. Still, I'm confident the Earth Jesters will save you. House Oxymid is an Earth House. Terra, the Earth God, always sides with Water. If we can convince the lady you're some sort of Water princess…"

But before he could say anything else, the man with the tenor voice entered the room. Six soldiers guarded the door.

"Most Blest by the Gods…the Lady Oxymid awaits!"

I took a cleansing breath before picking up the cat.

The audience chamber was filled with the most colorful people I'd ever seen. A throng of temple Jesters stood on the right, dominated by brown and red.

Why do they have to look so…I don't know…annoyed?

On the left were several courtiers. Wealthy merchants and guildsmen, I supposed.

There wasn't a single blue Jester.

Standing near the dais was a tall, aged man. Sitting on the throne was a cold, thin woman – an older version of the evil girl who frightened me.

Not good…

Othello studied the Lady Oxymid, expecting more from a noble born. The relic standing beside her was Lord Rance, the owner of the warship he saw that morning. Othello remembered his wicked deeds, admiring the ruthlessness of those birdlike eyes.

A hint of *ambrosia* filled the Air. Its presence was imperceptible to the drones in the room, but Othello could detect it with his keen sense of smell. *A clever trick,* he thought to himself, *but a risky one.* The same hallucinogen that pacified the courtiers would also muddle the sovereign's mind.

Though her mind's already been muddled. He could see it in her eyes. The widened pupils were perceptible to the trained eye.

Stealing from the Jesters to satisfy your endless cravings? What a dangerous game you play! The "miracle" drug, designed by the House of Wonders, was very addictive.

Curled in the arms of the man-cub, he took a moment to inspect his apprentice. She looked surprisingly regal, especially with that ridiculous silver "dress." *Glad I thought of it,* he thought to himself, never missing an opportunity to recognize his own brilliance. *After all, a well-watered ego is good for the soul.*

He warned the man-cub not to speak until spoken to. So he was pleased when she remained completely silent, staring boldly into the lady's eyes. Surprised yet again, he rewarded her with a calming purr.

"Most Blest by the Gods!" hailed Lady Oxymid. Her voice was loud, yet obviously troubled. "Welcome to Capro Bay. Our humble city is honored to serve your…munificent needs."

Completely lacks the confidence of an Alpha drone, he thought. *Betrays uneasiness, ignorance, and the stench of superstition.*

"Greetings and salutations!" Pallas announced. "I've come to you upon the Golden Egg, deep from the depths of the

Unquenchable Sea; as a blessing to the Good Earth, the Lady Oxymid, and the many peoples of your prosperous reign."

The cat was impressed. *She has a surprisingly theatrical quality.*

"My Lady!" shouted one of the Jesters. A Flame was cradled in his tiny brass lamp. "My Lady! This child speaks as if she were a God. She...is...not! Verily, verily I say unto thee – Mulciber, the Son of Fire, revealed to me this very day that she came to you as a sacrifice to the Goddess of the Eternal Fire!"

The astonished crowd murmured with interest. But the man-cub didn't flinch. Instead, she drilled her eyes into the lady...as if trying to cow her.

I must have taught her that, he thought with pleasure, with an assurance that cherished his enormous pride. *Isn't it amazing how clever I am?*

"Yes!" said the Jester, scouring the man-cub with murderous dislike. "Vulcana Herself demands she be sacrificed to the Flame!"

There it is: human sacrifice. What is Mulciber playing at?

Lady Oxymid frowned. "Why does Mulciber want this girl?"

"You ask why, my Lady?" said the Jester with surprise.

"Yes," the lady nervously replied. "It's unprecedented for a God to ask for a...human sacrifice."

The Fire Jester opened, then closed his mouth. He too, seemed confused.

An edgy murmur gathered around the chamber, one the *ambrosia* was powerless to subside. *And where are the Disciples of Poseida? They should be thrilled by their nautical guest.*

"What say the disciples of Earth?" said Lady Oxymid.

"My Lady," said a handsome young man. The polished stone he

carried was larger than the others, denoting him as the chief Earth Jester. "The Good Earth is friends with Water. Together Terra and Poseida gave birth to the world itself. Before the world was born, it was the union of these hallowed Gods…"

Othello was pleased to hear him recite the myth about the marriage of Earth and Water. *It's precisely why you should be welcoming her as a princess come from the Sea.*

The lady, however, seemed unimpressed. "Don't lecture me with your idle prattle. Leave it to the peasants you preach to so well."

Unabashed, the Jester continued. "But the Good Earth is also a friend to Fire, and the Son of Fire says that He has been wronged. That girl," he pointed at the man-cub. "Who is she? She is not a God, nor the daughter of a God. Yet she has earned the fury of Mulciber, and that fury must be avenged."

The cat could feel the terror in the man-cub's chest. *Earth and Fire are in league with each other? There's an unpleasant surprise.*

"You are advising me to sacrifice the girl to Mulciber?" asked the lady.

"If that is what the Son of Fire demands. For by this act, your Lady would seal a new alliance with Fire, allying House Oxymid with powerful, new friends."

That's why the Water Jesters are absent, thought Othello, intrigued by this new bit of information. *Mulciber's been very busy.*

"Enough!" said the lady, angry with rebuke. "Your tongue wags of things that are best kept silent."

"The fury of Mulciber is terrible indeed," said the Jester, "there is no God who exacts such swift, or brutal vengeance."

Othello could see that the man-cub's case was hopeless. *I was counting on the Earth Jesters to save her.* Yet the brown robed man was eager to hand her over to Mulciber. *And with the Water Jesters absent…*

"Most Blest by the Gods," said the lady, nervously fretting upon her throne. "Why did you come to Capro Bay?"

The man-cub didn't miss a beat. "Because...Poseida, Queen of the Unquenchable Sea, hath sent me."

Nicely done, he purred. *She doesn't know it, but she'd have made a fine actress.*

"And why did Poseida send you?"

"I am like a tree that is planted by the rivers of Water, that brings forth good fruit in its season. It is for mortal man to accept the gift that is given, and plant the flower where it can bloom. For who can tell the will of the Gods?"

This, of course, was another of Othello's practiced lines. In fact, it was his favorite. *The symbolism is particularly nice.*

"We hoped *you* could tell us," the lady replied, completely ignoring the flowery, blooming part.

Uh! And I spent so much time working that out!

"My Lady," said the Fire Jester. "Mulciber demands she be sacrificed."

What a boorish bumpkin! Have you no appreciation for the literary arts?

"Think of the reward the Son of Fire would give to House Oxymid," offered the Earth Jester, "if you were to offer Him this *thing* which He desires."

But of course! You can't read! None of you imbeciles can read! I keep forgetting how ignorant you are!

The lady popped something in her mouth. The sudden dilation of her chocolate eyes told Othello it was more *ambrosia*. "She...she says she brings good tidings."

"Yet how are we to know if the girl tells true? Indeed. She has brought ruin upon herself, cursed by the Son of Fire. To what lengths would such a creature go to protect her precious skin?"

The red and brown solemnly agreed, nodding their holy heads.

She's doomed, thought the cat. *They've decided.* But what should he, Othello, do now? He was already dangerously astray from his mission objectives. *I'll have to abandon her – wait until Mulciber arrives – steal away on his chariot – return to Volcano…*

The Fire Jester addressed the hall. "If she could only give us a sign, we might believe she is indeed 'Blest by the Gods.' But no, all I see is a girl who…"

He never finished his sentence. For just as he began his litany of hate, the man-cub reached into her dress, searching for a miracle. She grasped the strobe light, raised it over her head, and pushed the magic button.

The menacing orb panicked the crowd. Men whimpered; women fainted. Even the guards were terrified, dropping their weapons on the cold, stone floor.

The lady was particularly horrified, burying her nails into her throne. "Please," she begged, "make it…make it stop!"

The man-cub pushed the button again, glaring into the lady's eyes. Othello, who had just decided to betray the cub, afforded her a few more moments of loyalty.

I must admit…she keeps surprising me.

"Be not deceived!" shrieked Lord Rance, speaking for the very first time. His aged eyes were mad and cagey, haunted by the specter of his gory past. "She's a demon! Cast upon the lot of us from the depths of Tartarus! She must be destroyed. She…she doesn't belong!"

"Neither do you, dear Sir!" boomed a voice from the rear of the hall. Striding forward in proud career was a white-haired naval officer followed by three sea captains.

It was Lord Catagen, Commodore of the Three.

Curiouser and curiouser! thought the bewildered cat.

Chapter Six

Commodore of the Three

CATAGEN II – Lord of House Catagen, Lord of the Isle of Catagen, Commodore of the Three, Voting Member of the Zoo. Before the advent of the New Age, the second ruler of House Catagen was best remembered for his Machiavellian appetite for political victories; first of which was the culmination of his Voting Chair and the commission of the seven original warships, three of which he personally...

"Rise and Fall of the Pentathanon Gods"

Herodotus III

The mariner crossed the hall in a strident march. "Are you the one?" he demanded, ferocity wrinkling his weathered brow. "The one come from the Sea?"

"One what?" I asked, not knowing what to think. He seemed crazed with worry, furious with determination.

"That girl is not within your purview," snarled Lord Rance.

The Seafarer rounded on the ancient lord. "Neither is Capro Bay, my dear Lord. The Warden of the Southern Sea should be in the Southern Sea, I should think." Drawing uncomfortably close, he barked with flourish and pomp. "You, Sir, are out of bounds!"

Lord Rance took a step back. "I shall decide what constitutes the Southern Sea."

"Do not flatter yourself. I am the Commodore. You sail at my pleasure. That ship of yours could easily be given to Lord Zeliox."

This seemed to cow the aged lord. "My apologies, Commodore. I shall set forth to Arcadia with the coming tide."

"Quite right," replied the Commodore, "and my fleet with you, should you tarry." Then he stared widely in my eyes. "I shall collect the Mistress."

What? A thrill of excitement teased my soul. I even dared a hopeful smile...

"You will not!" hissed Lady Oxymid. "That girl belongs to me."

I gasped, my euphoria already foundering.

"No longer," said the Commodore. "The Mistress came from the Seven Seas. Triton's Waves, that's where I'm taking her."

"He wouldn't dare!" mewled the scarlet Jester.

"It would be totally unprecedented," said the brown Jester.

The Commodore brandished a zealous scowl. "Beware! The Lord God Triton, Son of the Unquenchable Sea, *ordered* me to collect the Mistress. Unless you wish to stand against the marriage of Water and Earth, you shall let me pass."

Oxymid quavered with doubt.

Rance retreated into a frightened corner.

The mariner seized his chance.

"I bid you adieu," he said with a bow. Then he took my arm and whispered, "Come with me. Now."

It wasn't a request.

"My Lady!" pleaded the Earth Jester.

"He can't!" said another.

"Mulciber demands!"

"Stand aside!" The captains cleared a pathway with menacing glares. One was tall with dark hair. The other two were younger, a redhead and a blond. The redhead had a parrot perched upon his shoulder.

"Coming through, coming through!" squawked the bird as they whisked me into a carriage.

"Drive," said the Commodore.

Another man, dressed in dungarees, jolted the carriage forward.

"Tell Dewey to ready the ship. We sail immediately."

To my vast surprise, it was the parrot who answered.

"Squawk! Ready the ship! Aye-aye, Matey!" Whistling with delight, it spread its colorful feathers and took wing.

"Teach that thing some military bearing," said the Commodore, "or I'll have the beastie on a plate!"

"Sorry, Sir," said the redheaded captain.

The carriage hurtled through the startled town, careening down the same streets I traveled just a few hours ago.

But…who are these men? And where are they taking me?

"Uh," I said to the Commodore, "I…uh, want to thank you."

"Don't thank me just yet," he groused.

What have I gotten myself into? The rampaging horses knocked over a fish stand, and then a vegetable cart. The owner threw a well-aimed tomato, splattering the side of the carriage. None of this fazed the stone-faced mariner.

After demolishing a fruit stand and a table full of linen, the Commodore reconsidered his words. "Sorry, Mistress. It's just…it's bad luck for a damsel to thank a sailor, before she's out of harms way."

I frowned, not knowing what to say.

"Nice friends," Othello whispered in my ear. "Out of the frying pan and into the Fire!"

"They're coming," said one of the captains.

I looked to the rear. Twelve knights were in hot pursuit. The Commodore stood and drew his cutlass. In unison, the three captains did the same. The driver spurred the horses, but the knights were faster.

"Stand down!" shouted the leader above the thunder of the hooves.

"We shall not stand down to the likes of you!" spat the blond captain. "You challenge the Commodore of the Three, Voting Member of the *Zoo!*"

The knight slowed his galloping steed. He seemed to be considering what was worse, attacking a Voting Member of the *Zoo*, or disappointing Lady Oxymid. Deciding he liked his chances with the Commodore better than with the lady, he slapped his sword against his chestnut's side.

It happened fast. The knights were on us, swords dancing through the steely Air. For a time, the mariners were lucky. The street was so narrow only two knights could reach us. But soon, our luck ran out.

64

"Cripes!" yelled the driver.

I looked around with terror. A table full of baskets completely blocked our way. Behind that; a crowded market, awash with shoppers.

"We're lost!" wailed the driver. "Must have taken a wrong turn!"

The Commodore turned and shouted, "Jump it!"

The driver spurred the horses into a reckless charge. Together, they leapt over the obstacle. But the carriage collided into the table, scattering baskets in an explosion of wicker and twine.

The knights were at a brief disadvantage. The rider on the left collapsed into the ruin, his steed coming to an ungainly stop. But the lead knight kept his seat, leaping his horse over the broken remains. As the knight circled right, we dove to the left. Sprinting down a narrow alley, we looked for a way to escape.

"Which way?" shouted the Commodore, his face red with fury.

"Don't know, Sir! Never been here before."

"We're doomed!" cried the driver.

"No, we're not," I shouted. "Follow me!"

To my enormous surprise, they did; following me to my new-found treasure…a manhole cover.

How many times have I gotten out of trouble by hiding in the sewers?

The mariners hesitated. "We'll be trapped."

"We're trapped already," swore the Commodore, hurling himself down the dark abyss. The rest of us followed. The redhead replaced the cover just as horses thundered passed.

We stood knee-deep in a river of filth. The stench was incredible, refuse floating past my newly-shaven legs.

"I think I'm going to be sick," said the blond captain.

"Don't even think about it!" I ordered, shocked again at my daring.

"They're going to figure out where we went."

"Someone's bound to have seen us."

"We're all going to die!" whimpered the driver.

"Move," said the Commodore. Picking a direction at random, he waded through the slimy muck.

We stumbled in the inky darkness, cursing the foulness and the gloom.

You idiot! I said to myself. Reaching into the harness, I produced the magic flashlight and turned it "ON."

I cast the light into their astonished faces. Ghoulish shadows marked their dread.

"Mighty Poseida!"

"Triton's Waves."

"How on Earth?"

The frightened sailors gawked and stared, flummoxed by the wonder of the sacred light. But their reverie was cut short by the opening of the manhole.

"Run!" barked the Commodore.

I sprinted down the smelly canal, briefly recalling my bizarre change of fortunes. *Galley slave to princess to sewer rat, all in a single afternoon!* As if to confirm this frank analysis, I saw some rats – huge ones – scampering up the narrow walls.

We came to a fork in the pipe leading left, straight, or right.

"Which way?" wailed the driver. The yells grew even louder.

Then I smelled something worse than the sewer...

"Oil!"

"They're pouring oil into the drain!"

"How dare they?" demanded the dark-haired captain. "You're the Commodore of the Three!"

A callous voice echoed from the void. "Commodore! This is your last chance! Give us the girl and you'll be free to leave."

"They must want the lassie pretty bad," muttered the redhead.

"That's enough, Mr. O'Brien," growled the Commodore.

"Which way?" pleaded the driver.

"We'll only get one shot at this," said the Commodore. "If we choose the wrong path, and they set the oil on Fire..."

No one needed him to finish that sentence.

I was absolutely bewildered. *Why doesn't he give me up? What makes my life so important that he would risk his own?*

"Uh!" I said. "I know which way to go."

"You do?"

"Sure," I said, beaming the light into the polluted stream. *Thank goodness for evaporation, and the entire hydrologic cycle.* "Follow the current!"

"Right," said the redhead, barreling towards the left.

"Why didn't I think of that?" said the blond.

Together, we raced down the infested pipe. The filth became oily and slick. Then came a terrible roar. The stench of the cesspool was hot and baking, choked by smoke and noxious gloom.

I gasped at the gathering heat. *My Gods! We're going to burn to death!*

The blond gruffly grasped my arm. "I can't believe it! I just can't believe it!"

The sewer turned left, then right, then…

It was the prettiest sight I'd ever seen, sunlight piercing through the grit and grime.

But the golden rays were nothing compared to the inferno behind. With a wince of pain I realized the Fire had reached us. My silver dress was now an oven. Flames licked at my naked legs.

The blond captain plunged me beneath the Water as the heat and Flames passed over me in a sordid haze. He dragged me by the scruff of the dress, his noble nautical coat ablaze.

Can I hold my breath long enough to make it? Will he burn to death before he pulls me out?

I felt the tug of the current in answer, propelling me out of the hellish pipe.

The mariners tore off the blond's burning jacket; my solemn rescuer, wincing with pain. The seven of us were treading Water, in the harbor, under a dock. Fire poured out like a river of lava, adding to the vileness of the pungent drain. Othello clawed his way onto my shoulders, disgust written on his sopping face.

By pure chance, the raft was only feet away, tethered to the pier. I looked into the harbor and saw another warship, just like the one that belonged to Lord Rance. Only something was wrong…

"I thought you were Commodore of the Three?"

"I am."

"But…there's only one boat out there. And you have three

captains with you."

"Ship," said the dark-haired man. "And we're not captains, I'm First Mate, and these two are lieutenants."

"The Commodore thought the lady would be more likely to give you up if she thought all Three were in the harbor," said the redhead.

"But how are we going to get to the ship?" sobbed the driver.

The Commodore gestured to the mystic raft. "Can you make that thing move?"

"Not really."

He frowned. "We'll never get to the gig, nor any other craft for that matter. We'll just have to swim for it."

"We'll never make it," moaned the driver.

"Archers will pick us off," said the First Mate.

"We'll swim as a group around the Mistress," he ordered, stern and grim and brave. "The Mistress is your only priority. Whoever survives, it shall be his duty to ensure she reaches the ship. You will not return for the others. Understood?"

"But Commodore," said the blond lieutenant, "it's you we should be protecting. House Catagen."

"That's an order, Mr. Rees. Pray it won't be me last."

The blond cast a murky frown. "Aye, aye, Sir."

I marveled at their desperate eyes. *I'm just a slave! The Commodore's one of the most important people in the world. Why would he sacrifice himself for me?*

"Wait. I just thought of something." *A really random, ridiculous idea.* "Wait here," I told them before swimming to the raft.

"I'm going to deflate it," I whispered to Othello as I reached its bulbous side.

"You are so vile! I can't believe you put me in that…that filth!"

"It was that or burn to death."

"I was perfectly happy in that castle."

"They were going to kill me!"

"Why is it always about you? Oooooh! I just knew I was making a mistake!"

I looked up through the slats of the pier. A multitude of soldiers scurried along the wharf.

"Shh!"

"Don't shh me! If I had any idea what trouble you'd be!"

The cat droned on and on. I ignored him, examining the deflation valve. There were two; one that lay above the Water, and one that lay just underneath. They both ended in a squat tube.

"What…what if we let the Air out? It would have to go somewhere. It would have to push against the Water." *Isn't that what Father talked about? Didn't he call it pneumatics?*

"So?" sneered the cat, just as stupidly as he could. "Listen! I am wet, and I am tired, and I am hungry, and…"

"Read this," I hissed, "what does it say?"

"I can't," he pouted. "It's too dark."

I grabbed him by the scruff of the neck, plunging him beneath the Water. The cat thrashed wildly, but my grip was firm. After a few seconds, I lifted him out.

"Read it!"

"Some…something about an emergency propulsion jet…one minute," he choked, "I…I can't make out the rest."

"What's 'propulsion?'"

"It sort of makes things go, I think." But then he regained his temper. "How should I know? I'm just a pet! Honestly, the things you want from me, as if there wasn't a brain in that ugly head of yours!"

The cat continued his ravings, but I wasn't listening. *Propulsion. Emergency. One minute.* I knew what a minute was, and this was an emergency. *I think it will work. The Air has to go somewhere.*

The mariners joined me despite my telling them to wait. It was just as well.

"I've got a plan. If we hide under this, their arrows won't get us."

"We can't swim under that," said the blond lieutenant. "We could never push it."

"I can make it go," I said, wondering if it were true. "But only for a minute. Then we'll have to swim for it."

"One minute. How far will that get us?"

"I don't know."

"Farther than we'll get if we swim," replied the Commodore. "Very well, Mistress, tell us what to do."

Wondering why a Lord of the *Zoo* was taking instructions from a teenage slave, I assigned a handle to each man. The Commodore and I would stay in the rear to provide the propulsion.

I hope!

The First Mate cut the tethered line. Othello jumped onto the raft with a soft pounce. He was *not* getting wet again.

71

I silently counted down with my fingers.

Five...Four...Three...Two...One...

I grabbed the handle under the Water, twisting it to the right. Nothing happened. I twisted left.

The raft exploded into action; the screeching defeating my own, startled scream.

The soldiers on the dock cowered and brayed, frightened by the high-pitched shriek. But the Jesters' found their wanting courage, chiding them to attack. A rain of arrows fell upon the raft, peppering the Egg like a mammoth pincushion.

But just as the manual had promised, the arrows punctured but did not tear its rubber sides. The jet of Air lasted sixty-five seconds before finally fizzling out.

But we've only gone a third of the way!

Another volley of arrows fell short. I studied the raft, realizing it was constructed of two doughnuts of Air. Now that the bottom tube was deflated, the second jet was under the Water.

A stab of pain rankled my arm as an arrow lodged beneath my elbow. Fighting to stay lucid – agony, sweeping through my frame – I twisted the second handle.

The torture made me swoon. Water pried my fingers from the handle.

But the Commodore caught me, grabbing me by the waist. "You scallywags shall never have her! Never!"

The raft sprinted across the bay as if it were behind in a one man race. After another frantic minute, it was totally deflated. Despite the pain, I swam for my life.

Archers tugged on powerful oars, rapidly narrowing the wet distance. The friendly ship was far away; powerless to help, no hope of assistance.

"Well, my Mistress," said the Commodore as we swam, "it was a good fight. There'll be Sea stories told 'bout this day – tall tales and legends of the deep."

Another volley of arrows fell, only ten yards shy. The mariners valiantly surrounded me now, protecting me like a coat of mail. Somehow, Othello was perched upon my shoulders, uttering a long, sad, plaintive wail.

"We'll never make it!" cried the driver.

An arrow buried itself in the blond lieutenant's shoulder, crimson oozing upon the sordid brine. The mighty ship was out of reach; our fey pursuers, close behind. Seconds now…all was lost, my bleak future coming to a fantastic, fatalistic end.

And in that hopeless moment, when death was full upon me, I dwelled not on a penitent plea. Instead, I thought of my beloved mother…at the irony that I'd would join her at the bottom of the Sea. "Hope you're happy!" I spat at Poseida, hating the Goddess for her cruel revenge.

But just then – as if in answer to my insolent prayer – a slick hide surfaced beneath me.

I gasped. The fin before me had that same, familiar notch!

The dolphins!

The First Mate gasped with shock and horror, brandishing a long, cruel knife.

"Stop!" I ordered. "Just hang on!"

For a third time, the mariners obeyed.

We slashed our way to the wooden warlord, each of us riding a dolphin of our own. The mariners were wide-eyed, aghast, humble – reverence stealing their salty tongues. The only one who dare speak was the intrepid Commodore.

"Aye, Poseida!" he sang with glee, "the mightiest of God of them all! And to Hades with all the rest!"

"HUZZAH!" sang the waiting warlord. The crew was waving, cheering, laughing, "HUZZAH!"

The Sea breeze swept my tangled hair, breathing life into my withered frame. I hushed my soul a pregnant moment; seeking, wondering, hoping...

How?

Oxymid's men halted their oars, muttering hymns and oaths and prayers. For it was obvious that – for whatever reason – I had Poseida's special blessing. Turning their boats quickly around, they retreated to the Earthen shore.

...for none dare test the Queen of the Sea.

Quick as lightning, the dolphins delivered us to the wooden ship. The mariners scrambled up the ladder, marveling at their good fortune. I, however, turned to say goodbye. For my steed was the same adolescent dolphin with the familiar notch.

"I love you," I cried, kissing her smooth, wet face.

"Oh, really!" scoffed Othello, digging his claws into my aching shoulders.

The dolphin winked her large liquid eyes, chirping happily at her two legged friend. I tried to kiss her again when someone pulled me away. Carried by a score of hands, I flew up the ladder to the wooden deck.

"Sway the main sail!" ordered the captain. "Prepare the rigging. Anchors aweigh!" Pointing at me, he rounded on a fat sailor wearing a red bandana. "Charlie, lend a hand! Take her to sickbay. Get Hebe in there at once."

I never got to my feet. Instead, I was carried inside a tiny cabin. My last glimpse of the outside was the mainsail rising majestically up the mast. With a sudden *Huff!* it filled itself with the glory of the Wind.

The sailors placed me on a narrow bed, cold and shivering like a drowned rat. Swooning from pain, tired and aching, I feinted while holding my sopping wet cat.

Chapter Seven

Birth of a Drone

In this world everything is upside down.
Joy is the serious business of Heaven.

Letters to Malcolm: Chiefly on Prayer
C.S. Lewis, English Author
circa 1945: Earth Standard

"I'm bored," sulked the God-child, "I'm tired of being perfect."

"But you *are* perfect," said the Goddess. "There's not a God or mortal as beautiful as you."

The praise delighted the eager child. Yet she ached for even more. "But why did you make me beautiful? You promised you would tell."

"So that one day, you'll become the Queen!"

The God-child hid her greedy smile. Flying across the starry void – jetting amongst the milky firmament – she cherished the wind that swept across her face…

…yet she craved for even more.

"Where are we going? Why won't you tell?"

"It's a secret."

She has so many secrets! thought the child. "But why is it a secret?"

"Our heavenly sisters would not approve."

"Even Poseida?"

The Goddess bent down and tickled her. "Especially Poseida!"

The God-child squirmed away, hiding a naughty grin. Stealing away from Atlantis, on a clandestine mission even Poseida didn't know about, she savored the joy of this brilliant adventure...

...yet she yearned for even more.

The Goddess flew the hovercraft to a third-story balcony of the granite castle. Beyond the glass-paneled doors was a large bedroom, crowded with midwives and Demes alike. A tall woman agonized on a large oaken bed.

Revolted by the suffering animal, the God-child said, "What *is* this place?"

"It is Castle Mare, home of House Catagen, a great House amongst the *Zoo*."

"But...why are we here? And why is that drone crying?"

"She is dying. The child within her will kill her."

"Eeww!" squealed the child. "Live birth? Like...like an animal?"

"They're *not* animals."

"Rhodes says you love them. She mocks you, she says terrible things..."

"I do love the drones...just as I love the lilies of the field, or the birds of the air. For they too, are my creation."

"Can't anything be done?" asked the child. The torment on the animal's face was, for some reason, troubling.

"All shall be done," said the Goddess. Then, as if remembering her pupil's tender years, she stooped down and caressed her. "For *you* have come to save her!"

"Me?"

"You're an Atlantian, are you not? That's what it means to *be* an Atlantian. To change the world, to save the helpless, to feed them on our hopes and dreams…"

"That's not what Poseida says."

"Never mind what Poseida says. *You* will save this woman, and her baby boy."

"How?"

"You must be clever, and you must be brave. Can you do that for me?"

The child's euphoria was like a drug. "I think I can!"

She rewarded the God-child with a daring smile. "I *know* you can." Reaching into her kit, she produced a medical scanner. She pointed the instrument at the writhing mother. "Imbeciles," she muttered, "it's a wonder the baby's still alive…" She made an adjustment to the delicate instrument and ran a few more tests. Satisfied, she changed her annoyance to a gentle coo. "Listen, love. When we walk into the room, there are going to be some very disagreeable men."

"Why will they be disagreeable?"

"Because they're men, little one. Men are always disagreeable when confronted with things they don't understand."

The God-child frowned. "They're such silly creatures, these men that you have made."

"Perhaps," she said with an impish smile, "yet we should pity them all the more."

"I suppose..."

"What's wrong?"

"That drone...her belly is so big and ugly. There's sweat upon her brow. There's blood and pain and..."

"Birth *is* blood and pain..."

"I know, but..."

"You promised to be brave."

For the first time in her entire life, the God-child suffered a moment of doubt. It was a craven shock to her perfect existence. "I'm trying..."

"I know you are," said the Goddess, wrapping her in loving arms. "But you *must* remember who you are."

"A child of heaven...an Atlantian God."

"Listen to what you must do."

The Goddess walked boldly into the worried room.

The midwives greeted her with a frightened shriek before sinking down to reverent knees. Recovering from their shock, they recited the sacred litany...

Glory be to the mighty Immortals,
as it was in the beginning, is now, and forever shall be,
world without end.

The Goddess acknowledged the holy words, gently addressing the midwives in turn. She smoothed their hands in the Aquarian fashion, whispering blessings for their noble work.

Then she turned on the men in Green.

The magic Demes, masters of the ancient science, retreated.

She marked them with a derisive laugh before examining the mother. "Why is she suffering? Why haven't you delivered the child?"

"Her water broke seventeen hours ago," mumbled the eldest of the Green. "But she's only dilated to five centimeters. She's exhausted now and..."

"Any fool can see she's exhausted. What have you given her?"

"*Ambrosia* for the pain."

"A hallucinogen? Why haven't you completed the dilation with a localized relaxant?"

"Drugs of that sort are not permitted to the drones. You know that."

The youngest of the Green interrupted. "I...I wanted to perform a C-section, your Holiness..."

"Shut up," scolded the elder. "We can't do that either."

"Why not?" said the Goddess.

"Our Magi doesn't allow it."

"Your Magi!" she snorted.

Another contraction wracked the woman. She whimpered with longing and pain. Emboldened, the youngest Deme approached the Goddess. "Please, your Holiness. Let me perform the C-section. I could do it in a moment. Repair the incision before they even knew."

"Hold your tongue," barked the elder.

"You hold yours," said the Goddess. "He's the only one of you who's making any sense…"

The midwives were captivated by the rapt divinity. The mother was crazed with pain. The little Goddess knew it was time. Gathering her courage, she tip-toed passed a tapestry of a swan and approached the misshapen drone.

The animal was writhing with agony. Her face was hideous, desperate. The God-child drew a revolted breath. *I don't know if I can do this!* Nothing in heaven prepared her for this…nothing even compared.

She touched the distorted belly. It was the bravest thing she'd ever done. Gliding her fingers upon the heat and sweat, she slid her hand to the pelvic bone. Holding her breath, she pressed the instrument against the uterine wall. The drug swept into the animal with a quiet hiss.

The Demes were arguing with the Goddess. The midwives were lost in prayer. The lonely mother gave a valiant push, arching her back against the sky. A head appeared amongst a trickle of blood, caked amongst gruesome purples. The mother pushed again.

The God-child almost vomited. Everything she'd ever known told her to run away. Yet she inched towards the gore, catching the baby in her arms.

Flailing against the sudden void, frightened by the cold, the babe let out an angry scream.

The little God-child laughed aloud, cradling the animal next to her heart.

The mother collapsed in a fit of joy. The midwives jumped with surprise. The youngest Deme rushed to the mother. The eldest turned on the God-child.

"What have you done?"

"She saved the woman," glowered the Goddess, "and the child."

"But...but...but," he stammered, "it's not allowed! She's broken the *Forms*!"

"When did mercy become a sin?"

He narrowed his aged eyes. "I'll report this to our Magi..."

"You do that," said the Goddess. "But not until you leave." Flourishing her arms, she ordered, "Go! Now! Return to your House of Wonders. You are no longer welcome as a Healer to these drones."

"You can't march in here, use the magic, dismiss *Zoo* appointments..."

"I just did."

"But the *Forms*!"

"To hell with the *Forms*!" she said with a huff. "Tell your Magi *that*."

The covey of Green grabbed the eldest before escaping the blessed room. All except the youngest, who tended to the mother.

"What is your name?" asked the Goddess.

"My...my...my name is Hebe, your Holiness."

"Hebe. You are now Healer to House Catagen. Tend to your charges well."

"I...I shall, your Holiness."

The midwives chanted the sacred rites that accompanied the birth of a drone...

As he came from his mother's womb,
naked shall he return.
The dead cannot praise the glorious Gods,
they walk, instead, in the shadow of the living.

The mother ignored the glum prediction, transfixed by the beautiful babe at her breast.

The Goddess bent to her knees to hug the God-child. "Do you see that?" she whispered. "*That* is the most important thing in the entire universe."

The little Goddess gazed at the mother, admiring the smile on her radiant face. So ugly and worn a few minutes ago, the creature looked almost human. Her babe was soft and smooth, feeding greedily of his mother's bounty. "It's the most gorgeous thing I've ever seen."

"You did it," said the Goddess. "*You* gave both of them life!"

The mother stole a look from her baby. Lilting her voice like a song, so different from her throes of agony, she said, "Your Holiness is lovely and mercifully kind. Thank you, thank you so very much. House Catagen is forever in your debt."

The God-child looked at her mentor, not knowing what to say. She'd never been spoken to by a drone this way.

"Tell her she is welcome."

"You are welcome," said the child. It felt strange to speak to an animal, yet liberating all the same. "What will you name him?"

"Please, your Holiness. I beg you. Bestow your sacred blessing by giving him a name."

The God-child touched the infant's brow. She liked these drones, surprising herself...she liked them quite a lot.

"Dewey," she said, "I read it in a story once..."

"Your name is Dewey," said the mother to the child.

Chapter Eight

Twins

"She is safe, mighty Poseida, and in the care of Lord Catagen."

"Yes, I can see that. Announce to the others that I claim her as my new Token. Make a special effort to ensure that Mulciber is informed."

"I shall, oh mighty Queen. But...who is she?"

I woke to the sound of a young girl's voice.

"Just a little more. Wait! No!"

A sailor fell in from the porthole which served as the only window. I sat up with a jolt, wincing at my arm. Othello, asleep on my lap, tumbled to the floor.

"Hello," sang the intruder. Only it wasn't a sailor, but a pretty girl with light brown hair cut short like a boy's. About fifteen, she wore a uniform of dungarees. "Don't mind me. Were you sleeping?"

I heard giggling behind the porthole. A pair of naughty eyes darted away.

The cabin was very small. By its green walls, I knew it was a sanctuary of Deme, the Goddess of Life. As if to confirm this, a short thin man wearing green robes appeared at the door.

"You!" he said with a look of surprise, "I might have known!"

"Please, Hebe," cooed the girl, charm oozing out of every pore. "Please don't tell the Old Man."

"And your other half? Is she hanging out the side of the ship?"

The pair of eyes returned, playful and curious.

"Well, well, come in before you fall into the Sea," he said. "You'll be expecting dolphins to rescue you as well."

From the porthole, a second girl emerged, a blond twin to the sailor on the floor.

"Really. If the two of you spent half as much time with your lessons as you do playing scallywag and spy…"

They rolled their adorable eyes in answer.

The Healer smiled, turning his attention to me. "Brave Mistress, how are we this morning?"

"Fine," I nervously replied. The man wasn't gawking, but the girls certainly were. And I didn't like the term "Mistress" everyone kept using. "Where…where am I?"

"You, dear friend," declared the blond, "are on the mightiest warship of them all! Flagship of the Commodore, Sovereign of the Seven Seas."

"Rescuer of intrepid, young princesses," added the brunette as she picked Othello off the floor. "And pretty little kitties. I'm Lucy," she said as she sat on my bed, "and I'm rather pleased to meet you."

I found I could not answer. Her delightful smile intimidated me. *I know plenty of delightful girls in Kelly Tree. None of them ever liked me before.*

"Sorry," said Lucy, stroking the purring cat, "you *do* have a name, don't you?"

"Pallas," I muttered, huddling my arms to shield me from the precocious girl. But the slicing pain returned, souvenir of my audience with Lady Oxymid.

"Now, now, Mistress," soothed the Healer, propping some pillows behind me. "You mustn't move that arm just yet. Pray, give it a day to heal, and it'll be as good as new."

"Thanks."

"My name is Hebe. I am a servant of Deme, and the Commodore."

"I'm Casey," said the blond. "Tell us all about your adventures, Pallas!"

"Yes, do tell us," said Lucy. "We're just dying to hear."

"I...I don't know where to begin."

"Begin at the beginning, silly."

"O'Brien says you can make magic light."

"Can you really talk to dolphins?"

"What were you doing on that strange, orange Egg?"

"And where did you get that silver dress?"

"Did you really hatch from that Egg?"

Hatched? I thought, bewildered.

"Oh my Gods!" said Lucy to her twin. "We must tell her about Prince Triton!"

"Triton?" I gasped. "What about him?"

"As if you didn't know," chided Casey.

"We were sailing north to Turner Hill," said Lucy, "when all of a sudden the Lord God Triton comes crashing out of the Sea on a silver chariot flanked by mermen, dolphins, and whales!"

"Really? What did he say?"

Othello seemed interested as well.

"Commodore of the Three!" bellowed Lucy in a funny baritone. "I speak to you as the voice of the Seven Seas. Glad tidings of unspeakable joy! For lo, the realm of Atlantis, throne of Mighty Poseida, Queen of the Unquenchable Sea, finds favor in House Catagen, mortal though you be."

"Glad tidings," said Casey, "but also those of peril. For I have sent you a girl-child, Mistress of the Sea. Chosen to live in the land of mortals – to live the life of mortals – so that she might do wonderful deeds!"

"Tarry not, and sail through the Misty Straights before you." Lucy pointed out the window. "Go to Capro Bay, and deliver there the child from mine enemy."

"Then he sank back into the Sea."

"Oh, I do wish they'd stayed," Lucy sighed, dreamily collapsing into a chair. "The mermen were just divine."

I was stunned. *I don't even believe in the Gods! Yet one of them ordered the Commodore to rescue me?*

Then I glared at Othello. His smug expression was absolutely infuriating.

"So?" said Casey. "Tell us about Triton."

"Tell us about that Egg," said Lucy.

Nervous, I stuttered an incoherent reply.

Luckily, Hebe came to my rescue. "Now, now. Both of

you…out!”

“Oh, but please,” said Lucy.

“We promise to be good,” pleaded Casey.

“Now, now, my princesses, I must insist. This is a sanctuary of Deme, not a playground. Off with you, that's it.”

“We're very pleased to meet you!” they chorused as he chased them out the door.

The cabin seemed immediately dull and empty.

“My apologies,” said the Healer. “They're quite excited, as you might guess.” He approached my bed, waving some sort of humming thing over my head. “No fever, that's lucky. How do you feel?”

“Uh…groggy, I guess.”

“The drugs do have that effect. Let's have a look at that arm.” He gently unwrapped my bandage. I gasped at the hideous wound.

“Now, now, you'll be fine. The powers of Deme are wondrous. You'll feel much better by tonight's mess. I promise.”

“Someone's going to make a mess tonight?”

“My apologies,” he said. “You must forgive me. I've been in the service of the Commodore for over forty years. 'Mess' is dinner, and we shall be eating it at the Captain's table, in the wardroom.”

Oh, I thought, confused by the strange words. “Please, Sir…where are we?”

“You are aboard the *Hornet,* temporarily the flagship of the Commodore of the Three,” he said as he soothed ointment on my arm. The searing pain instantly vanished. “We're sailing south towards Turner Hill where we'll rendezvous with *Yorktown* and *Enterprise* before we journey to the Isle of Catagen.”

"Catagen?" I gasped. *The Isle of Catagen is at the other end of the world!* It would take a whole week to sail there. *How will I ever get home?*

"Swallow this, please." He offered me two pills and a large cup of Water. I drained the cup, so he poured me another which I drained as well.

"Now, now, Mistress, you must rest if you want to be fresh tonight."

I wanted to ask more questions, but I was fading fast. Dreamily, I saw Hebe exit the cabin.

A sharp pain awoke me, needles piercing my wounded arm.

"I haven't been fed!"

"Neither...neither have I," I mumbled, sinking back to sleep.

"That's not my fault! If you wanted to be fed, you should have asked. I, on the other hand, am a cat. It's your solemn duty to provide for me."

"Go away."

"If that's the way you want it. Only I haven't sharpened my claws today, and wouldn't it be a pity if I soiled that pretty harness?"

"Oh, all right," I said, stumbling out of bed. Half asleep, I got a can of F-I-S-H and opened it. "That's the last one."

"Not my problem," he said with his mouth full.

I wearily plopped back to bed. But the claws found me again.

"What!"

"You can't go home. You must never tell them you're from Kelly Tree."

"Why not?" I gasped.

"Because...your father will be *murdered* if you do."

My heart skipped a horrid beat, the sleep I fought a moment ago – a distant memory. "What...does this have to do with my father?"

The cat smirked, enjoying my terror.

"Answer me! What do you mean, I can't go home?"

He seemed to measure his morbid response, patiently toying with his evil words. "Those priests in red robes didn't like you very much, did they? Nor the ones in brown. Nor the Lady Oxymid..."

"So? What'd I ever do to them?"

"Beats me," shrugged the cat. "You seem to have a people problem."

I wanted to argue, but the drugs stole my consciousness. Unable to stay awake, unable to do anything at all, I collapsed onto my pillow.

"Promise you won't tell them."

"I promise," I mumbled, drifting off to sleep.

But in my dreams, I dreamt of home.

∞

When I woke again, it was late afternoon. Othello was asleep, of course, but I was fresh and curious. Rising from my bed, I stole a glance at the mirror.

Oh my Gods! My hair! The Sea and sewer had reaped their havoc,

91

turning the Oxymidian creation into a frightful ruin.

I looked at the sleeping cat. His peacefulness somehow annoyed me. "Thinks he's so smart," I muttered, "just because he can read and knows the Gods and…"

"Jealous," he said from his snoozing nap.

"Shut up," I said, mortified that he'd heard me. "The day I'm jealous of a stupid animal…"

"Speak for yourself."

"How long have you been awake?"

But the cat ignored me, solemn in his slumber.

"I'm going out."

"Not dressed like that, you aren't."

"Watch me."

"Fine. Only please, just so you don't embarrass me, do something with that mane."

He's right, of course. I should brush it out. But to spite him, I did nothing of the sort, gathering it in a pony tail instead. Wrapping a shawl over my nightdress, I opened the narrow door.

"Such an idiot," he drowsily opined.

The Sky was painted with ginger and pink as the sun collapsed in the indigo Sea. I didn't step a foot outside when a fat sailor wearing a red bandana stopped me.

"There now, Missee, best ye get back in," he said as he barred my way. "There, there, thas a gem. The Old Man, he wants to see ye."

I retreated inside the cabin.

"Bob, lend a hand. Fetch the Old Man, 'nd be quick about it!" he shouted as he closed the door. "And get that blasted tailor, the Mistress be needin' proper clothes, she does."

"I told you," said Othello from his nap. "Have you not an ounce of dignity? Don't you *care* how you present yourself...especially in the company of a great House?"

"Great House? What so great about them?"

He huffed, raising his alabaster brow to mock me. "You truly are a nightmare. You know that, don't you?"

"Takes one to know one."

"How very clever," he said with a tinny laugh. "Did you learn that retort when you were three?" Then he curled himself into a different position so he could watch the door. "Remember what I told you; I don't talk, and you're not from Kelly Tree. Reveal nothing about your past. Nothing."

With that came a knock at the door.

"Come in."

The door swung open to reveal the Commodore. With the excitement of yesterday's events, it was the first chance I had to really study him. The old man wore a leathered face, tanned too many times, layered with work and care. His muscled frame stood perfectly straight despite his many years. Snow-white hair topped a cheerful, nervous brow. "Mistress," he announced, performing a solemn bow, "you've awakened. I pray this day sees you well?"

"Uh...yeah," I stammered. "I'm like...uh...OK."

Othello uttered a plaintive wail, as if ridiculing my pathetic response. The Commodore seemed confused as well, though he at least attempted to hide it.

"I trust you'll join us for mess. Or...do you take your meals alone?"

"Oh, no." I hated eating alone.

"Good," he beamed. "We shall see you at 1900 hours sharp then, if that's quite convenient. And you shall wear..." He turned around, cracked the door open, and barked, "Charlie, where's that tailor?"

"Coming, Sir, straight away, he is."

"Very well." He closed the door again. "How is your arm, my Mistress?"

"Better, much better." In fact, it was so much better, I completely forgot about it.

"Ah, that Hebe's a sorcerer, one of Deme's own best."

"Uh...yeah."

There was a long and painful pause. The Commodore was obviously on edge.

He wants me to say something — tell him who I really am. But that stupid cat won't let me!

"I've heard you've met the girls."

"They seem...nice."

"Ah, girls — all girls. Such is the fate of my sons. But they make fine sailors, and I can give them no higher praise than that."

I managed a weak smile.

The mariner seemed determined to avoid my gaze. Instead, he looked out the tiny porthole. The horizon had swallowed the sun, strokes of ginger melting into streaks of purple and blue. "You shall be as comfortable as we can make you, so I want to hear if there's anything you need. This ship is a man-of-war, of course; not meant for royalty or..."

He stopped himself. As if in an act of sheer will, he looked straight into my eyes. The reverence on his face was disturbing.

Unable to hold my gaze, he immediately looked down at the floor. "Still, we do what we can. On the Isle, my servants shall attend to your every need. And I think you'll find Castle Mare quite satisfactory," he added, as if he *hoped* I'd find it satisfactory.

Dumbfounded, I just stood there, leaving the Commodore to his doubts.

"Right then," he said with false bravado. "We shall see you at 1900 hours then...and where is that confounded tailor?" He quickly escaped, barking at Charlie again.

A moment later the tailor arrived, surprising me with a nearly-finished dress. It seemed to fit just fine, but the tailor insisted on a few nips and tucks, "And take up the hem line, just a bit." He left with a bustle to finish his creation.

The cabin was silent again. Wondering how to occupy myself, I thought, *if I'm not allowed out, I might as well do something with my hair.* I sat at the mirror, steeling myself for battle. "Ouch!" I griped, muttering at the injustice of long hair.

"Serves you right, after that ridiculous episode with the dolphins."

"We're alive, aren't we?"

"Humph!"

"Ooow!"

"Would you please be quiet? I'm trying to sleep."

"Sorry," I sniped. But I intentionally raised my voice, cursing all the louder.

The cat raised his head. "Do you see that green bottle sitting next to the mirror?"

"Yeah."

"Use it on that mane of yours."

I frowned, reluctantly uncorking the bottle. I took a cautious sniff. It had a fragrant odor I didn't recognize.

"You're not supposed to drink it."

"I know that!"

"Only don't use too much. A smidgen is all you need."

I glared. *It's so embarrassing. An animal knows more about hair products than I do!* Still, I did what I was told, placing a dab on my hair. It was tangle free in no time.

Delighted, I favored him with a smile. "Thanks."

The cat didn't answer, flicking his tail instead.

"Coming?" I huffed.

"No, I have things to do. Though you'd better bring me something to eat."

"How about a nice piece of toast?"

Othello got up, stretched, leapt onto the warm part of my bed, and lay down again. "Remember what I told you."

"But why can't I tell them? Why can't I go home?"

Othello enjoyed an evil smirk, with the pitiless playfulness of a cat with a captured mouse. "Because the Fire God wants you dead!"

"But why?" I pouted.

"Why indeed?"

"You are so stupid…and mean. Why won't you just tell me?"

"Because you're far too ignorant to understand."

But I had had enough. I stood in a flurry and stomped my foot, using my height to leer over the creature. "I'm not listening, do you hear? I'm done playing your stupid game!"

"Are you?" he replied. "Then it shan't bother you, when your father and the entirety of your smelly little village goes up in Flames. For the horses' heads were like the heads of lions, and out of their mouths issued Fire and brimstone…"

"You are so lying."

"Yes, and do tell the Commodore you're nothing more than a fraud. I'm sure he'll be quite impressed…"

I gasped, realizing for the first time the trap he'd placed me in. *He's right! The Commodore thinks I'm some sort of – I don't even know. If he finds out I'm a slave…*

I stared at the lounging cat, comfortably licking his paws. If I'd ever wanted a pet before, I didn't anymore.

But this cat can read! Somehow, I knew that was important.

"Fine," I stated. "What *do* I tell them? They're bound to ask."

"Oh…I don't know," he yawned. "Tell them you came from the Golden Egg, an Egg spawned by the Unquenchable Sea. Pretend that you hatched from the Egg – fully grown – with no history and no education. Never reveal who you are. Never disclose your primitive past. The pretense of innocent naivety will, perhaps, gloss over your obvious ignorance. And you might as well throw in the Mulciber part, as it certainly adds drama to your perilous predicament."

I paused, struck at how quickly he came up with such a complicated answer. Obviously, he'd thought of it a long time ago. I continued to wonder why, when he made me recite more of his practiced lines. "Just so you don't make a fool of yourself."

This, I took quite seriously. For despite the friendly faces, despite the reverent stares, I was painfully aware of how out of place I was.

I've never gotten along with popular, important people before. Why should these be any different?

π

The man-cub's dress arrived an hour later. The tailor complained he didn't have enough time, but Othello thought he'd done a passable job – considering the prehistoric tools with which he labored.

"Well," she said, "wish me luck."

"Humph," Othello sardonically replied. "If wishes were fishes, we'd all cast nets."

"Whatever," she snorted, opening the door.

Lucy and Casey were waiting for her. Leaping forward with the exuberance of a sprite, Lucy grabbed her hand.

"All right, Pallas! Slept enough today?"

"Yeah," she sheepishly replied, "I…uh, ya know…kinda had a big day yesterday."

"We heard!" said Casey as she took her other hand. "We heard all about it from Mr. O'Brien."

"Were there really twenty knights chasing you?"

"Tell us about the magic light!"

"Where did you get that silver dress?"

Othello exploited the girlish din to slither out of sickbay.

"Girls, girls," said the First Mate, the brown haired "captain" from yesterday's adventure, "why don't you show the Mistress to the wardroom, and we can hear all about it?"

"Right you are, Mr. Gridley," said Casey.

"Capital idea!" said Lucy. With that, they escorted the slave with the importance of a royal honor guard.

Othello followed with the stealth of an assassin.

The wardroom was small but well appointed, with bold nautical flair. On one end of the crowded table sat the Commodore, on the other, the captain of the ship. The blond and red haired officers were there as well, along with a handful of younger males. The man-cub, of course, would know none of the ranks. But Othello knew all their titles, both nautical and familial.

The officers rose as the girls entered, Captain Dewey performing an elegant bow. He was tall for a drone and handsome for his species.

"Mistress, the *Hornet* salutes you, and is deeply honored by your magnificent presence."

"Here, here!" the drones agreed, toasting their guest with blood-red wine.

The man-cub blushed, with an innocence so shy they toasted her again.

She's a canny range of theatrics, thought the cat. Hiding in the rafters, he was grudgingly impressed by her unschooled abilities. *Of course, considering the moronic intelligence of these so-called officers, they'd probably be impressed with a chimpanzee.*

"A round of introductions, I think, is in order. I am Captain

Dewey, son of Lord Catagen, commanding officer of *Hornet.*"

"The finest ship on the Seven Seas!" chorused the girls.

"Here, here," the officers agreed, drinking to this as well.

The cat sniggered at their dog-like loyalty.

"Quite right," said Captain Dewey. "My intelligence informs me you have already met my lovely daughters – a doting father's thorn and pride."

"I'm the thorn and she's the pride," said Casey.

"Ha!" said Lucy with mock outrage. "That's just like her, hoarding all the fun for herself!"

Dewey gave them a playful wink. "You've also met my senior officers; Gridley, Rees, and O'Brien," he said with gestures towards the brown, blond, and red-haired officers who participated in the rescue in Capro Bay. "Though I'm faced with the unenviable task of demoting them back to their proper ranks."

"Either that, or face certain mutiny," said Casey.

"Who ever heard of four captains?" said Lucy.

"Quite right, quite right. Mr. Gridley is my First Mate, while Mr. O'Brien and Mr. Rees are lieutenants. With any luck, Mr. Gridley and Mr. Rees shall be captains of their own ships some day; though I'm afraid Mr. O'Brien is a completely hopeless case."

The table roared with laughter. O'Brien donned a daring grin. "Aye, captain," he said, "but tell our Mistress the truth. You're just jealous of my dashing good looks!"

Dewey snorted. "Aye, the lassies love you. That I can't deny. But what good is it having a lady's man aboard my ship, when the only ones wearing skirts are my very own daughters!?"

"Who's wearing a skirt?" said Casey with a huff.

Lucy wagged an accusing finger at Hebe. "See? I told you we were ladies."

"Did the good Healer suggest otherwise?" asked Mr. Gridley.

Casey turned to her father, a petulant pout on her cherubic face. "He called us scallywags and spies."

"Did he?" said Dewey to the Healer.

Hebe gave a willowy reply. "Captain, I only meant..."

"Truer words were never spoken!" he said with a laugh. Next, he introduced the junior officers as well as a young midshipman training to become an officer.

The man-cub looked confused by the blizzard of names. *A shame*, thought Othello, *as some of those Alphas are very important, especially Dewey and that midshipman named Oliver...*

The captain turned to the Commodore. "And finally, I present to you, Lord Catagen, Commodore of the Three."

"Here, here!" shouted the officers, draining their glasses and slamming them on the table.

"Aye," scowled the Commodore, "enough of that nonsense. Let's eat."

Spirited conversation danced about the cabin as stewards in white uniforms served dinner in five courses.

The food smelled excellent; the talk, lively and fun. The table was covered with dozens of plates, each with a pair of blue lines circling the circumference. There were seven utensils for each, obviously surprising the man-cub. Othello was nervous, sure the barbarian would ruin everything with one of her ignorant displays, when Lucy quietly showed her which utensils to use.

"I still can't believe she attacked us," said the First Mate.

"There must be a raid," said Rees, his shoulder still in bandages. "Some sort of reprisal. Oxymid can't…"

"Just say the word, Commodore," said O'Brien, as if thrilled at the prospect of another adventure.

"No, no. I want *Enterprise* to handle it. It'd be best if *Hornet* stayed away from Capro Bay for a fortnight or two. Dewey, speak to Tiberius about it."

"Aye, Father," sighed the captain, disappointment written on his face.

How bold the Catagen's have become! thought Othello. *A far cry from their humble beginnings.*

He looked at the vacant expression of the man-cub, knowing she had no idea what the drones were talking about. *Of course. Her Neanderthal "school" would never have told her about the feuds of the great Houses, the landed nobility of her tiny, fractious world.* The cat uttered a long-suffering sigh. *Politics is another subject I'll have to teach her.*

The highlight of the meal was dessert, velvety chocolate ice cream. The man-cub gobbled hers up and then looked around the room as if hoping for more. Lucy picked up on this, ordering another bowl for herself, "and my friend."

"Thanks," said the man-cub, casting a smile at the Catagen princess.

Be careful, thought Othello. *Perhaps she acts like an angel. But that princess has the cunning of a Venetian spy.* Indeed, it was Lucy who popped the question that he knew was coming.

"Pallas," she cooed, "won't you tell us where you're from? Everyone's just dying to hear."

A hush descended upon the chattering room, everyone focused on the dolphin rider. Even the stewards halted their service, hoping to hear the extraordinary account.

Othello flicked his silken whiskers. *Let's see if she can do this.*

"I came from the Golden Egg," said the man-cub, "begotten – not made – by the mysterious Sea."

Othello purred. It was the first of his practiced lines, and she delivered it perfectly.

"You actually *hatched* from that Egg?" asked Casey.

"Do you remember the moment you were born?" said the man-cub.

Casey drew back. "Uh... no."

"Then what can I tell you of my own nativity?" She said the words with surprising authority, commanding the cabin with solemn, gray eyes.

Casey tried again. "But...why were you in Capro Bay? And why were you all alone?"

"Alone?" said the man-cub. "When have I ever been alone? If I ride the wings of morning, or dwell in the farthest Sea...*She* will always be with me."

The cryptic statement – an obvious reference to Poseida – caused the officers to quake. *The poetry is particularly brilliant,* thought the cat, *never mind that I stole it from an Israeli king.*

"Mistress," said Captain Dewey. "You are more than welcome. You're presence among us is nothing short of a...a miracle. Never before have the Gods..." He faltered, as if burdened by the weight of his own startling words. "But...won't you tell us...*why* you are here?"

"Have you walked the depths of the Ocean, captain? Have you bathed in the wellsprings of the Sea?"

The captain looked stricken. "No, my Mistress."

"Can you cause it to rain on the fields of man? Can you make

103

the lightening fall upon the wilderness?"

The mariner was silent.

"Can you bind the sweet Pleiades, or loose the belt of Orion? Can you guide mighty Arcturus, or any of his celestial sons? When the stars sang their glad jubilee, and all of nature shouted for joy, were you there, my Captain?"

The mariner whispered a hushed regret.

"That which is done, is that which *shall* be done. For there is nothing new under the sun." The man-cub paused with dramatic flair. "All I can tell you is that I come from the Sea. And that Mulciber has vowed his wrath upon me."

Absolute silence.

In the stillness of the once-vibrant room, Othello felt the swaying of the rolling waves. Slowly, he toured their vacant faces, studying them for traces of skepticism. But the fearless officers, men of reckless adventure, wore speechless, anxious stares.

He turned his attention to his budding actress, with the pitiless scrutiny of a stage director. She was unnerved, he could tell, though hiding it well.

He bit his tongue, hoping she'd have the sense *not* to break the morbid silence.

She didn't. The quiet lingered: unending and cruel.

"Well!" roared the Commodore. "It'll be a cold day in Volcano before Mulciber sets his greedy hands on ye!"

"Here, here!" the officers gallantly agreed.

But their haunted eyes betrayed them.

Chapter Nine

Three Brothers

HOUSE CATAGEN – Catagen was the second most powerful Water House. It held the offices of Commodore of the Three (a position Catagen II created through shrewd diplomatic maneuverings) and Voting Member of the Zoo. Located on the Isle of Catagen, its only source of income came from its poor fishermen...

...the Isle was subject to many pirate invasions. In the beginning, House Catagen, with its meager resources and small population, was ill-equipped to combat the well-provisioned marauders. The incursions became a life-and-death struggle when Catagen I died defending the village of Piraeus...

...in the year fifty-eight, young Catagen II avenged the massacre of Piraeus. Assembling a tiny squadron of merchant ships and fishing boats, he surprised and defeated the pirate fleet...

It was later discovered that House Excelsior was secretly financing the pirates in an effort to eliminate House Catagen. Thus began the bloody feud that embroiled these two great Houses well into the New Age...

"Rise and Fall of the Pentathanon Gods"

Herodotus III

I woke to the sound of scurrying sailors. I tried for a moment to do something with my hair, quickly gave up, and hurried out.

"You forgot to feed me!"

I slammed the door with an impish giggle, pretending not to hear.

The Sky was a brilliant blue, the dazzling sunlight stinging my eyes. Raising my hands like a visor, I looked to see what everyone was pointing at. In the distance were two tiny specks. *Oh, no! Not more trouble on my account!*

"Smashing, isn't it?" said Casey as she bumped me from behind. "All Three! Together!"

"Good morrow, Mistress!" popped Lucy from my other shoulder. "Sleep well last night?"

"Uh…yeah," I answered. *Why are they always so cheery and bright?*

"I rather thought you might be lonely in that room by yourself."

"She's got that cat, you know. I expect he keeps her company."

"Want my cat?" I said, feeling oddly surrounded. "I'll sell him. Cheap."

"No thanks," said Lucy, winking at her sister. "Have you got a looking glass? Would you like to see?"

"Thanks," I said, trying to keep up with their racing minds. Casey handed me a telescope made of expensive brass. I'd never seen one before.

"Right. Just look here."

I put the lens to my eye, but all I could see was black. "Are you sure it's working?"

They doubled up with rude laughter, howling with boorish delight. Watching sailors gawked and stared at the apparently hilarious sight.

But Oliver silenced them with his angry arrival. The guilty girls scurried like rats as Oliver pulled me inside my cabin.

"What are you doing?" I huffed, confused.

Then I saw my image in the mirror. My right eye had a thick black ring around it. Unwisely, I tried to wipe it off. But the oily black smeared across my face.

"Bearing grease," Oliver said with a frown, as if he'd seen this prank before. "The only thing'll cut it is mineral spirits."

"Thanks a lot!" I spat, much harsher than I wished. *Those pampered twits don't like me! They're just like those snotty girls in Kelly Tree.* "Do we have any mineral spirits on board?"

"Yes, Mistress. I'll go and fetch it." With that, he mercifully left.

I snarled at the unforgiving mirror. *Dolphin rider?* I hissed. *More like a mangled boxer!* Vulnerable, humiliated, and suddenly sad – I was stunned by how much they'd wounded me.

"My, but you're a pretty sight," said Othello. "Is that what they're wearing in Greenstone?"

"Shut up!"

"Fashion these days," he said with an Air of exasperation. "I just can't keep up. And the makeup girls are wearing! Well, it's just frightful."

I didn't know what makeup was, but if I could have found that cat, I would have kicked him. Instead, I closed my eyes, willing myself not to cry.

You're just a slave! An unpopular one at that. Did you think all of that would change, just because you climbed into a stupid raft?

Yet my life *had* changed. It was different now. *Everyone seems to like me. Everyone except those two savage beasts.*

"Serves you right," said Othello. "You'll think twice the next time you forget to feed me."

Make that three savage beasts...

But before I could answer, there was a knock on the door. When I bid him open, Oliver strolled in with an odd smelling handkerchief in his hand. "May I, my Mistress?"

"Yeah," I scowled. "Why not?"

The sailor took a tentative step, as if frightened to get too close to me. I shut my angry eyes. Smoothly, gently, he caressed the cold cloth over my scowling face. "Now, now, Mistress. It'll be all right."

"Don't worry about me! It's those two princesses you'd better watch out for."

"They only did it because they're curious. See what sort of stuff you're made of. You know."

"I'll tear the stuffing out of them."

"Full of spirit, they are. Yet no truer friends shall you ever find."

I'll reserve judgment on that. Soon my face was clean, and I was ready to go outside again. *But...do I really want to? Wouldn't it be safer, just to stay inside?*

Oliver seemed to know what I was thinking. "A bird that refuses to hatch from its egg can never learn to fly. It spoils instead and dies."

I paused. He sounded just like my father. *Isn't it odd how they talk alike, a blacksmith and a young midshipman?*

But thinking about my father intensified my loneliness. *How he must be missing me...*

"Come, Mistress," said Oliver. "Better to face them now than to skulk about in this cabin."

"Fine."

Oliver led me to the very front of the ship. The Twins took no notice of me. Instead they leaned over the crowded bow.

"Good morrow, Mistress," Lucy said. Neither of them even favored me with a glance.

I frowned, focusing my attention on the horizon. The two specks had grown into mighty warships, lily white sails billowing in the Wind. I'd seen boats all my life, of course, but those were sad imitations compared to these majestic vessels. "What are they?" I asked.

I instantly wished I hadn't.

"You mean you don't know?"

"Miss Casey," said Oliver. "We can't expect the Mistress to know everything."

I angrily stared at my feet, reminded – yet again – at how stupid I was. But Casey was right – I didn't know anything. *Ignorance is bliss,* my father used to say, *but knowledge is power.* Suddenly, it seemed like my "blissful days" were far behind me.

"The one on the left is *Yorktown,*" Lucy bragged. "She's commanded by Captain William Catagen."

"The one on the right is *Enterprise,*" said Casey with a know-it-all glare. "She's commanded by Captain Tiberius Catagen. They're our uncles."

"Precisely. William is the oldest..."

"Then our dad, Dewey."

"And finally Tiberius."

"You really didn't know?"

"She knows a great deal about some things and perhaps not as much about others," said Oliver. "We learn from each other."

But I knew he was only being kind. *These girls are witty, cultured, and smart. Compared to them, I'm just a moron.*

The two ships were now within shouting distance, a wooden mermaid decorating each massive bow. *Yorktown's* figurehead was a brunette, while *Enterprise's* was a redhead.

"Ahoy there Mateys!" shouted a gruff voice.

"Scallywags off the starboard bow!" bellowed *Enterprise.* Sailors on all three lined the decks, casting cheers at raucous friends.

"Look!" said Lucy once the ships had passed *Hornet's* stern. "They're going to make a race of it!"

"Won't that be exciting?"

"Two bits on *the Lady.*"

"Four bits on *'er Prize.*"

Soon the deck was full of wagers, money passing from hand to hand. But above the din of the cackling sailors, I heard the strong, crisp voice of a young, red-headed captain. "Stand aside, Sir! And let good men pass!"

"Not on your life, little brother!" retorted *Yorktown.*

"Then you shall see naught but my stern, Sir! And the rear of my britches!" Then he blew a whistle.

In unison, *Yorktown* and *Enterprise* heeled lazily to port. At least I thought it was lazy, though the others remarked at how tight they turned.

"Come on, *my Lady*," whispered Oliver.

"Well, it's really hers to lose, isn't it?" Lucy said. "*Enterprise* is on the leeward side. She'll never catch up."

"Leeward?" I asked.

"Downwind," nagged Casey. "*Yorktown* is upwind. Her sails will cut off the Wind to *Enterprise*."

"Oh."

But to everyone's surprise, *Enterprise* reefed her sails and shot oars out the waist of her ship. The starboard oars pulled forward while the port pushed back, spinning her quickly to the left.

Too quick, the crew of *Yorktown* realized. For her bow was pointed straight at *Enterprise's* midships. *Yorktown* tried to tighten its turn, to no avail. She was heading straight for the middle of *Enterprise*. In a minute she would ram her.

"Turn to starboard!" cursed Oliver. "Before you knock Brandy right off!"

I didn't know who "Brandy" was, but even I could see *the Lady* was going to hit *'er Prize* if she didn't change course. I felt a sick feeling of disaster as the frigates crept closer and closer.

The captain of the *Yorktown* must have been feeling the same thing. "To starboard, you fools! To starboard!"

But it was more than the helmsman could do to throw the enormous rudder around. The First Mate and a lieutenant grabbed the helm as well, swinging the rudder to the right.

Yorktown halted her leftward drift, sailing straight at escaping *Enterprise*. The brunette mermaid crept inches from destruction. Then slowly – agonizingly – she corrected right.

Too late! I heard a loud CRACK as *Yorktown* cleared her sister's stern, seeking the refuge of the open Sea. She floundered behind on the leeward side, pointing in the wrong direction.

"Huzzah!" shouted *Enterprise*. Releasing her reef lines, retracting her brazen oars, she quickly raised her mainsail. The rushing Wind filled her sails, adorning her with the splendor of a royal wedding.

Oliver was fixed in a dumbfounded stare.

Casey slapped him on the back. "Now there's a fine bit of sailing, lad. A fine bit indeed."

"The Bull shall be furious," Lucy laughed. "He absolutely hates losing."

Enterprise howled as *Yorktown* limped shamefully behind. Sailors did pull their britches down, just as Captain Tiberius warned – but that was far from the worst of it. As *the Lady* pulled closer, I saw that the head of the brunette mermaid was completely shorn away.

"Poor Brandy!" crowed the twins, smiling with wicked delight. Oliver wore an embarrassed frown as the Commodore and Hebe sauntered towards the group.

If the ancient mariner was angry about the near-miss of his priceless warships, he hid it well. "Argh!" he growled. "Now that's what I call sailing! That's what I call guts! And you've got to have 'em if ye want to be in *this* man's navy!" Putting his arms around both of his granddaughters, he squeezed them lovingly tight. "Showed the Mistress round the ship, have ye? Given 'er a tour?"

"Not yet," Lucy squealed. "Please, Grandfather. Won't you please let Pallas sleep in our quarters tonight?"

"Well now, depends on what she likes. Maybe she's keen on having a bunk by herself."

"Please, Pallas," said Casey. "It would be *so* much fun."

Really? I thought. Evidently, she'd forgotten about the black eye she'd given just a few minutes ago. But I managed a non-committal smile and mumbled, "That would be, uh…fine."

"Right, then!" said the Commodore. "Oliver, see to it. If she's fixed up, that is. What 'bout it Hebe?"

"She's quite well," said the Healer. "In fact, I think the company would do her good. Give her time to...acclimate."

"Quite right, quite right indeed!" he merrily pronounced. "Very well. I shall see ye at mess, my lassies. And I want to hear that you've shown the Mistress every square inch of this ship." But then he paused, looking very stern, "And none of your confounded jokes!"

"No, Sir!" said Casey with a look of shocked denial.

"Grandfather!" Lucy pouted. "What a dreadful thing to say."

"All right, all right," he chuckled. "All the same..."

He paused, lingering on their faces, his jolliness contorting into a vicious scowl. "Have these two, have they...done...anything, Mistress? Anything at all?"

I studied the fidgeting princesses, still smarting from their malicious joke. They looked nervously pensive, yet curious all the same. *I bet that teddy bear of a Commodore would turn into a grizzly if I told him the truth.* "No, Sir."

"Grandfather," said Casey, her look of dread turned to innocent denial, "we have totally outgrown that silly prank stage."

"We're right little princesses, we are," Lucy said, "and on our very best behavior."

"Right," said the Commodore, hesitating. He seemed to know something was up, but didn't want to pursue it. "I'll see the lot of you tonight, then. *If* we can all fit in the wardroom!" he joked before striding away.

The twins took a moment to breathe again.

"Thanks," said Casey.

"Anytime," I threatened, wondering why I'd defended my tormentors.

The girls showed me the entire ship. Though the tour was meant to make me comfortable, it actually had the opposite effect.

I don't know this much about anything!

After inspecting the lower decks where the crew lived, they led me to the wardroom.

"They call this officer's country," Casey explained. "The crew's not allowed past this hatch."

Such funny words, I thought. *They sound like utter nonsense.*

Mr. Rees was inside the wardroom working on a treasure I'd never seen before. "Parchment," he said, revealing a map of our tiny world. "We use it to make charts."

"How do you get parchment?" I asked.

"Lady Gemello has people who make it," said Lucy. "No one else has anything like it, not even *Hood, Bismarck,* or *Yamato.*"

"Though we don't know about *Argo,*" Casey mused, "as Lady Gemello probably shared her secret with Lord Tel."

"Why would she do that?"

"They're Air Houses," Casey sniped. "My word! You don't know anything about anything, do you?"

I instantly squared my shoulders, threatening Casey with a furious glare. Intellectually outwitted, awash with shame, I was angry. *Angry at my ignorance, angry at my loneliness, angry at this stupid charade!*

Casey laughed. "Sorry. Call it Pax?"

I growled, not knowing what she meant.

"There's a brick," said Lucy. "Mr. Rees, show the Mistress where we are."

The lieutenant looked nervous, yet he obediently complied.

He's probably thinking about those dolphins, I thought. *And about my magic light. Isn't it odd how the officers revere me, while these two impish pests…*

"This is a chart of the entire world, my Mistress. Or, at least the entire *known* world."

"What do you mean by that?" said Casey.

"Well, there's bound to be places we haven't discovered," he said, waving his hand towards the edge of the parchment, "there beyond the Western Sea."

"Wherever did you get that idea?" said Lucy.

"Well, it just makes sense, doesn't it? I mean to say, haven't you ever thought the world might be larger than we know?"

"Honestly, no."

"Not once," said Casey.

"Just a school-boy's dream, I suppose. Discovering new people, exploring undiscovered country." He seemed ready to say more when he checked himself. "This is our current position, just off the coast of Aulis. Tonight we shall pass Turner Hill."

But I wasn't looking at Rees' finger or Turner Hill. The coastline I longed for was on the far side of the parchment, somewhere near his elbow.

For Kelly Tree lay on the gentle shore of the Eastern Sea.

The last stop was the twin's bedroom, a huge cabin at the stern of the ship. Appointed with plush carpet and over-stuffed chairs, it was practically a mansion compared to crew's quarters. Looking through the jeweled window that bathed the cabin in a mosaic glow, I could see *Enterprise's* redheaded mermaid following close behind. I felt oddly sorry for the headless Brandy, wondering what caused to me have such thoughts.

"Do you like it?" Lucy said, crossing the floor to pet Othello. He lay upon the windowsill, enjoying the sunshine through the many-colored panes. "Normally, Father sleeps here."

"It's beautiful." Despite my anger, I marveled at the wealth. It was easily the finest place I'd ever been.

"Well, it's certainly fit for a captain or a princess," challenged Casey, "but...will it do for a Goddess?"

"Listen," I snapped, "I'm not a Goddess, or anything like that..."

...when I was interrupted by a screeching caterwaul. Othello arched his alabaster back, baring cruel, malignant fangs. Horrified, I placed my hands over my guilty mouth.

"What?" said Casey, confused.

Oh my Gods! I almost gave it away! I almost told them who I truly am! "I...uh..." I pathetically stumbled, transfixed by the cat's evil eyes, "I...uh...only know the Gods sent me...sent me to you."

Casey stood defiant, challenging me with her vicious stare. But Lucy, puzzled, strode over to the cat.

"Poor Kitty," she said, gathering Othello in a loving embrace. "Must have spotted a rat." She flopped herself into an overstuffed chair, cooing the monster into a gentle purr. "Yes, Pallas...but *why* did they send you?"

"Who can guess the will of the Gods? It is for mortal man to accept the gift that is given."

116

"Don't give me that rubbish," Casey flared.

"It isn't rubbish!"

"Why, it's absolute rot, from beginning to end!" shouted Casey. "And you jolly well know it!"

"You heard what Triton said," said Lucy. "You saw the dolphins."

"Of course I saw them," Casey scowled.

Lucy laughed at her twin. "Don't worry about her, Pallas. Jealous, really, don't you think? Jealous *she* didn't ride a dolphin."

"Humph!" snorted Casey, storming to the corner of the cabin.

Lucy took me by the hand. "A bit edgy, isn't she? Or, hadn't you guessed? Still, she's a rather charming girl, once you get to know her. Just not very…trusting. Had a very bad spell when she was rather young, you see, and…"

I breathed a welcome sigh of relief. For I saw Casey's retreat and Lucy's confidences as a victory.

That would change.

"We only want to be your friend," Lucy soothed. "Your mates, you know. We wouldn't want you to tell us anything you wouldn't tell a friend."

"Yeah," I said. "OK."

"Of course, we are rather curious. I'm bound to say that, aren't I? I mean…your mystical birth from the Golden Egg; your magic light from the depths of the Sea; a thrilling rescue by a pod of dolphins…"

"It was great, wasn't it?"

"Great? Why it was absolutely smashing! We even heard they

drove the Egg into Capro Bay while you were wearing that spectacular, silver dress."

"Yeah, only it wasn't my idea…"

But before I could say another word, Othello leapt upon my chest. His razor claws were particularly sharp.

"Whose idea was it, love?"

I stared into his pitiless, snake-like eyes; shocked, and suddenly afraid. A horrible realization sprang into my head. "You're trying to trick me!"

Lucy wore a look of hurt denial. "Honestly, darling, what a thing to say!"

But I *knew* it. *They're trying to trick me! They're trying to discover my terrible secret.* "I'm not telling you anything!"

I wrenched away from the precocious girl to stare hatefully at the ruthless Sea. The faces of my childhood – the popular peasants of Kelly Tree – seemed to reveal themselves in the mosaic haze. Each of them scorned my sad pretense; each of them mocked my stupid charade. *These princesses are just the same! They don't like me, and they never will.* Defeated, I cried a hopeless tear.

"Muffed it," said Casey, frowning at her twin.

"Oh, bother," Lucy smirked. "Only I told you it wouldn't work. She's much too smart for that sort of nonsense."

"Well, we jolly well had to try," said Casey.

"I suppose. Only I'm certain we looked like mindless idiots. Do tell us, Pallas dear, what do you think of our beastly little game?"

I didn't know what to think. Neither twin was insulted, or even sorry. They just looked annoyed, as if they'd lost a silly bet.

"I want them to like me," I mouthed to myself, my longing for friendship cowing my pride. *I desperately need a friend…*

Humbled by a lifetime of suffering – loneliness, my only loyal companion – I wandered to the refuge of my beleaguered soul. Searching for a source of courage, hoping for a bulwark of strength, I stumbled instead upon my mournful rage.

"My mother died when I was very young," I said. I wielded the tragedy like a peevish weapon – to hurt these girls, just like they'd hurt me. "And that's all I'm going to tell you." Then I collapsed upon a solemn chair, expecting them to exploit my weakness.

Instead, a shadow clouded their faces. "Our mother died too," Lucy whispered. "Just when…just when we were born."

I suddenly shivered at the familiar chill, the frost that defied the hot humidity: the cold that haunted my tragic dreams, clutching me with its fatalistic frigidity. "I'm sorry. What was she like?"

"Elena won't tell us," growled Casey, glaring at the welter of the Western Sea.

"Who's Elena?"

"Our dear older sister," said Casey.

"Everyone says she was really beautiful," said Lucy.

"Beauty's not everything," spat her twin.

Her reply gave me a moment of clarity. *She's jealous! Jealous of the time this eldest sister spent with their mother.*

Lucy sighed. "You must understand, Pallas. Losing our mother… It's been like a curse."

"I know." And without knowing why, I took her trembling hand.

The loss of a mother – we girls shared. A void had been carved out of our vibrant female souls; an abyss the shape of our mother. It was a sacred place – a place our fathers had tried to fill, yet…were powerless to even enter. We'd be mothers some day; perhaps bear daughters of our own. Yet we'd never been mothered – cheated of this priceless treasure.

Lucy and I traded furtive smiles, sharing in the cold of bitter understanding. I felt the stirrings of deep emotion, familial kinship and female bonding.

Then Lucy turned to her womb-mate.

But Casey stood alone, grim and sad. Too hurt to join us; too wounded to care, she silently glowered like a remorseless sentinel.

"We hate Elena," said Lucy, "and…well…when our mother died…"

"I don't hate Elena," retorted Casey, "and I certainly can't blame my mother for dying."

Yet she hated and blamed them both.

Chapter Ten

The Bull

"Your daughter is dead, my darling. She didn't survive the crash into the Sea."

"Indeed, so are my parents, and my grandmother. Tell me love, why does everyone in my family have these…unfortunate accidents?"

"I don't know," she tittered, "you do seem to have that effect on your kin."

"Yet the Water-witch remains, whole and unblemished."

"Not for long."

The Twins helped me "unpack" or, rather, they found a uniform I could wear. Though the coarse fabric wasn't much to look at, I eagerly donned the blue dungarees. *At least I won't be the only person in the fleet who's wearing a dress!* The uniform gave me a feeling of freedom, and a false sense of anonymity.

Ding, ding! Ding, ding! Ding, ding! The noise came from a brass tube that wandered through the ceiling. "Mess call! Mess call! First division report to mess. Second division, man your duty stations. Knock off all ship's work." The nameless voice paused for a moment, and then said, "That is all."

Lucy leapt out of her chair. "We'd better get going. We'll be heading to *Yorktown* soon, and we haven't shown you the bridge."

I flashed the cat a dirty look before doggedly following the precocious Twins.

π

Othello followed them to the bridge on the fantail, at the very stern of the ship. The Healer and half a dozen mariners stood near to the helm, the wooden wheel that turned the ship's rudder.

Captain Dewey scanned the horizon. "So, Midshipman. Is our course true south, or do we need to make a correction?"

Oliver studied the setting sun, the coast, and the twin moons. After making a calculation on a plate-sized chalkboard, he said, "We need to turn a bit starboard, Captain."

"Good," beamed Dewey, "very good indeed!" He slapped the midshipman on the shoulder before reciting a poetic phrase. "When I consider the heavens, the work of thy fingers, the moon and the stars which thou hast ordained."

Why are you quoting the Psalms? thought Othello. *A bit impertinent, don't you think?*

"Aye!" said Gridley to the man-cub. "Didn't know our captain was such a bard, did ye?"

The crewmen shared pleasant chuckles, glancing respectfully at their learned captain.

Yet Dewey seemed alarmed. Not at the crewmen – but at the unexpected presence of the man-cub. "Aye!" he said with too much bravado. "I'll tell the Bull he needs to Fire that navigator of his."

Everyone laughed again. The man-cub looked perplexed.

Lucy explained. "We're following *Yorktown,* who is in the lead. Her course ought to be due south, but she's off by a small jot."

"Oh," she said, fetching the compass from her pocket and lining it up with the bow. "Yeah, you're right; we need to come thirty degrees to the right."

The cat dug his claws into the gunnel. *What are you doing!*

"Thirty degrees?" said the First Mate. "How on Earth d'ya know that?"

"Easy," she said, showing the mariner his very first compass.

"Triton's Waves!"

"Davy Jones' locker."

"Holy Poseida!"

"What *is* that?" Casey asked.

"It's a compass," she idiotically proclaimed.

"A what?"

"It shows what direction you're heading. You put the arrow on the 'N.'"

"What's an 'en?" asked Lucy.

"North – this marking, here," she explained. "The needle always points north, so if you line the needle up with the 'N,' you always know…"

π

God or drone? He couldn't decide. But it was clear that this careless girl, *whatever she is,* had no idea what she held in her hand.

Before that moment, sailors had to calculate their heading using angles formed by the sun and the moons and the stars. But these angles constantly changed, making navigation difficult and inaccurate. *Which means they must stay in constant sight of the shore. For if the mariners ever strayed too far from land, they could become lost forever.*

Yet here was something that always pointed the right direction, rain or shine. To her salty companions, the compass was a priceless treasure.

Yet she acts like it's a toy.

He bit his narrow lip. All his years of patient secrecy, all of his benevolent deeds…had they led him to this sordid crux?

I knew it! he complained. *I knew it the moment Triton rose from the Sea.* The brazen God had foolishly disturbed the balance that kept the world at peace.

But what truly surprised him was that Triton proclaimed her as Poseida's new Token. *That weak, silly girl?* He flinched when he remembered Poseida's last Token, at the agony he'd seen on the dying man's face.

Does the child have any idea how dangerous her life has become? Does she realize what Mulciber is capable of?

For a moment, he wallowed in introspective doubt, his compassion eclipsing his solemn duty. *Can I handle the pressure when put to the test? Can I do what must be done?*

π

He stared into her sacred eyes. Guilt robbed the warmth of his body.

He thought of the Goddess he once had loved.

He remembered her vengeful fury.

Had happiness been worth it? Was lost ecstasy a willing price?

To this day, he did not know.

One thing he did know – the arrival of this teen had changed his life forever.

He took a breath and swore an oath, quoting the writings of a Spanish soldier. *"For you was I born, for you do I have life, for you will I die, for you am I now dying."*

π

"May I...touch it?" whispered Oliver, as if seeking the grace to handle a holy relic.

"Of course," I said, handing him the instrument. "Keep it."

The boy looked crushed. "Oh, no, my Mistress, I...I couldn't."

"Go on." The wonder on his face filled me with unexpected pleasure. "It's a gift! Besides, you'll get more use out of it than I will."

He swallowed at the enormity of my sacred largess. "You are...too kind, my Mistress. I shall cherish the...the compass...forever, as I cherish your worship, deep in my heart." Then he knelt to his humble knees.

Embarrassed! I thought as he kissed my hand. Bathed in the warmth of blissful belonging, my cheeks scalded red in the cool summer breeze.

I'm just a peasant, after all, a stupid, disobedient slave. Yet everyone thinks I'm special…now that I can read.

Then it hit me: like a tsunami upon a village of bamboo and twine. *I am powerful…because I can read!*

Plagued by my ignorance, cursed by my dismal education, I still didn't understand the artificial nature of my plastic world. Yet I'd caught a glimpse at a larger reality; a vast, infinite cosmos. A universe in which I was no longer a slave, but master of all I surveyed.

Because I can read!

No one noticed my wandering thoughts. Instead, they focused on the divine arrow that always pointed north.

"I told you she was a God," Lucy whispered to her twin.

Casey solemnly agreed. "How else could she know such powerful magic?"

∞

"Why do they call her *the Lady*?" I asked as we boarded the gig. Tonight, mess was to be held aboard *Yorktown*, as she was the flagship and better equipped for large parties.

"They call her *the Fighting Lady*," Casey said.

"Why?"

"Oh bother," said Casey. "How should I know?"

"Now, don't let the Bull scare you," said Lucy, "as he's nothing but a cow."

"The Bull?"

"It's a nickname Captain William fashioned for himself," said Casey, "one of which he's quite proud."

"It's the most spectacular joke, really," said Lucy. "The entire fleet thinks it's simply idiotic…everyone except the git himself."

"Imagine making up your own nickname!"

"Of all the self-important things to do!"

Yorktown was exactly the same size as *Hornet*, but with much fancier trimmings. Ornamental work of rope and lines had fancy names like "Turk Heads," "Coxcombing," and "Fox and Geese." Casey told me that a proper sailor knew at least a hundred knots. I hoped she was exaggerating.

I met the oldest Catagen brother, William, and the youngest, Tiberius. William, "the Bull", was stocky with black hair and a brow that furrowed in a constant scowl. Tiberius was just the opposite, a tall redhead with eyes that sparkled with mischief and mirth. William, Captain of the *Yorktown*, looked every bit the Senior Officer; Tiberius, Captain of the *Enterprise*, a dashing swashbuckler.

I was introduced to a line of officers, each favoring me with a reverent bow. I was far too distracted to remember any of their names. I did notice that Oliver had an auburn-haired uncle named Fletcher who was just a few years older than he. Greeting each other with bearish hugs, they shared handsome smiles and muscular chests. Soon, they were grappling with each other; trading playful, boorish jokes.

I was strangely miffed. *How typical: tall, dark…and immature. Why do men have to act that way?*

After the round of introductions, the Commodore invited everyone to retire to the wardroom, where he would join us shortly. "Just want to say hello to some of the men."

"Very well," huffed Captain William. Irritated, he turned to his First Mate. "You heard the Commodore! Reconvene in the wardroom. Order the stewards to start the mess."

"Aye, Aye, Captain!" said the nervous officer before saluting and sprinting away.

"You have that man wound tighter than a spring," Dewey joked.

"You run your ship as you see fit, dear brother, and leave me to my own," scowled the Bull.

π

Othello watched from the rafters as the officers took their seats. *Yorktown's* wardroom was slightly larger than her twin aboard *Hornet*; the magazine was a bit smaller to accommodate the large, mahogany table.

"Captain on Deck!" shouted the First Mate.

The Bull swaggered pompously into his tiny realm. "Seats!" he commanded.

What a jerk, thought the cat.

Stewards in white jackets flurried around the table, bearing delicacies that made Othello lick his lips. The drones had barely started their soup when Casey began the night's theatrics.

"Uncle Tiberius," she said with wicked delight, "*Enterprise* certainly was the cock of the walk this morning! How long have you been waiting to try that trick?"

"There now, lassie," he smoothly replied. "Just something I dreamed up the other day."

128

"Must have been drilling your crew for weeks," groused the Bull, mashing his bread into his ox-tail soup. "Those of us aboard *Yorktown* have more important things to attend to."

"Jealous, I'd say," said Dewey a grin. "Jealous the flagship was defeated by her youngest sister."

The gathered officers chuckled appreciatively.

"And what has *Hornet* been up to?" said the Bull, "Besides causing political catastrophes?"

Dewey laughed. "Quite right, dear brother, hadn't had a spot of bother in a while and wondered what sort of mischief I could get into."

Undeterred, the Bull charged recklessly ahead. "Yes, but at what cost? What if father died rescuing…" He pointed at the man-cub. "Well, really?"

A sudden pall descended upon the room. *Finally,* thought Othello, *a shred of doubt.* He knew, of course, this moment would come – knew that someone would question her story. *This is the part she was born to play. But can my actress convince them of my divine masquerade?*

"Oh, balderdash," said Tiberius. "It was a grand adventure and a damn good story!"

"Just how long do you think we can keep her out of Mulciber's reach?" said the Bull, feeding on their frightened stares. "Dare we flout the Prince of Fire?"

The mariners were unanimously crushed this time; the stench of fear, spoiling their wine.

Othello narrowed his emerald eyes. *Perhaps I'll have to eliminate this William, crown prince of House Catagen.* He studied the officer's dog-like faces, hoping their canine sense of loyalty would overcome their sense of dread.

But the sailors looked dismayed, defeated and cowered.

129

Just like at the court of Lady Oxymid, Othello thought his pupil might be trapped. But again, the man-cub surprised him with her canny sense of defiance.

"Seeing how we're floating in the middle of the Ocean," she declared, "I should wonder which is worse: thumbing your nose at the Prince of Fire...or disobeying the Queen of the Sea?"

The rampant laughter was loud and thick as the merry sailors drained their flagons.

Othello purred. *Perhaps her sass does have it's uses.*

The Bull's face was loud and raging as he toured the laughing men. "It'll take more than dolphins to elude a God!"

The man-cub narrowed her steel grey eyes; opened her mouth to retort. But Captain Dewey beat her to it. "As long as there is Water under my feet and breath in my body, the Mistress shall be welcome on my ship." Turning purposely to his steak, he added, "If the Old Man says we keep her, then we keep her."

"Maybe it's time Father stepped down," threatened the Bull, "before he destroys House Catagen altogether!"

Dewey stood, slamming his fist...

...just as the cabin's hatch opened.

"Commodore on Deck!" yelped the First Mate.

"Seats, please," said the Commodore, unceremoniously sitting in the empty chair. "Sorry. Did I miss anything?"

"Oh, no, Grandfather," said Lucy. "Uncle William was just saying how he was going to do whatever he possibly could to make Pallas feel at home."

"Quite right, I dare say. Quite right. Good for you, son."

The rest of the meal was much nicer, as the Bull was too angry to say another word. Jokes abounded everywhere, the mariners laughed and sang and roared.

My feelings were wild and rangy. After hurling my nervousness on that hateful uncle, I mellowed to the comforts of friendship and wine. I won many adoring glances from the handsome faces, acting more confident than I really was. The sailors all favored me with flattering stares; all except Oliver, who seemed timid and frightened.

"Look who's got a crush on you," whispered Lucy.

"Come off it. He hasn't said a word to me all night."

Yet it was Oliver who brought me back to the center of attention. Speaking for the very first time, he stood at the table; his coal black eyes, anxious and bright.

"Kind Sirs and gentle Ladies. I propose a toast, and I pray I offer it with words fitting the occasion. To our fair Mistress. Fair winds and following Seas. And may she grant Godspeed to us all."

The entire table rose except for me. I felt both honored and humiliated. "To our Mistress," they chorused.

∞

After dinner, I followed the Twins to the main deck for a special treat: the first official telling of the Commodore's epic rescue. Since no one in my world could read or write, storytellers were responsible for recording what little history we had, a toil in which they labored with consummate flair.

To my surprise, the storyteller was none other than the fearful driver of the escaping carriage…though he was certainly fearful no more. The twelve brown knights had quadrupled into fifty, and each mariner dispatched ten knights apiece before climbing down the fateful manhole. In this rendition, the Commodore knew exactly which way to go, and the oil was replaced with another army of soldiers. I still powered the Golden Egg, but I did so with magic sent by Poseida herself, as was witnessed by the dolphins' dramatic entrance. The bard was superb, adding details I could never have remembered…*or even invented!*

After the heroic account, the sailors produced hornpipes, drums, and tiny guitars. Soon, we were singing merry yarns about beautiful mermaids and the sorcery of the Sea. One of the crew, a brutally handsome young sailor, asked me to dance. I accepted, feeling an odd and unexpected yearning.

The handsome young sailor was sharp on his feet; his rugged smile, ensnaring me even further. We danced a jig so well that the others formed a happy circle. Clapping to the rhythm of the quickening chantey, the crew cheered the musicians faster and faster. I gleefully kept up my nimble prance, my feet alight with joy.

Our caper ended in a brilliant crescendo, followed by a round of boisterous praise. Lapping up the bawdy applause, I regaled the sailors with a triumphant bow.

π

Othello considered the ignorant cub, narrowing his emerald eyes. Irritated as he was by the barbaric music, he was even more annoyed – perhaps even jealous – of her innate abilities.

Never in my wildest imagination did I expect her to play her part so well, his budding actress exceeding his own, impossible expectations.

132

It would make what he had to do much more dangerous.

And much more entertaining.

∞

I was asleep, dreaming about a handsome young sailor, when I was rudely wakened by my least favorite set of claws.

"Ouch! Is that the only way you know to get my attention? Why don't you 'meow' or something?"

"We need to talk!"

"Can't it wait?" I yawned.

The razor-sharp needles returned.

"Ooooww!" I hissed, hitting my head on the top bunk. "That hurts!"

"My, but you're accident prone. I'd be more careful if I were you."

"What do you mean by that?" I said, massaging my head.

"Not here," he whispered, "follow me." Alighting from my bunk, he pranced to the door.

I slumped to me feet, thinking, *Why do I let that little monster boss me around?* Feeling insolent, I stopped just shy of the door, wondering what he'd do if I didn't open it.

The demon leapt upon my shoulders. Again, the needles returned.

"Open it!"

I did. Othello bounded to the deck and slinked around a bulkhead. I followed, surprised at how well he blended into the shadows. Soon we reached the bow of the ship.

I huddled behind the gunnel, shivering in the sharp breeze. The Wind caught my hair, blustering it aloft like a tattered flag.

"Do something with that mane of yours!"

I gathered my frazzled strands, clenching them like a rope.

"I heard about the compass."

"So?"

"Uh!" he mocked. "How did I know you were going to say that?"

"What do you mean?"

"You need to be very careful, man-cub. Reveal too much, and their going to figure out who you are; a brainless drone from a smelly hovel."

"Come off it. They love me."

"That's because they're not thinking," he said, curling his angry tail. "Though I find it utterly incomprehensible, it's possible you've discovered a species of drones more idiotic than yourself. They're all so impressed after you got rescued by that pack of tuna."

"They weren't tuna! They were dolphins."

"Same thing."

"Why do you care? In fact, *you* were Mulciber's pet. How do I know you aren't some sort of spy?"

Othello frowned. "Mulciber's daughter. And if I was a spy, do you think I would have taught you how to read?"

"How should I know?"

"Exactly my point, because what you *don't* know could fill an encyclopedia."

"Encyclo-what?"

He pleasured himself with an evil laugh, smarming his whiskers with derisive delight. "If I ever catch you showing those idiots anything else from that raft…"

But I was tired of being lectured. *My own father doesn't talk to me like that. Why should I let some stupid cat?* "If you'd just tell me what's going on!"

"And let everything we've worked for, fall to ruin? Not on your life."

"Who's we?"

"Not telling!" he sang. "As you're far too ignorant to understand."

"I'm a lot smarter than you think, you flea-bitten mongrel!"

"Call *me* a mongrel? Your whole species is nothing but a collection of mutts and half-breeds."

I still didn't know what a species was, but I knew it was pretty bad. Losing my patience, I sprang at the cat.

A wild scramble ensued. It ended with my hand bleeding from a savage rake.

Othello sprang onto the gunnel, the very edge of the ship. "How dare you? Don't you understand? You're pathetic life is completely in my hands! I could destroy you in an instant!" He paused for a moment, lowering his voice to a malignant whisper. "But no. That would be far too easy. Instead, I'm going to teach you a lesson."

I lanced forward to grab him again. "I'll teach you a lesson!"

Surprised, Othello jumped with a shriek of shock, carrying him over the side of the ship...

No!

I threw myself against the gunnel, horrified. Staring into the inky darkness, I prayed I'd see a white ball of fur.

I saw nothing – the blond of *Hornet's* mermaid, the farthest thing the light would show. Beyond and below was as black as death.

I called his name a million times, begging Othello to magically appear. But the ruthless Queen had taken the cat, just like she'd taken my mother.

Why? I whimpered. *Why did I do that?*

But the hateful waves mocked me, lapping against the reproachful bow.

Overwhelmed by guilt and loss, I suddenly needed to confess my sins. Crashing into the cabin, I woke the sleeping Twins.

"I killed him! I killed Othello!"

"Who?" Casey mumbled, half asleep.

"My cat!"

"Of course you didn't," Lucy soothed. "What a thing to say!"

"It was an accident," I said.

But I knew it wasn't true. *I killed him! I murdered Othello!*

Lucy got me to sit down, stroking my tangled hair. "Not to worry, Pallas, dear. Not to worry. We'll get you another cat."

"But...I don't want another cat," I sobbed. "I need him."

"What happened?"

"I…I didn't do it on purpose. He made me angry, and I…"

But I couldn't continue, burying my head into a pillow.

∞

The Twins stayed up with me most the night. They tried to cheer me up with their soothing words, but I was simply inconsolable.

No amount of contrition could cleanse my guilty heart. For I alone knew the burden of my crime. I alone knew the cat could speak.

But then I had a horrible thought, one that truly terrified me. *I can't do this without Othello! I can't fool them by myself. What will they do when they find out who I really am?*

I suddenly realized my wretched plight, the trap that now ensnared me. I couldn't continue this divine charade.

Not without Othello!

The sun leapt boldly above the thin horizon, lighting the cabin through the multi-colored panes. The Twins patted my back and departed, leaving me to my rampant shame.

After hours of tears, after a nighttime of mourning, I wept yet again – crying like the day I lost my mother. I buried my face in my sodden pillow, brutally reliving that odious day…

…when something fluffy tickled my arm.

I looked up, astonished. Inches from my nose were those evil, emerald eyes.

Othello chuckled with malicious delight. "Enjoy my little lesson?"

I jumped back with alarm. "You're...you're alive?"

"Noooo!" he leered in a spooky voice. "I'm the ghost from Christmas Past, unearthed from Hades to haunt you!"

"Uh! But...didn't you fall in the Water?"

"Of course not," he scowled. "Didn't want to lose another life on your account, thank-you very much. I'm down to five already. Besides," he said as he inspected his tail, "it'll take weeks to properly clean my coat after that ridiculous episode in Capro Bay."

"B-b-but..." I garbled, "I...I thought you'd drowned."

"Precisely."

I gasped. *I can tame a team of dolphins, fool a fleet of sailors, but not this wicked cat.*

"Now...let's remember our little lesson, so I don't have to repeat it."

"W-what," I said through bleary eyes, "what lesson is that?"

"Do not fool with me."

∞

The next day was very strange. To my vast dismay, the entire fleet was talking about the sacred compass. Outrageous rumors flurried about, helped along by a very superstitious crew.

"They call you a Water princess," Lucy said.

"Beguiling dolphins, steering the stars..." said Casey.

"Guiding the planets..."

"Aligning Jupiter with Mars..."

"Where did you hear that?" I said, annoyed.

"Just this morning," Casey said.

"The lads are on and on about it. I've never seen them in such a state."

"*Are* you from Atlantis?"

"I told you," I scolded. "I came from the Egg...and...and that's all I can tell you."

But whispers followed me wherever I went, murmurs about a Mistress come from the Sea. Cultivating my already legendary strangeness, they added to my unwanted mystique.

"They think I'm from Atlantis!" I riled at the cat. "Like I'm some sort of...some sort of God."

"What's wrong with that?" he said over his tuna and cream. "It's certainly better than being a slave."

"I liked being a slave."

"Don't be ignorant. No one likes being a slave. For the poor is hated even by his neighbor, but the rich have many friends."

"Whatever," I said, feeling moody and cross. "Look...I absolutely hate the Gods, Poseida in particular. And you want me to pretend that I am one?"

He licked his lips with syrupy delight. "You know, you're absolutely right. I have been rather unfair. Why don't you march into

139

the wardroom and tell those barbarians you're nothing but a fraud."

"I...I can't. They'd probably...hang me if they knew."

"Nonsense!" he laughed. "I thought they loved you."

"They love this *myth* you've created."

"Then you'd better do as I say."

"But...what about my father? When will I get back home?"

"Mulciber will *murder* him if you return."

"But why?" I said, exasperated by the convenient quality of his many tales. "Why does Mulciber even care?"

"Humph!" he snorted. "Why, indeed?"

∞

I woke a few days later to the call of the crow's nest.

"Land Ho!"

I hurried to the lonely bow, desperate to glimpse my foreign cell. For though the Twins bragged about its many delights, I knew the Isle would be a prison – exiling me forever from my father.

Sharp crags serrated the treacherous coast like a tangle of broken glass. I remembered endless beaches of sugar-white sand, realizing how much I missed my home.

The Three sailed to the fortress of Piraeus, guardian of the tiny Catagen River. As the fleet neared the seafaring village, her citizens flocked to its stony shore.

"Why are they so excited?"

"You're laughing!" gasped Lucy.

"Because of you!" said Casey.

I felt even more abashed. I didn't like all this attention.

Lucy seemed to sense my sadness. "It's not about you, silly. Honestly, you think the whole world revolves around the very spot you're standing?"

"It does, doesn't it?" Casey teased.

"Well, I certainly thought so," I joked, feeling better somehow. The Twins were having that effect on me. Turning my head to the salty breeze, I gazed again at my island jailer.

As *Hornet* passed the fortress of Piraeus, the river current slowed her to a halt. "All divisions muster to rowing stations," ordered Oliver.

"Aye, all divisions muster to rowing stations," repeated the First Mate.

"Oliver's guiding us in?"

"Yep," Casey smirked.

I was impressed. The river looked quite narrow. "Has he ever done it before?"

"Nope."

"Very first time," said Casey.

"Well," said Lucy, "we might as well go in. It'll take most the day to reach Catagen City."

"Really?" I said. "I didn't think it was that far."

"It's only an hour going down stream," she said, sounding bored, "but going against the current...well, it takes ten times as long. And I hate this trip. If you're going to be on a ship, I want to see the Sea. Looking at all this..." She waved her hands in dismay. "I'd just as soon be there."

With this, the Twins returned to their opulent cabin. But I stayed on deck. I wanted a better look at my gilded cage.

The low, brown hills gave way to large, pretty ones as the Three slowly crawled up the river. Groaning with their labors, the crew dragged *Hornet* through the rolling moor. The brackish Water became clearer and clearer until we finally rounded a rocky bend.

The scene was absolutely gorgeous, the bristling river opening into a crystal blue lake. On the right was a massive cliff. On the left, nestled behind a luscious lawn of green, was Catagen City. In the center was Castle Mare, the ancestral home of House Catagen. The cliff and the cottony clouds were mirrored on the glassy lake, a beautiful foreground to the bright blue Sky.

"Well," said Lucy as the Twins rejoined me, "what do you think?"

"It's spectacular. Really."

"Not quite Atlantis," Casey said, "but...I think you'll like it."

A huge crowd greeted the warlords, sporting Catagen banners and colorful bits of cloth. Children waded in to the lake as a little brass band played a spirited song.

Everyone was smiling. Everyone except the Twins.

"Oh, great," Casey snarled. "There she is."

"What did you expect? Think she'd get married before we got back home?"

"A girl can hope, can't she?"

"Who are you talking about?" I asked.

"Little Miss Perfect."

"Her most excellent highness."

"I get the idea. Any relation?"

"Not really."

"Just our sister."

Oh yeah...I completely forgot. "An older sister, right?"

"The only older sister, thank-you," said Casey. "I don't think we could take any more like her."

Lucy strutted across the deck while Casey narrated. "Yes, lords and ladies, I have the distinct privilege and highest honor of presenting to you for your viewing pleasure: the unquenchable beauty...the gorgeous hair...the sapphire eyes...the porcelain face."

Lucy waved to her make-believe audience. "Thank you, thank you, to my adoring fans...and all the little people who wish they could be just like me."

"Humph!" Casey snorted, "As if!"

"She can't be that bad," I giggled.

"Just you wait."

The crowd moved to the wharf where *Yorktown* was making its approach. As there was room for only one ship, the flagship normally took the dock. But the mighty ship suddenly turned to the left.

From the bridge of *Yorktown* came a booming voice. "Ho, there *Hornet!*" shouted the Old Man. "The port is yours!"

Word spread across *Hornet* like wild Fire.

"The port is ours! The port is ours!"

"Grandfather's honoring *Hornet* for rescuing you!" said Lucy.

"Bet the Bull will hate that!" said Casey. Then the Twins galloped to the bridge. Embarrassed, I timidly followed.

The First Mate frowned at Oliver with concern. "The port is ours, Captain." It was obvious he didn't want the young midshipman to steer the ship into the dock.

Oliver faced Captain Dewey, rendering a sharp salute. "Sir, the port is yours. I shall certainly understand if…"

Dewey didn't bat an eye. "Take her in, Mr. Oliver."

"Aye, aye, Captain," said Oliver, resolve plastered on his handsome face. Pacing towards the side of the ship, he planned his very first approach.

"Captain," said the First Mate, "the entire city is watching, and the Three. Perhaps…"

"Mr. Oliver has the con," said Captain Dewey. "You should address your concerns to him."

"Aye, aye, Captain," said Mr. Gridley. "Let's bring her in, Mr. Oliver."

Even I knew that docking a ship this size was difficult. Such things as the current of the Water, the direction of the Wind, and the drift of the ship had to be taken in to account. Added to the fact that *Yorktown* and *Enterprise* were watching, along with the entire city… It was easy to see why Oliver would be nervous.

"Helmsman, quarter turn to port," he ordered. "Rowers, slow to one third."

"One quarter turn to port, aye," the helmsman said.

"Rowers, one-third," shouted the First Mate into the sound-powered phone. Listening for a reply, he reported, "Speed is one-third."

"Very well," said Oliver. He looked to the dock and then at the Captain. Dewey watched in stoic silence.

Oliver turned back to the dock. "Helmsman, quarter turn to starboard. Port rowers, hold steady."

"One quarter turn to starboard."

"Port rowers hold steady." The bow turned slowly right as the surrounding hills pivoted left.

"Port rowers are steady," the First Mate said.

"You only get one chance at this," Lucy whispered in my ear.

"He's got the angle too sharp," said Casey. Indeed, the *Hornet's* bow jutted at the dock nearly head on. The dock grew larger and larger. Gridley's eyes grew wider and wider.

"Mr. Oliver," he pleaded, "if you please."

Oliver waited a moment, and then said, "Hard turn to port, steady on my command. Rowers, withdraw your oars."

"Hard to port, aye."

"Rowers, withdraw your oars," yelled the First Mate.

The bow of *Hornet* pivoted left as the hills swung wildly to the right. The force of the turn slowed the ship somewhat, but the dock kept getting bigger.

"On my mark, stop your turn…mark."

"Aye, Sir. Steady as she goes," said the helmsman.

Hornet slowed to a graceful crawl, happy grins littering the anxious deck. The sharp turn slowed the warlord perfectly.

"Helmsman, quarter turn to port," ordered Oliver in a much steadier voice.

"Quarter turn to port, aye."

"To anchor, port side only. Linemen, throw your lines."

The crew scurried to obey. *Hornet* glided gently to the right, stopping a few feet from the dock as the ropes became taut from the anchors on the left.

"Well done, Mr. Oliver!" said Captain Dewey. "Well done, indeed!"

The young man beamed with pride.

"That landing was as good as any I've seen the Bull try," said Casey, slapping him on his back.

"Honestly, Oliver. It was brilliant," Lucy agreed.

"Thanks," he said with a modest smile.

"That was great, Oliver. Really great," I said, reaching out to shake his hand.

But the triumphant mariner jumped with alarm. Evidently surprised that I'd been watching, he tripped on his sword and fell on the deck.

A chorus of rude guffaws followed.

"Aye, Mr. Oliver!" chided the First Mate. "Impressed the Mistress, ye did."

"Maybe she'll put in a good word to Poseida for ye!" squawked Lieutenant O'Brien.

"Maybe she'll fix you up with a mermaid!" teased Lieutenant Rees.

"D'ya think any mermaid wuld 'ave im?" asked the helmsman.

Chuckles surrounded the sheepish midshipman as he quickly sprang to his feet.

"Mr. Oliver, may I have the con?" asked Captain Dewey. "So I might leave you to attend to your...adoring fans?"

"Aye, Sir," he saluted, turning from a picture of pride, to that of pink embarrassment. "You have the con, Captain."

"I have the con. Mr. Gridley, set the in-port watch. Record the draft of ship, fore and aft. Prepare for liberty call."

"Aye, aye, Captain," saluted the First Mate.

I caught the gaze of the burly midshipman as the hounding mariners continued their jibes. The quiet Oliver ignored them all, staring instead into my inquisitive eyes.

He likes me! Or does he just...worship me?

Cackling with raucous, ferocious delight, the Twins took both my arms and led me down the gangway.

"I've never seen Oliver in such a state," said Lucy.

"Honestly! He's usually cool as a cucumber," said Casey.

"Oh, bother Oliver," Lucy said. "I can't wait to show Pallas the castle."

"You'll stay with us, in our father's wing, won't you?"

"I guess." I hadn't considered where I would stay, or that the castle had more than one wing.

"Excellent. We've lots to show you."

"There's the Waterfall, and the secret passages."

"And don't forget the caves."

"And the beaches."

Tagging along like a lost puppy, I tried to keep up with their playful banter. Their musical voices were blithe with pride.

But their happy conversation died a sudden death when confronted by the most beautiful girl I'd ever seen. Magnificent and tall, her elegant face was decorated with delicate strands of blond.

Sapphire eyes glared at me, ruby lips, curling with dislike.

Oh my Gods! She's absolutely gorgeous!

I suddenly felt ugly and small, brutally aware of my every flaw: eyebrows that were too bushy, lips too thin and skewed; cheeks that could have been rosier, eyes that should have been blue.

I wanted to say something, and certainly expected the Twins to. But my boisterous friends were strangely mute. Lost amongst the lively crowd, their silence carried a deafening din.

Finally, the splendor spoke. "I *expected* you to be taller."

"Hello, Elena," Lucy scowled.

Chapter Eleven

Elena

I of course fell in love with her the moment we met, and did everything in my power to make her feel at home.

"My Life, Reflections of Elena Catagen"

I could instantly see why the Twins hated their older sister, for she was everything they were not. The Twins were tomboys who loved the Sea and couldn't care less about looking pretty. At a glance, I could tell Elena was totally pre-occupied with looking beautiful.

And she was beautiful, there was no denying it. Yet it was a cold beauty. It was obvious she didn't think much of me.

"Of your courtesy," she said, as if bound by etiquette to do so, "I am Elena, eldest sister of these two urchins you've had the misfortune of spending time with."

I sniggered in answer and turned to the Twins, waiting for their bold reply.

It never came. They seemed wary, flustered...defeated by a foe who'd crushed them before. I'd never seen anyone tame these two, not even the Bull. Yet they dare not to test the tall beauty.

Elena straightened to a regal pose, peering down her flawless nose. "You must be the Mistress, the one they've all been talking about."

"This is Pallas," growled Lucy. "We're best friends."

"Indeed?" she said with a falsely bright voice. "How...perfect. But honestly, children, why are you wearing those ridiculous uniforms? And what, pray tell, happened to your hair?"

"Hebe cut it," said Lucy. "I think it's fabulous."

"You would," she scoffed, scrunching up her nose. "And what is that smell? Please, tell me it's not you. Off with the lot of you; into the carriage! We shall have you properly bathed and dressed before the whole of Catagen sees you in those stinking rags."

I followed the Twins into the carriage. Elena followed in a carriage of her own, embossed with silver and pearls.

The Twins were uncharacteristically quiet. We rode in silence through the charming town.

"What's up with her?" I said.

"Simply intolerable!" Casey fumed.

"Honestly, she's a nightmare," said Lucy.

"But, why..." I asked when we arrived at Castle Mare.

Much larger than the keep in Capro Bay, the Catagen home was built with pale granite stones, gingerbread woodwork crowning its high-topped walls. Instead of gargoyles, mermaids smiled from the tall battlements.

Lucy pointed at the ornamental moat which wrapped around a lawn of green. "Notice how clear the Water is? It's fed by a lovely Waterfall behind the castle."

Over the drawbridge and into the courtyard, I wondered at the flowing Sea of blue and green. An army of pale cobalt pavers separated thick, manicured grass. The effect was warm and cheering, serving as a nautical foreground against the high gray walls.

A host of attendants was waiting, bowing before Elena. But they bowed even lower to the mythic princess. This did not improve the tall beauty's temper.

"If you please! Take them to the manor this very instant. I want them bathed and dressed straightaway."

"Bloody hell, woman!" Lucy protested. "We're already dressed!"

"Blimey," said Casey. "People'll 'ave seen us like this plenty of times!"

"Where did you learn to speak like that?" said Elena with a sharp, staccato voice. "Three months at Sea, and you come back talking like insolent slaves!" Rounding on the trembling servants, she commanded, "I want the three of them painted and dressed, *before* the lord arrives!"

A burly woman grabbed my arm, practically carrying me inside the castle. The Twins came scuffling after.

"I want every square inch of them bathed and lathered," said Elena, hounding us with proud career. "And don't forget to look for lice. I want them smelling like princesses, not sailors."

"Shut up," said Casey as two attendants dragged her down the hall. "You can't boss us around."

"Speak to me like that, shall you?" she said with a smile. "A good scrubbing will take the sauce out of you."

I'd never had a hot bath in my entire life, so I marveled that this was my second in a week. Though the Twins howled at the injustice of it all, I almost enjoyed the royal treatment.

Except for the beauty's malicious stares.

Elena kept prodding the servants with orders like, "Make sure you wash behind their ears," or, "Don't miss between their toes." The bath ended too soon for my liking when we were taken to another room to apply the paint.

The painting at Oxymid's had been kind of fun, *at least till she tried to kill me!* Shocked by the memory of that near-death experience, I shared in the Twin's indignation.

Elena was obviously enjoying herself. Her first victim? Me. First, she tormented me with rose blush, coloring violet hues above my eyes. Next, she turned on the Twins. Casey was tortured with peach and Earth tones, while Lucy endured pink blush and baby-blue eye powder.

Then Elena introduced me to mascara.

"Don't blink," she scolded. "Keep your eyes open."

Too late. Tiny paw prints circled my eyes.

"You are a mess, aren't you? Haven't you ever done this before?"

I kept my jealous silence, vainly searching for a single flaw. *Her face, her lips, her eyes: they're all so...perfect.* Her beauty was surreal, impenetrable and threatening.

The next indignation came in the form of hot rollers, though Elena was at a loss with Lucy's short hair. "Quite the cherub. Did Hebe take a bowl and cut it off against the rim?"

"You're just jealous you didn't come."

"And miss Lady Gemello's visit to Catagen? I don't think so."

"Well...you didn't get to see Pallas ride a dolphin."

"And you didn't see Prince Borelo on his dappled palomino. Harness lined with feathers, his breastplate a splendid silver mantle." Elena looked dreamily into the mirror. "I could have died."

"All right by me," said Casey.

"Maybe we need to tighten those curlers a bit, Abbey," she said as she gave Casey's hair a sharp twist.

"Ouch! That hurt!"

"And I don't think that blush will do, Martha. It's not the right shade for her delicate eyes. It will have to come off, and we can start again from scratch."

"All right, all right!" Casey surrendered. "I give in. Call it Pax?"

"Why certainly, darling," she said with an angelic smile, "after we re-apply the blush."

The makeover lasted longer than I could have imagined, each application more torturous than the one before. Though the Twins continued their protests, I uttered not a single word.

Why bother? She'll ridicule anything I say.

"You're a quiet little mouse," taunted the tormentor.

I bit my lip, stifling a response.

"What," she jeered, "do the Gods have nothing to say?"

Unable to help myself, I unleashed one of Othello's cryptic lines. "I do not speak for the Gods," I said, glaring straight into her sapphire eyes, "I let them speak for me."

Elena stared, opened her mouth to respond, and then thought better of it. "I rather think we're finished, Abbey."

"Yes, Ma'am. Let me get their dresses."

A dozen gowns paraded into the room. The Twins were fitted quickly, Lucy in Sky blue and Casey in pale pink. The attendants

153

spent more time with me, trying mauve and purple before settling on a lovely jade green, a slender creation of delicate silk.

Finally escaping, the Twins led me down the many halls. I felt jittery in the expensive dress, though the Twins seemed just as comfortable in delicate gowns as they were in dungarees.

"Ooooh, that girl!" said Lucy. "I'd like to tell her a thing or two."

"Don't worry, Pallas," mumbled Casey, "it's a big castle and an even bigger island. We'll just stay out of her way."

"Besides," Lucy said, "we know lots of hideouts. The castle is absolutely full of them!"

Casey rounded a corner, gesturing to an open door. "This will be your room."

My jaw dropped. Twice the size of my entire house in Kelly Tree, it was breathtakingly beautiful. The scrumptious furniture was bright cherry, whimsical conch shells carved into the wood. A cheerful pour of joyous light embraced lush carpet in a warm, welcoming glow. The bed was enormous, the wardrobe, a masterpiece; limitless sofas sprinkled to and fro. But the crowning jewel was a soaring mirror, buttressed by a marble-topped bureau.

I savored the splendor of the opulent spread...until a white monster alighted on my bed.

"Where have you been?" I mumbled, peevishly angry at his unwelcome intrusion. For he was a constant reminder of problems I'd rather forget.

"You mustn't be cross with poor kitty," said Lucy, gently stroking his back. "You'll hurt his feelings."

"I doubt it." Then, thinking I ought to *pretend* to like him as well, I reached out to pet him. But he sprang from the covers, briskly pattering across the carpeted floor.

"See, you scared him," Lucy said. But she didn't dwell on it.

"Do you think we have time to show her the tunnels?" asked Casey.

"Look at what you're wearing. Miss Perfect will kill us if we get dirty."

"Why do you let Elena boss you around?" I asked.

Lucy flopped in an overstuffed chair. "We were quite chummy, really, before...well...before Grandmother died."

"That changed everything," said Casey.

"I'm sorry about your grandmother," I said, "but...what does that have to do with Elena?"

"The Gods have not been kind to the Catagen wives," said Lucy. "Aunt Martha, Uncle William's wife, died long before we were born. And, of course, our mother..."

"Yeah," I whispered.

"Grandmother was the matron of the House. But then she died as well. So Miss Perfect managed the manor."

"You know, plan social engagements, supervise the many meals."

"Boss us around, tell us what to wear, when to go to bed."

"Anyway, Father let her. Thought it was good for her. She took Mother's death quite hard."

"Who hasn't?" Casey scowled.

"Sorry," I said. *There isn't a single day I don't think about my mother.*

155

"What was your mother like?" asked Lucy.

Othello leapt into Lucy's arms, meowing with dramatic interest.

"Oh, look. Poor thing's starved," I said, steering the conversation away from my past. "Can we get him something to eat?"

"We can bring him back something from the party," Casey said.

"Who's going to be there?" I asked.

"All sorts."

"Mostly people from the Isle," said Lucy, "though Borelo and his crowd are here as well."

"You mean 'Bore-us-loads,'" Casey giggled. "Worthless Windbag! That Gemelleon prat would be the perfect match for our prig of a sister."

"Who's Gemelleon?"

"House Gemello, the most powerful Air House. Lady Gemello is the ruler of Geminus."

"I just love watching them talk," Lucy said. "Oh, Bore-us-loads, you're *so* handsome!" Pointing her nose high into the Air, she started duck-walking round the room. "You make me want to swoon." Swaying ridiculously backwards, she collapsed on the sofa with theatrical flair.

"More like throw up," said Casey.

"So...what's he like?"

"Well," said Lucy, "he's rather tall."

"Gangly," Casey corrected.

"Blue eyes, and thin, white hair."

"Balding."

"Delicate hands."

"Weak, she means."

I giggled. "Sounds like your type."

Casey answered by throwing a pillow. I jumped onto the bed before launching one in return. Lucy clobbered me with a well-aimed cushion, screaming with naughty, raucous joy. I shrieked with impish, wicked delight; losing my troubles to the happy brawl. Soon the room was littered with feathers, our laughter carrying down the granite halls.

The Twins peppered me with their fluffy crossfire. I rained thunder from my heavenly height. It was only a few minutes before...

"What are you doing?" roared Elena. Her arms were crossed, her eyes were cruel, and indeed, she had her nose pointed higher than any nose ever had a right to.

"Uh..." said Casey, feathers falling on her head, "is that a trick question?"

"Three months at Sea, and you come back acting like urchins? Father insisted that you go, and see what he has wrought!"

I shamefully slid from my lofty perch, hardly knowing what to say. The princess made me feel childish and small. But then I reconsidered. *We're just having fun.* It wasn't a crime to have fun, *not even for a slave.*

"It's my fault," I said. "I started it.'

"How very sweet," tittered the beauty. "Re-living your life in your heavenly abode?" Then she rounded on the Twins. "Out with the both of you! Go on. Out!"

They lowered their heads as they made their escape.

But Elena remained, transfixed with pleasure. "Tell me, do they pillow-fight in Atlantis?"

I paused a moment to size up this nemesis. *Should I pay homage to this conceited girl?* That's what wolves did; showing servitude to the leader of the pack, begging to be included in their cherished inner-circle. *It's certainly what the pretty girls in Kelly Tree would do.* But my dignity wouldn't allow it. Instead, I relied on my old standby: blunt antagonism.

"Only when they want to have fun."

"Is that what the Gods do to enjoy themselves? I thought they listened to harps and drank *ambrosia.*"

"Only when they're bored," I said, stalking forward with cruel intent. Nose to nose with my beautiful foe, I continued, "Most of the time, they sit around, planning creative ways to ruin people's lives."

Elena stared right back, pretending to be confident. But the flush in her cheeks betrayed her.

"It's not very wise to upset a God," I threatened. "Did you know that?"

The sapphire eyes darted to and fro, fear encroaching upon their elegant splendor. "I'll…I'll just go then," she bleated before squeezing out the door.

I watched her retreat, balling my hands into angry fists. I tried to be happy with the meaningless victory, but knew that it was hollow.

I need to make friends, not enemies.

Othello, slinking around the armoire, pounced upon the dresser. "That went well."

"Yeah…she absolutely hates me."

"You seem to have a people problem. Can't we all just get along?"

"Shut up," I said as I picked up the pillows. "Where have you been?"

"Working."

"Yeah, right…as if you've ever done a moment's work in your entire life." I tossed the pillows onto the bed. "By the way, nice of you to jump away like that. Don't you think they'll get suspicious?"

"I don't like you petting me."

"You let Lucy pet you."

"I like her. She's sweet."

"I'm not sweet?"

"If you have to ask."

"Never mind," I grumbled, arranging the pillows. Changing the subject, I spun around and posed. "How do I look?"

"It's…fine," he shrugged. "Of course, I am partial to green."

"I'll take that as a compliment."

"If you feel you deserve one."

"Well I do!" I said, stamping my foot. "It's not enough I was nearly eaten by a shark and sacrificed to a God! Everyone around here thinks I'm some sort of…I don't even know…and you insist I let them! Their uncle hates me, and that sister can't wait to catch me doing something stupid!"

The cat seemed to savor my anger, lapping it up like a bowl of cream. "If you'd be more careful, they wouldn't catch you doing something stupid. On the other hand, with your limited intelligence and sub-standard breeding…"

"Ha, ha! Very funny. Any more enchanting things you'd like to say?"

"Ah! Now you demand to be enchanted? Princesses are enchanted, not mere Gamma drones. Are you to be a princess now? A far cry from the peasant who crawled into my raft."

"Worst mistake I ever made."

"The Commodore doesn't think so."

"The Commodore?" I pleaded, rolling my guilty eyes. "Look at all the trouble I've caused him! A daring rescue, burning oil, the wrath of Mulciber...and for what? I don't even know *why* I'm so much trouble!"

"Indeed. We need to work on your people skills."

"I need to work on my right cross," I said, punching at my image in the mirror. "All this rich living's making me soft."

"And fat."

I knocked him off the dresser with a furious pillow. Scurrying on the slick marble floor, he scrambled behind the leg of a chair.

"My word!" he savaged. "A bit testy, aren't we?"

I studied the girl in the mirror, wondering if she *had* gained weight. "You're so mean," I whispered, the defiance I sported a moment ago, melting into cheerless doubt.

Othello sighed. "I know."

I looked at him, surprised.

"Teenagers," he said. "So vain, so vulnerable."

"Then why do you..?"

"Because I want you to think," he purred, a sympathetic twist upon his emerald eyes of green. "Look at yourself. Go on, look in the mirror. Tell me. What do you see?"

160

"All I see is a girl," I pouted, "a common peasant, pretending to be a princess."

"Ah…but I see a princess pretending to be a peasant."

I blushed, genuinely touched. "Thanks."

"Yes, well," he said, as if flustered by his own, unexpected generosity. "Don't let it get to your head."

"Fine," I huffed. "I'll be off."

"And where do you think you're going?"

"To the party, of course. It must be nearly time."

"Yes, about that. Though I'm sure to be bored at the Neolithic affair, I'm afraid it'll be necessary to bring me along."

"What? You can't go!"

"Well, yes, I can. And in fact, I must. This party is an incredible opportunity to see what intelligence I can gather."

"Intelligence?"

"Lady Gemello is going to be there. So is her son, Master Borelo."

"So?"

"It's going to be much more difficult to fool them, than those simpleton officers."

"Ugh!" I gasped. "Is lady whats-her-name a follower of Poseida?"

"No, Zephyr, the Air God. In fact, she's the most important Air House in the *Zoo*. That's why the Commodore brought her here. Now that Earth has sided with Fire, Lord Catagen must equalize the balance of power by forging an entente to counter this new threat.

He's trying to shore up a Water-Air alliance."

I didn't know what an entante was, but I was not bringing that cat. "No. If you want to hang around and pretend you're chasing mice…"

"I do not chase mice."

"Fine, squirrels. Whatever. But if you think I'm carrying you around…"

Chapter Twelve

Secrets Behind the Mist

There is a magic in names,
and the mightiest of these is Atlantis.

H. G. Wells
English Author
circa 1900: Earth Standard

I met the Twins with the monster in my arms, and a scowl that rivaled Elena's nastiest looks. Though they thought bringing Othello was a "capital idea," I secretly hoped Elena would demand I take him back.

As luck would have it, I met the Commodore first. "There she is, and what a vision! Turn around, and let an old man see."

I nervously obliged – a little embarrassed – smiling all the same. I couldn't help but like the ancient mariner. *He always knows just what to say!*

"Mistress," said Elena with sweet displeasure, "surely you'd be more comfortable with your pet back in your chambers."

I was about to wholeheartedly agree, when the Commodore came to my unwanted rescue. "Nonsense, Elena. If the Mistress wants to bring that cat, let her bring it."

"Of course, Grandfather, if that's what the dear wants. I just thought…"

"Hell's Bells! I'll have none of it! Tonight, I'll be seen with the prettiest girl in town. If she wants to bring her cat, so be it." Gallantly taking me by the arm, he whisked me out to the terrace.

The back of Castle Mare was, if anything, more spectacular than the front. A Sea of flagstones descended upon a luscious lawn of green. Tables in white linen sprawled upon the twilight, candles perched upon a hundred iron stands. A Waterfall cascaded upon a crystal moat, graced by a chorus of regal swans.

Scores of guests filled the lawn, chatting with happy delight. When the Commodore made his entrance, the band stopped the ballad they were playing to perform a triumphant march. Every head turned to see the Commodore, the Mistress...

...and that stupid cat.

The applause was rapturous, the Commodore waving a happy salute. The exuberance died to attentive silence as he swelled his ample chest.

"Ladies and Gentlemen! Lords and Ladies! I present to you – the holy girl-child – proclaimed by the Lord God Triton! Chosen to live in the land of mortals – to live the life of mortals – so that she might do wonderful deeds. Princess Pallas, Mistress of the Sea!"

The cheers made me blush. I'd never been more embarrassed, more honored, more special in all my life. I felt a nervous urge to flee when the Old Man squeezed my hand.

"Aye, Mistress," he soothed. "They love you, they do. Right proud I am." Looking upon my trembling form, he offered a reassuring smile. "Ye can do this. I know ye can. Wouldn't have ye out here if it was more bite than ye could chew."

I took a deep breath, clamping my teeth into an artificial smile. *Why in the world is this man, this wonderful man, doing this for me?*

The applause slowly died when the Commodore signaled for quiet. "The Mistress comes to us from the wellspring of the Ocean –

born upon the Golden Egg – foretold by the Lord God Triton, voice of the mighty Sea. By Holy Poseida's generous bounty, we dedicate House Catagen – and the entirety of Her faithful subjects – to our fair Mistress…and her fateful coming."

Rabid approval. The people seemed delighted with their strange, new visitor. Awed as I was by the Commodore's oratory, I couldn't help but notice that he used Triton's exact words.

"But the Mistress is not our only important visitor tonight. Indeed, all of Catagen is honored by my trusted friend and devoted ally; the Lady of Geminus, Lord Protector of the Twins, Voting Member of the *Zoo*. Ladies and Gentlemen, please welcome Lady Gemello."

Polite applause greeted the lady and her son as they ascended the terrace, but it died more quickly than it had before. After kissing the lady on both cheeks, the Old Man shook the forearm of her son. Curious, I tried to get a better look at "Prince Bore-us-loads."

The lady blocked my view, embracing me with a formal hug. "It's so lovely to meet you," she said, pretending a smile. "Promise you'll tell me all about your adventures."

"Uh, yes, Ma'am," was all I could think to say.

The lady beamed at me nonetheless, embracing me again for good measure. She was a delicate, cultured woman with long silvery hair wrapped in a complicated beehive.

The Gemelleon prince looked sulky and bored, but he bowed just the same. I didn't know how to curtsy, or even that I should. This seemed to confuse the prince. Looking even sulkier, he kissed my hand before backing away.

Borelo was thin as well, dressed in a tight suit of yellow leather. He shared his mother's aristocratic polish and silver-white hair, its thin strands held aloft by a magic I didn't understand.

Again the Commodore raised his hand. Brandishing a winning

165

grin, he gazed upon his charges. "As you know, the Three have returned from…well, a rather extraordinary adventure!"

His subjects roared in reply, raising proud tankards in the Air. The feeling of victory was infectious; all Three home from a gallant voyage in which they rescued…

…they don't even know what they rescued, I thought. I supposed that made me even more exciting.

"So I say to you all! To the sailors, and the officers. To the wives, and the sweethearts…and I pray they never meet…"

Raucous laughter. The people loved their boisterous lord.

"House Catagen isn't strong because of its riches, nor the mighty warlords we sail. House Catagen is strong because of you – the iron sailors who sail these wooden ships!"

The crowd erupted into applause again. This was the Commodore at his best – praising his loyal shipmates, playing upon their sense of camaraderie. Waving at the band to start a merry tune, he led me into the eager throng.

He introduced me to hundreds of people. Everyone provided reverent bows, addressing me with praise and adoration. I managed a timid smile, trying to keep the flickering tail out of my face.

Why do you have to be so annoying?

Finally, the Commodore whispered, "Now, Mistress, permit an old man do some politicking, won't you?"

"Of course," I said, disengaging from his arm; grateful, really, to be left alone.

But soon the moment passed. All at once, I felt lonely in the crowd.

A minute ago, I was the epicenter of the Isle – masquerading as a mythic princess. Now, I was alone and friendless. Though the multitude awarded me a thousand curious stares, only in the Commodore's presence did they dare address me.

I felt surprisingly abandoned. Hoping to find the Twins, I looked around...

...straight into the cold, cruel eyes of Elena.

Her faultless face was spoiled with rage. I curled my lip in a vicious sneer when Bolero arrived to take her arm. Looking to see who it was, she transformed her scowl into an affectionate smile.

"Borelo," she cooed, "the delight of my eyes. Wherever have you been?"

"Mother," he sulked. "Making the rounds. You know."

"Ah, but she's so proud of you, my handsome prince," she said, pulling him even tighter. "You know how she adores showing you off."

I scoffed. *Reminds me of a toddler with a toy, crying, "Mine!"*

"I hate her," he whimpered. "Parading me around like a dog through its paces. Mingling with this rabble. Such a bore, the things I put up with."

"It's simply horrid," agreed Elena. But even she looked embarrassed by his whining.

I retreated from the multitude, seeking the solace of the gentle pool. Admiring the swans from a marble bench, I envied their sense of belonging. Swans mated for life – it was something my father once told me.

How I miss him! I thought, watching the handsome pairs amongst the floating candles. The Catagen's wealth was impressive. They'd been nothing but charitable and kind. But if I'd had my way I'd be home with my father, cooking a simple stew.

π

"What are you doing?" scorned Othello. Both irritable and hungry, he was supremely frustrated by the ignorance that surrounded him. *I'm a genius compared to everyone here; a repository of infinite knowledge. Yet I must keep my silence while this fool of a cub mumbles incoherent sentences.* "I can't learn anything over here!"

"What do you want me to do?"

"Mingle. Party. You know…meet people. For a man hath no better thing than to drink and be merry."

"You've got the wrong girl, Othello. I was never good at these things."

"Jupiter's Moons! What I have to work with!"

"Who is Jupiter? And does he really have moons?"

He looked at his pupil with utter disdain. *At least she's honest,* he thought to himself, *at least she realizes her limitations.* But in Othello's line of business, honesty was rarely the best policy. "You wouldn't understand."

"Try me."

"Maybe later. I need you to talk to that Borelo character."

"Why?"

Why indeed, he thought.

Lord Gemello, Borelo's grandfather, was an unabashed troublemaker, disliked by many in the *Zoo*. Indeed, his abusive behavior nearly lost his family's charter of Protector of the Twins when he declared war upon House Catagen. The Commodore answered with a daring raid, destroying the store houses of Geminus.

Immediately after the expensive fiasco, Lord Gemello died a mysterious death. Further disaster was averted when the lord's eldest daughter, Lady Gemello, salvaged her Houses' fortunes by cutting a deal with House Catagen.

Othello knew the man-cub, with her miserable education, would know nothing of the small war. But to him it was priceless knowledge. *For it shows how desperate the Commodore has become…and what a cunning schemer! Now that the Earth has turned against him, he needs to form an alliance with the Air.*

"Master Borelo comes from a very important House," he said. He could have told her more, of course, but his training wouldn't allow it.

"No! I won't."

"You'd rather sit here and pout."

"Yes, I would."

π

"There you are," said a voice behind me. "I've been looking for you all night."

Borelo stood before me in all his amber glory. In a single motion, he took my hands, staring longingly into my eyes. "Really Pallas, you should be more kind. It's wrong to hide your beauty amongst the shadows of the night."

"What?"

"Please, my Lady. Allow me just one dance. It pains me to look at you and not be by your side."

"You looked pretty content with Elena at your side," I said, liking the prince of Geminus less and less. *Lying to all these people is one thing. Escaping the wrath of a God, I can handle. But I'm not going to play nice with this insolent prince!*

"Elena?"

"Yeah…like the girl who was dripping all over you a minute ago?"

"Oh, her. She's…nice. But you, Pallas," he said with a dashing smile. "You are a woman of distinction and flair. I can see adventure glowing in your brilliant, blue eyes."

"They're gray," I retorted, seeing in his eyes, two orbs of deceit. *Why is he acting this way? Just a minute ago, he couldn't care less about me. Now I'm a woman of distinction and flair?*

"So they are," he cooed. "Very rare. Very rare, indeed."

I wanted to pull away, but the Commodore spotted us together. He gave me a jovial thumbs-up, as if happy we were getting along. The band started a waltz. Borelo insisted we dance.

"Please, my Lady. For my honor."

Othello pounced to the ground, looking happy. Grateful to be rid of one pest, I reluctantly followed the other.

We danced. I knew how, as my father had taught me. I'd never considered how he, a slave, learned to dance like the nobility. Yet now I wondered amongst the suits and gowns.

If Borelo didn't like being a show dog, he certainly didn't mind being the trainer. The prince of Geminus dazzled the crowd, twirling his famous partner for everyone to see. I smiled, pretending to enjoy myself, when I fell upon the malevolent gaze of Elena.

For a moment, I savored my sweet revenge.

Yet the hurt in her eyes left me empty and cold.

As the band finished the waltz, the Gemelleon prince made the traditional bow. I didn't know I was supposed to curtsy; my father never taught me that part. Instead, I turned and raced away. Borelo tried to follow but Elena intercepted him, urgently waylaying her wayward warrior.

π

For some reason the man-cub was hiding behind a tree.

Ah-hah! thought Othello. *Perhaps she told Borelo to meet her there, using her feminine wiles to seduce him. How exquisitely clever.*

Othello thought humans gangly and pale, *with so little fur to hide those horrible wrinkles!* But from years of studying the species, he knew the cub was attractive for her kind...

...*until she opens that adolescent mouth.*

"So," he asked, "what did you find out?"

"I found out he's a stuck-up jerk."

"Yes, yes. But when are you going to meet him? Later tonight?"

He had to scamper up the tree to avoid being kicked.

"Meet him?" she snarled. "I told you! He's a jerk!"

"So?" he growled, perched upon a limb. "Whether you like him or not is completely beside the point. Do you think I help *you* because I enjoy your company?"

"I have no idea!" she riled. "Because you won't *tell* me!"

"There you are!" said Casey.

Oh great! thought the cat. *Tweedle-dee and Tweedle-dum!*

"Honestly," Lucy said. "We've been looking everywhere. Why don't you join the party?"

"I don't know," she demurred.

"I'm not much for these either," said Casey.

"At least the grub's good," Lucy said.

"I'm not hungry."

"Maybe your kitty is. Weren't you saying...?"

Why yes, man-cub, what a marvelous idea. Think about someone else for a change... He pounced from the limb onto his pupil's shoulders, careful to extend his razor-sharp claws.

"Ouch!" she winced. "Why do you keep doing that?"

"Maybe he's hungry," cooed Lucy.

"Oh...all right," said the slave, following the princesses to the opulent tables. "Let's see if there's anything his majesty would like."

Of course, there were quite a few things Othello liked – yards and yards of marvelous wares.

"Here's something he might fancy," said Casey as she pointed at an ornate bowl.

"Eew," said the man-cub, scrunching up her nose. "That's disgusting."

"It's caviar," Lucy announced. "It's rather dear. I've a mind your puss would like some."

"Meow!" *Now that's more like it!*

"I don't think so," she frowned, turning to a pyramid of oranges.

172

Excuse me? Uttering a warning growl, he wrestled to rid himself of her arms.

"Stop that!"

"Meeeooow!"

She planted a hand on his head, trying to push him back into her arms.

He met her hand with a savage rake.

The man-cub winced with pain, crimson streaking across her thumb. "Mangy animal!"

Othello ignored her, springing over the halibut to bury his head in the caviar.

People stared. The man-cub grew red with embarrassment.

Let that be another lesson! thought Othello. *After your schooling aboard that ship, I'd have thought you'd learned by now.*

"Look what you've done," said Lucy. "You've hurt poor kitty's feelings."

Humph! he thought. *Not likely.*

He allowed Lucy to collect him in her arms, along with the bowl of caviar. Casey filled a plate of fish.

They're a bit precocious, he thought of the princesses. *Still, they do make adequate servants.*

The man-cub made a plate for herself, containing mostly fruit.

Pathetic.

π

I followed the Twins to a solitary bench. The little monster dove into his feast; I merely picked at mine. I was furious with shame, certain that everyone was talking about my unmanageable pet. The Twins wisely kept us separated, trying to cheer me up by pointing out people they knew. But the kaleidoscope of faces made me feel homesick.

Lucy seemed to sense my sadness. "I know, Casey. Let's show Pallas the Waterfall!"

"Capital idea!" said Casey, grabbing me by the arm. In a moment we were racing through the castle, Lucy carrying the horrible fury.

"I thought we were going to the Waterfall," I said.

"Behind the Waterfall," Casey explained. "There's a secret passage."

We stopped at a tapestry of a woman holding a swan.

"Who's that?"

"Grandmother," Casey told me.

"She absolutely adored swans," said Lucy.

Checking to see that no one was coming, we slid behind the thick cloth. Casey smoothed her hands along the stone, looking for a secret protrusion.

"There!" she whispered. "Help me push."

I doubtfully obeyed. To my astonishment, a hidden door slid noiselessly open.

"Hurry in before it closes."

I jumped inside just in time. Surrounded by the sudden darkness, I was mesmerized by a tiny, blinking light.

"What's that?" I asked, amazed.

"A key-pad lock," said Casey. "A gift from Poseida. *You* of all people should know about that."

But I had never seen a key-pad before, as I had never been to Atlantis. Intrigued, I touched the fascinating light. It magically illuminated a small panel. Twelve buttons appeared, each with a different number: 0 through 9, and a # and a * symbol I didn't recognize.

"You *have* seen one before!" said Lucy. "Look, Casey. Pallas knows how to work it."

But I wasn't listening. In the top right corner of nearly all the buttons were three tiny markings...

"Do you know what these are?" I said, pointing at the "ABC" on the number "2" button.

"No," Lucy said. "No one does."

"They're letters! Letters of the alphabet!"

Othello catapulted out of Lucy's arms, landing on my chest.

I gaped in sudden horror. "Sorry!" I apologized, wincing at his claws.

"Sorry?" said the Twins.

"Yeah...I...I just meant, uh...shouldn't we be going to the Waterfall?"

"Hang on," said Casey. "You just said..."

"No, I didn't!"

"Yes, you did! You said these were 'letters' – and something about 'All fall bets.'"

175

I nearly cried with frustration. *How could I be so stupid?*

Then I looked at the ferocious cat. I'd forgotten how poisonous those eyes could be; his snake-like pupils bathed in the low, red light. *It's like holding a viper,* I thought, nearly dropping him out of pure fright.

But the fear of dropping him was even greater.

"Look..." Casey started.

But Lucy interrupted. "Call it Pax," she said, stroking Othello's back. I didn't know if she was trying to calm the cat or me. "We jolly well know there are all sorts of things you can't tell us at the moment. When it's quite convenient, you'll tell us the whole lot, won't you?"

"Yes," I said, grateful. "Yes, I will. I promise."

"Come on," said Lucy, gathering my arm. "Let's tour the Waterfall."

But Casey gave me a suspicious glare.

The tunnel went on for about two hundred yards before opening into a cave. The Air was thick and cool, with a delicious wet fragrance I couldn't quite describe. The cascading roar was like the breaking of the waves, tossed upon the gentle Eastern shore. I closed my eyes, pretending I was home...

"Isn't it amazing?" said Lucy. Lights from the party shone eerily through the mist, the veil of the Water separating us from another reality. "It's one of my very favorite places."

"Yeah," I whispered.

π

The Alpha females talked for hours, sharing stories about their ancestral Isle. Giggling over their mischievous tales, they told the man-cub how to avoid Elena, what to do if Borelo was pestering her, and how to soften up the Catagen lord.

Othello pretended to nap. In truth, he harvested every fact, fascinated by the princesses' clandestine prowess. *Just proves the power of genetics,* he reminded himself; cataloguing every scrap of information into his endless repertoire of covert intelligence.

When they seemed talked out, Lucy suggested they rejoin the party. "All the nobility will be gone by now, and we can have the run of the place."

Sleepy-eyed, the man-cub agreed. She stood up to leave when voices interrupted their solitude.

"What are we doing? Mist is collecting on my new dress."

The girls hid behind some rocks. Elena and Borelo appeared in a rowboat, concealed within the Watery curtain. Despite Elena's protests, they were both quite dry.

"I thought you wanted to be alone," said Borelo.

"Not *this* alone," scolded Elena.

"I'll tell you my secret."

The princess pretended a sullen pout, rolling his hair around her delicate fingers. "It's naught of thee to use me so. Take heart of grace, dear prince, and tell me truly."

Remarkable! thought the cat, impressed.

Borelo trembled with eagerness, feasting his eyes on the most beautiful girl alive. "All right. But first, you must give me a kiss."

She withdrew her hand from his wispy mane. "You're a rum

little dreamer."

"It's about Pallas," he tempted, "and the Egg."

The man-cub gasped with terror.

Othello purred.

Elena raised her pencil-thin eyebrows, as if making a political computation. Her calculation complete, she addressed the prince of Geminus. "Tell me, dear Borelo, and I'll give *you* a kiss."

Jupiter's Moons! thought Othello. *She's using him like a tool!*

"I'll tell you!" he cried with boyish glee. "Mother heard it this afternoon, shortly after the Three arrived. She said it came from a spy."

"How perfectly thrilling!" she feigned with delight. "Do say on, dear prince."

Borelo crept closer, so close his silver locks mingled with her golden strands. "It's a prophecy, sent from the Gods. A prophecy about a girl."

Othello twitched his whiskers with eager anticipation. *It will be interesting to see if he gets the rhythm right…*

"What…kind of girl?" Elena growled.

"Born of the Sea, hatched from the Egg – child of Atlantis, God with us. For she shall herald a glorious Age, and they shall call it…Aquarius."

Othello smiled. *Quite charming, if I do say so myself.*

Elena's eyes grew large as saucers, sapphire spoiling to jade. "And you think…you think this prophecy is about Pallas?"

"She rode on a dolphin, didn't she? The Egg came from the Sea. Isn't it obvious she's a child of Atlantis?"

Her eyes changed from green to a loathsome crimson sheen. "Take me back! This very instant!"

"What about my kiss?"

"Bosh! You can forget about that!"

"But...you promised," pleaded the prince.

"Here," she said, roughly seizing his hand. She gave it a spiteful peck before flinging it in his face.

Chapter Thirteen

A Day at the Beach

Prophecy is an odd thing. Until it is accepted it is nothing more than idle prattle, an incoherent guess better described as nonsense. Yet once it is believed it takes on a life of its own, an indomitable juggernaught even the Gods are powerless to stop...

Kassan

A prophecy – about me?

My mind whirled at the consequences of this unwelcome message. *"For she shall herald a glorious age..." Who came up with such nonsense?*

But one look at Othello told me all I needed to know.

We waited for the quarreling lovebirds to leave.

"Can you believe it?" said Lucy.

"How perfectly wonderful!" said Casey.

"How is this wonderful?" I said, crushed by the cryptic revelation.

"Oh, what nonsense," Casey grinned. "You *are* a funny goose."

"I told you she was smart," said her twin. "She's been pretending all this time, making us believe she's a blithering idiot."

"Well, she's certainly a jolly good actress."

"I mean to say," added Lucy, "we knew you were important when Triton popped out of the Sea..."

"...and now we know why!"

"You *did* come from Atlantis!"

I kept my anxious silence, too frightened to say a single word. *Yeah...blithering idiot. That's what I do best.*

"Oh, bother," said Lucy. "Back to that, are we?"

"Mum's the word," laughed Casey, a little more pleasantly now that she knew I was from heaven.

"Borelo knows," Lucy said.

"Bother, that is a problem."

"Loose lips sink ships," Lucy said. "If Lady Gemello knows, she's sure to tell Lord Tel."

"Why?" I asked.

"Because," Casey chided, "they're Air Houses, silly."

∞

I was absolutely furious by the time I went to bed. *Isn't my life complicated enough without all these stupid lies?* "Did you know about this prophecy...thing?"

181

"Not telling!" sang Othello in his tiny, tenor voice.

"*You* did this!"

He danced his tail in a spirited jig. "Me? Why would I make up such a nasty little lie?"

"Because...you're a manipulative little monster."

"Monster?" he laughed. "Now there's a compliment."

"Yeah, well...you deserve it," I said, biting my nails.

"I suspect Poseida started the prophecy. Wasn't it she who ordered the Commodore to protect you?"

"No. It was Triton, didn't you hear?"

"Triton is just a mouthpiece, nothing more. Remember that, young man-cub. Poseida is the brains behind Atlantis."

"But I don't even believe in the Gods!"

He laughed again. "The fool hath said there is no God."

I angrily punched my pillow before placing it behind my head. "Listen! I hate Poseida. I want nothing to do with that stupid wench."

"A rather inane idea, as you've obviously been chosen to be her new Token."

"Her new what?"

"Token. Puppet. Crusader. Pawn. Call it what you like."

"What are you talking about?"

He seemed ready to scowl a shrill response when he suddenly stopped himself. Instead, he recomposed his face into a patient frown. "Like it or not, your fate is tied to Poseida – ever since you climbed into that raft."

"Tie me to some other God's fate! I don't care who. Maybe Zephyr, or Terra, or…"

"Poseida is your future. There can be no debate. You will love her, worship her, cling to her powerful side."

"You are so stupid! I hate her, didn't you hear?"

"You'll do as I say," he warned, "or you'll end up as an epitaph." Then he leapt out of the open window.

I jumped from my bed and called out to the night. "I hate Poseida! D'ya hear? I hate her, and I always will!"

∞

I lived like a princess the entire summer, enjoying the friendship of the raucous Twins. Our adventures took us all over the Isle, climbing mountains, playing on beaches, riding horses on the rambling moors. I loved our daily jaunts. Soon, we became quite close.

Othello seemed happier in his pampered surroundings, so much so he actually mellowed enough to be marginally tolerable. Every now and then, he even forgot to be mean to me, though he did insist we read every night.

Elena was worse. She continued, as always, to harass the Twins. For me, however, she harbored a long-suffering hatred.

And there was so much to hate me for. Prior to my coming, the Isle had been suffering from a three-year drought. Yet this summer they had plenty of rain. And the rains didn't come during the daytime when farmers were working, but at night when everyone was safe in their beds.

The sheep grew larger, their wool was softer, and several ewes had twins. There was plenty of corn in the fields that year, and the fishermen's nets were full to the brim.

Even worse, the great oak in front of Castle Mare – planted in honor of the old dead lord – whispered riddles in the night. Invisible fairies spread their splendor; singing songs of magical delight.

The reason for these miracles? Me…of course! So said the vapid Water Jesters. Their fawning homilies added to my aura, and the jealous venom in Elena's eyes.

The Catagens were odd about their worship. They visited the Water Temple at least once a week, revering Poseida more than anyone I'd ever known. Yet they kept the Jesters at a guarded distance and never imbibed their sacred *ambrosia*.

I asked the Twins why.

"The Old Man doesn't like it," said Lucy. "Says it clouds the mind."

"It's for slaves," said Casey. "You know. To control them."

It was funny. Father had told me the very same thing.

The only time I felt self-conscious was when I mingled with the slaves. After all, I had been one of them – *was* one of them – but for the clever lies of the duplicitous cat. But I shelved my qualms within my joys, savoring the delicious life of a princess.

As for the boys in my life, they completely disappeared. Thankfully, Borelo left a few days after the party. But Oliver was gone as well, at Sea aboard *Enterprise* with Captain Tiberius. The Twins pleaded like lost kittens to go as well, but Elena insisted they stay, "…to take the salt out of your tongues."

"Blimey!" Casey swore. "What did the broad mean by that?"

"Bloody hell!" said Lucy. "You know what these landlubbers are like."

So I spent an entire boy-free summer, the nobility working their magic on the slave from Kelly Tree.

Yet as happy as I was, I could never stop thinking about my father. *How lonely he must be! He lost his wife and his daughter on that same, hateful shore.* How the villagers must be taunting him after what happened that horrible, wintry night.

My only solace was Othello.

He was also my greatest curse.

He was the only one who understood my inner conflicts, my desperate desire to go back home. Yet I couldn't help thinking that it was *because* of Othello that I couldn't return.

Was the cat the author of all my problems, or had he truly saved my life? I couldn't decide.

So I hid from this disturbing paradox as if hiding from myself. For it was easier to live a handsome lie than to struggle for a difficult truth.

If I felt a pang of guilt, it was at night when I lay in bed. Sometimes, as I lolled off to sleep, I said a silent vow...

Tomorrow I'll do it. Tomorrow I'll escape.

But tomorrow never came, as each morning found me lost in another carefree day.

But stories have a way of making pleasant times hurry while difficult ones seem to linger. Summer swept by in a blissful haze until something interrupted my happy recess.

Unexpectedly, the offending party was the arrival of *Hornet.* Though the Twins were ecstatic about the return of their father,

Hornet's cargo also contained the Prince of Gemello.

Borelo would be staying at Castle Mare for a week.

We girls would be staying away.

∞

It was a wet, wintry night. The toddler lay safe in her father's arms, giggling at his funny faces. Her mother sang a sad and lilting lullaby, a song she hadn't heard before.

But her singing was cut short by a blow to the door. Merciless soldiers, cold and cruel, roughly seized her father. The toddler cried, torn from his embrace, as they dragged him out into the freezing rain...

"Father!" I cried, leaping out of my bed.

π

Watching from a corner was a cunning pair of eyes. Observant and calculating, they followed his pupil like a pitiless predator.

"That nightmare of yours is getting stronger, isn't it?"

"Yes," whispered the man-cub.

"That's the sixth one this week."

"I...I know," she panted, clutching her pillow in a desperate hug.

"Why don't you tell me what it is? Maybe I can help."

The nervous teen curled her lip. "I'll never tell you. Never."

Never? he snorted, amused. *What a delicious challenge!* "Just remember, young man-cub. Never is a very long time."

∞

We did a spectacular job for an entire week, hiding from Borelo and the love-sick princess. It was something of a game, seeing how far we could stay away from the insipid pair.

But the Commodore wrecked our plans when he announced he wanted all of us to go to the beach together.

"Now, now," he said over breakfast, "I want you lassies to put a good face on it. Tomorrow, the lot of them are going back home, and you haven't spent a lick of time with them."

"We hate those flighty Wind-folk," Casey complained, "Borelo in particular."

"Do ye think I like them any better? The whole point of having them here is so you'll all get along when you get to be my age."

"What, a hundred and sixty-three?"

"Lucy," scolded her father.

"Nay, lass," said the Old Man, "I'm not a day over a hundred and sixty-two, and don't ye forget it!"

The whole table laughed.

"Not made of skin and bones, ye know, but rope and steel. Wooden ships and iron men...aye, that's what's needed 'round here."

"Speaking of iron men, Father," Dewey said, "I understand *Enterprise's* 'tour' of Capro Bay was quite successful."

"Aye, Tiberius! Now there's a lad who knows how to sail a ship!"

"Father is the best sailor alive!" said Casey.

"Apart from you, Grandfather," Lucy added with a wink.

"Quite the charmer ye are, my lass. And in a few weeks ye shall all be sailing as well, all the way to Greenstone."

"But Grandfather," Lucy implored, "you *are* going to let Pallas come to University, aren't you?"

The Commodore seemed sorry he brought up the tender subject. "Now, now...let an old dog lie. Ye know my mind on that."

"But it's *so* unfair," Casey said. "How is she going to learn about politics if she doesn't go to University?"

"Ye know those Fire fools. The Mistress is much safer here on the Isle."

"You can't keep her here forever!"

"Not forever," he said to his sausage and eggs. Then he stared my way, wide-eyed, with the same deference he always used when speaking to me. "Poseida told me to protect you, Mistress. Triton's Waves, that's what *this* sailor's going to do."

Elena chose this moment to join breakfast. Sauntering to the table, she gave both her father and her grandfather a kiss on the cheek. The cold, angry glare she reserved for me was firmly in place, though it melted into a pleasant smile when she asked her father for the jelly.

"There was a yellow canary in the foyer this morning," sang Casey. "Dead, just like the others."

"We've had a dead canary every morning since those flighty Wind-folk arrived," said Lucy.

"You know what the servants are saying," chided Casey. "They're saying Poseida is causing those canaries to die – as a warning to those worthless Gemelleons."

"What an idiotic superstition," said the beauty.

I lowered my eyes to hide from Elena, to discover her reflection in the silver chaffing dish. Her face was murderous, her cheeks were Flame...as if *I* was the cause of these unexplained portents.

When I know very well it was Othello! I rued. *He's been doing all sorts of crazy things to convince these people of that stupid prophecy!* I didn't know how he could possibly control the weather, but was sure the "fairies in the tree" were nothing more than the deceitful cat.

"Sounds like the prophecy about Aquarius is already coming true," laughed Lucy. "What do you think, Grandfather?"

He rumbled an incoherent response, stuffing his mouth with a large wedge of cheese.

We ate in quiet conversation until Lieutenant O'Brien marched into the room.

"Mr. O'Brien," huffed the Old Man. "Can't it wait till after breakfast?"

"Commodore," he said with a sharp salute, "*Enterprise* just arrived from Greenstone...with some very important news."

"Very well," he growled. "Go on, Lieutenant."

"I, uh..." he stammered. "Perhaps in your office, Sir?"

"Nonsense, man," he said with a wave of his fork, "we're all family here. Out with it."

"Yes, Sir…well," he paused, "it's, uh…it's about the Mistress."

"Triton's Waves!" the Old Man swore, bolting out of the room.

∞

The three of us reluctantly meandered to the stables. Unfortunately, Borelo and his friends were already there. The Gemelleon prince was never without these five "friends" that Casey called "bodyguards," all of them much older than he. Personally, they gave me the creeps.

Oliver, who had just arrived on *Enterprise*, was there as well. Nor did he look happy about it, staring at Borelo with rude dislike.

I wonder if the Old Man made him come?

That's when I saw him – the tall, dark stranger. Muscular and strong, short dark hair perched upon graceful shoulders, he locked his hazel eyes on mine.

I wrenched away from that perilous face to harbor in the shelter of my harmless friend.

Oliver greeted me with a halfhearted smile. "My apologies, Mistress. Allow me to present my good friend, Liam."

"Liam?" I laughed, hiding my surprising insecurity with a careless jibe. I'd never ever fallen for a boy; I'd never given them a second thought. Yet the stranger's stare was a sharp scalpel…deep, cutting, precise. "Just Liam? Isn't he the son of some nobleman, or crown prince of a great House, or some such rot?"

"Liam's…a friend," said Oliver. His voice retained its steady quality, yet his eyes were strangely amiss. "A friend who is, um...serving aboard *Enterprise*."

"Is he a servant or a friend?" I asked, annoyed with Oliver's evasion. I'd never known the forthright midshipman to be anything less than honest with me.

"Both," said Liam with a wide, handsome grin. Haughty beauty poured from his eyes, dazzling my eyes in a glorious aurora. "I no longer call you servant, for the servant knows not what his lord doeth. Henceforth, therefore...I call you friend."

I stood there and stared, my mouth idiotically open. The stranger sounded like Othello and my father all at the same time.

Borelo seized upon my distraction by laying a prying hand around my waist. "Servants are, I'm sorry to say, the only friends Oliver has."

I escaped the arrogant prince with a brusque of my shoulders, pointedly striding towards my favorite saddle. Picking up the heavy burden, I struggled over to my favorite horse.

"Let me help," said Liam, attempting to take my saddle.

"No," I growled, heaving the leather on her withers. The handsome stranger scared me somehow, frightening my heart into a pattering pace. "I can do it myself."

"Of course, Bright-Eyes. I meant no disrespect. It's just...I find that many hands make light work."

"Is that right?" I drawled. "Well, I find that boys who think girls can't do a thing by themselves are obnoxious jerks."

Casey laughed out loud. Lucy rolled her elfin eyes. But Liam broke into a happy grin. "A sharp-witted damsel who's hardly in distress! Are there more of your kind on this little Isle?"

"There are three in this barn," mocked Casey.

"And we're all good shots," said Lucy. In unison, both the Twins twanged the string on their bows.

The bold splendor laughed. "Then I shall resign myself to your Amazon race, to the elixir that flows through your cloven breast!"

I coughed rudely at this weird remark, unsure what to think of the mysterious stranger. Dressed like a stable boy, he spoke with the tongue of kingly nobility. Muscles bulging with gorgeous hair, he sported the physique of a Pentathanon God.

My heart pumped wildly as I retreated to the Twins. Casey, who had a gift for horses, was helping Lucy tighten her horse's girth. A quiet tension permeated the stable as we girls ignored the boys and the boys refused to talk to each other.

Her golden hair tied in an elaborate bun, Elena finally arrived. *I bet she spent half the morning arranging that.* She wore a pink silk shirt which gathered around her features and leather riding pants that accentuated her long, shapely legs. Taking a moment to acknowledge the stranger, her smile turned lovingly towards uncaring Borelo. The Air prince turned disdainfully away. I didn't know or care why.

Liam brought Elena her horse, saddled and ready. No one expected Elena to saddle a horse. We wordlessly set off, Oliver and Liam in the lead. Elena kept near Borelo, who ignored her completely, while the Twins and I held a distant rear. After riding the moor a few hours, we arrived at a rocky cove.

The pebbly shore the Catagens called a beach made me long for the sugar-white sands of Kelly Tree. *A "beach" implies sand,* I thought, and there was no sand upon the Isle of Catagen. After swimming in the cold brisk Water, the Twins and I gathered our towels, climbed a low cliff, and lay in the sun.

"I can't believe he made us take those Wind Bags," Casey bitterly complained.

"Which Wind Bag are you talking about?" I asked.

"Borelo, of course!" said Casey.

"Oh," I said. "Well…Elena doesn't seem to mind."

"He's such a twit," said Lucy. "What can she see in him?"

"He is a prince," I said.

"Don't even start," Casey warned.

"Those bodyguards are so unnerving," said Lucy.

"What do you think Oliver is?" said Casey. "I think you're right, Pallas. The Old Man ordered him to come."

"I think he fancies you," teased Lucy.

"If he does," I said, "he has a funny way of showing it."

"What about that Liam?" asked Lucy.

"He is absolutely divine!" said Casey.

But before we could discuss the subject further, we heard someone climbing up the rocks. Poking his head over the low cliff was Borelo, his silver hair curled into delicate locks any girl would be proud to own. "Ladies, of your courtesy. May I join you?"

"If you must," said Casey. As if on cue, we closed our eyes in unison, laying our heads on our towels.

"Marvelous view," he flattered. "The waves, the rocks, the sunlit Sky, and three bathing beauties."

"I thought the view you were interested in was down on the beach," I quipped.

"Quite the wit, my Lady. Your intellect is rivaled only by your radiance."

I didn't answer.

There was a long silence before he tried again. "Perhaps you'd like to stroll with me. Just the two of us."

"I don't think so."

"Come. You'd be surprised what I could show you."

"With or without your bodyguards?"

"You wound me, my Lady. They are my cherished friends."

"OK. With or without your 'friends?'"

"Without, of course."

"I don't think so."

"Fine," he sulked, "suit yourself." With that, he mercifully left.

∞

We lay there for over an hour, the Twins falling fast asleep. But I was wide awake, unable to force Borelo out of my mind. *Why is he so interested in me?* As I did my best thinking on my feet, I decided to go for a walk.

Again, I rued the absence of the sugar-white sand. The shore on the Isle was impossible to walk along as it was interrupted by high, jagged rocks. So I left the tiny cove, walking inland towards a stream that gurgled down a ravine. I carelessly ambled along, turning left around a fig tree, when I heard a girl's voice.

"Stop it!" she cried. "Get your hands off me!"

"Give me a kiss."

"No! Get your filthy hands…"

I heard a slap, then a splash of Water. Rounding the corner, I found Borelo standing over Elena. She was prostrate in the stream, her pink shirt ripped asunder, covered in mud.

I charged without thinking, reckless and brash. In three angry strides I was on him. He looked up with astonishment, too late to avoid my punishing right cross. Flying backwards, he landed clumsily into the brook. I nearly fell in as well, but managed to right myself above the fallen princess.

"How dare you!" seethed Borelo, wiping blood from his mouth. "Leave now! Or the fury of Tornado…"

"Shut up!" I shouted, reverting to my street-fighter antagonism. "*You* leave."

But Borelo remained, sitting in the stream, making absolutely no effort to stand. He seemed to be waiting for something.

I helped Elena out of the Water. The princess was crying, holding her mangled shirt together with her hands. She was almost on her feet when she slipped on a stone, nearly falling in again.

That's when Borelo's "friends" arrived; four were in front, one behind. Now that he outnumbered me six to one, the prince finally rose, popping something in his mouth. Dirt and blood clotted his hair. The look didn't really suit him.

"You should have left," he sneered. "Now…I'm going to teach you a lesson."

I was scared. Quickly, logically, I considered my options. I could run, but I knew Elena wouldn't follow. *And I'm not going to leave her to that despicable prince!* I could fight. *Still – six against one – all of them bigger than me.* I looked down. Out of the corner of my eye I could see Borelo step towards me. Best do what I had to do quickly…

I turned as if to flee, then wheeled around to plant a savage kick in Borelo's stomach. The prince groaned in reply, crumpling back into the stream. I picked up a stone and threw it at the one behind me. His nose blossomed red as he fell upon the ground, holding his face in agony.

I wheeled around again. The four were almost on me. *I can't handle all of them!* They were simply too big. Still, I resolved to go down swinging as I braced for the coming blow.

The blow came, but not from the direction I expected. Flying from atop the low cliff came Liam, kicking two of the bodyguards with heavy boots. They toppled to the ground and writhed in the dirt as my savior tumbled to his nimble feet. Quick as lightning Oliver appeared, ferociously pummeling the other two. Then he turned on Borelo.

"Worthless waif!" he snarled, with a ferocity I hardly believed of the boy. "How dare you?"

Borelo considered his new opponent. Sporting a wicked grin, he grabbed a knife from his boot.

Oliver laughed. "Put that down…or I'll cut you up like a jigsaw puzzle."

A blank stare washed over Borelo's face. Reconsidering, he dropped the knife.

Oliver spat in disgust, apparently disappointed. He turned to face me when Borelo erupted out of the brook. A new knife in hand – I didn't see where it came from – leapt at Oliver's back.

"Oliver!" I screamed.

Borelo thrust his knife…

But Oliver was ready. He spun left just in time, making Borelo miss badly to the right. Grabbing his exposed shoulder, the sailor plastered the prince into the stream. Oliver howled with maddening rage, brandishing his fists, ready to pounce…

"Stop!" Elena shouted.

To my vast surprise, he did, checking his savage attack. "You," he huffed between heaving breaths, "you…all right, Mistress?"

"Yeah, I'm, uh…thanks," I said.

"Elena?" he grunted.

"I'm fine," she said as she closed her eyes, willing herself into a state of composure.

Liam bowed his head, sensing Elena's shame. "I'll just go and…look after the Twins."

"Yes," whispered Elena. "Yes, of your courtesy, please do."

"Oliver?" asked Liam.

"Good idea," said Oliver. "I've got it from here."

Liam nodded to Oliver before sprinting towards the beach.

Elena bowed her head for a long moment, looking as if she might cry. Then, with all the dignity her beleaguered state would allow, she raised her chin in her trademark display of superiority. "Fie for shame, Oliver! Fighting like a common street urchin."

I gasped aloud. *You have got to be kidding!*

Oliver pretended to ignore her. "Fury of Tornado!" he spat at the prince. "You're nothing but a putrid draft."

The prince huddled shamefully in the Water. "I'll remember this, Oliver. Borelo doesn't forget his debts…or his debtors."

"Arrogant to the end. That's what I like about you Wind Bags."

"Stop it, Oliver!" Elena ordered.

The mariner fell ruefully silent.

You're not telling Borelo to stop! I thought, resenting the princess

197

more than ever. *How can you defend that Gemelleon beast?*

"Come, Oliver," said Elena, as if speaking to a dog. She started walking towards the beach, holding her head as high as she possibly could.

"Here," said Oliver, pulling off his naval jacket and handing it to Elena, "I'll be right along."

"You'll come now," she commanded. "I don't want any more fighting."

"I'll wait to let you put that on, then I'll be right along."

Elena paused, nodded, and then strode towards the beach.

I hesitated. Oliver was surrounded by six felled foes.

"Go on, Mistress," he said. "Stay with Elena."

I reluctantly obeyed, hurrying to find the tall beauty huddled behind the fig tree. Quivering with rage, she was trying with difficulty to put the jacket on over her torn silk shirt.

"Here, let me help you," I said.

"Don't touch me!" she snapped.

I fell sadly silent, not knowing what to say.

Elena was so upset, she couldn't get her arms into the sleeves. Fumbling like a toddler who didn't know how to dress herself, she wrestled with the jacket for an agonizing minute before furiously tossing it to the ground. I picked it up and followed, checking to see that Oliver was coming. He was dutifully shadowing us, staying about a hundred feet behind.

We finally reached the cliff where the Twins were sunbathing. Only they weren't there. I looked anxiously about to find them playing in the surf. Liam was on the beach, evidently guarding them.

I bit my lip as I turned to Elena. *I know she absolutely hates me.* I knew I couldn't heal her wrong. Still…I wanted to say something, *anything,* to soothe her hurt. But the princess' haughty face wordlessly demanded she be left alone.

Sighing, I turned to go…

"*I* used to be the prettiest girl in town."

"What?" I faltered, certain I'd misheard.

"Grandfather. At the party. He said he wanted to be with the prettiest girl in town."

I had to think. *The party was months ago. What could she possibly be talking about?*

Then I remembered. *The Old Man did say that, just before he introduced me to the crowd.*

I huffed, still smarting from months of vicious stares. "You *are* the prettiest girl in town."

My nemesis turned to face me, her porcelain cheeks streaked with tears. Her clothes were torn and filthy, her makeup was smuged and smeared. She clutched her shirt defensively, her delicate hands trembling with rage. Her sapphire eyes were sad, and for the first time…honest. "You're…you're just saying that."

"I'm not. In fact, you're the prettiest girl I ever saw." I didn't like admitting this, even to myself.

Elena frowned, quickly changing tack. "But you are ever so brave."

"Brave?"

"Away from your home, battling lords and ladies and childish princes. Look at me. I'd be nothing if I wasn't surrounded by my family, its power and its wealth."

"I'd trade if I could. I didn't ask for this."

"I know," she said. "You could pout and whine…like I do. But you don't, do you?"

"I guess," I said, unused to fetching compliments from the teenage matron.

Elena stared dejectedly at the ground. "I really admire you, Pallas. I wish," she sighed, "I wish I could be more like you."

"I wish I could be more like you." I'd heard it was the sort of things girls said to each other at times like these.

"Petty, self-conceited, proud..."

"No. Elegant, cultured, smart." I turned from the princess to stare at the Sea. "I wanted to be friends. It's just, you were always so…"

"Evil?"

I shrugged.

"I've been absolutely horrid," she confessed. "Jealous, I shouldn't wonder."

"Jealous of what?" I brandished. "You're an incredibly beautiful girl who lives in a gorgeous home full of wonderful people who love you." Again, I turned mournfully to the lonely Sea. "I have none of those things."

"Yes you do," said Elena, featuring her first true smile. Grasping my hands, she shrugged, "You have us."

I gazed into the tear-stained face, still wary of the teenage tyrant.

But before I could think of anything to say, she graced me with an earnest embrace – the princess' tears falling gratefully upon my peasant shoulders.

Chapter Fourteen

Rising Sophomores

In the early days, most great Houses considered the 'New Age' myth to be just that, a fabrication created by the Aquarians to destabilize the delicate Balance of Power. But closer research reveals that it was not the Aquarians who floated the myth, but an obscure source...

"Rise and Fall of the Pentathanon Gods"

Herodotus III

The ride to Castle Mare was somber. The Twins were curious why we were leaving without "Bore-us-loads." Oliver explained that Elena wanted to go home early to prepare his farewell feast. He and Liam rode a horse length behind Elena who led our solemn way.

Elena spoke not a single word.

I busied myself with the Twins, yet my mind lingered on the despicable prince. Eventually I couldn't stand it any longer. *I've got to talk to her,* I thought as I led my horse abreast Elena's.

A single tear drained down her porcelain face.

"Don't worry," I said, "the Old Man will set Borelo right."

"Oh, but Pallas," she said. "We mustn't tell Grandfather."

"Why not?"

"If I have to explain," she said. "Pallas, please. Promise me you won't breathe a word…not to anyone."

"Elena! I can't believe you!"

"Promise!" she ordered, the teenage tyrant suddenly reborn. "Swear it!"

I spurred my horse in answer, galloping recklessly away.

The Wind streaked past my heated brow, flaying my hair upon the mocking Breeze. I was absolutely livid, Borelo's sneer branded upon me like the cut of a knife. If something like that ever happened in Kelly Tree, the villagers would have thrashed the boy within an inch of his life.

Not the proud nobility!

I rode the Arabian harder than I ought, dismounting as soon as I got to the stables. Not bothering to unsaddle my horse, I ran straight up to the castle. I was nearly through the gates when someone grabbed my shoulder. I rounded on the offending hand to glare into the coal black eyes of Oliver.

I roughly pulled away. "Get off!"

"We need to talk," he growled.

"We can talk later."

"We'll talk now."

I brandished a malevolent stare, sure it would cow the reverent boy.

He didn't even flinch.

"Fine," I said. "Talk."

"You *will* respect Elena's wishes."

"Why?"

"Because…she's the daughter of House Catagen, and that filth you waylaid is the son of House Gemello."

"So?"

"If the Commodore finds out, he'll probably kill Borelo."

"Good."

"And then Gemello would go to war against Catagen. Water would gather her allies, and Air would gather his. Fire would fight for Air. And Earth …"

"What are you talking about?"

"The Gemelleons are the most powerful Air House. The Fire Houses are itching for a fight."

"So?" I mocked. "Let them fight!"

"Do you want the whole world to go to war over Elena?"

No, I paused, *of course not. That would be stupid*. Still, I was furious. "Let the Air gather his friends. The Water can gather hers."

"The Commodore doesn't have any friends," he grimaced, "now that you've arrived."

I frowned in startled disbelief, flinching at the evil omen. Something quivered within my chest, something hurt and sad and solemn.

The mariner's face was rancid…as if embarrassed to say the

words. But he said them anyway. "The Good Earth used to be friends with the Water. But the Old Man offended two Earth Lords when he rescued you: Rance and Oxymid. They're seething now…want retribution. They look to Gauntle to teach Catagen a lesson."

The flurry of names meant nothing to me, as I was completely ignorant about House politics. But one thing I understood. *The Old Man put himself in a very dangerous position when he rescued me from Lady Oxymid.*

"If Elena wants to tell the Commodore, let her. But it's her decision, not yours."

"But Borelo…"

"I'll handle Borelo."

And he was as good as his word. The next day, the prince left the Isle with a wicked black eye, and a very bruised ego.

I returned to the stable to find a groom tending to my steed. I cooed to the exhausted Arabian, feeding her carrots to salve my guilt. In a few minutes, Dewey's daughters would arrive. So would Liam. For some odd reason that made me feel giddy and nervous.

But my thoughts were interrupted by Lieutenant Rees. "Mistress," he announced with grave formality, "the Commodore kindly requests your presence in his office…if it's quite convenient, of course."

He knows! I trembled. *He knows about the fight!*

Alarmed, I followed the lieutenant into the Commodore's office.

It was the first time the man-cub had ever been into this inner sanctuary. Othello, of course, visited every day, spying on the Commodore and the fools he called officers. The chamber dripped with masculinity, mahogany walls meeting ancient heart-of-pine floor. Leather sofas were tossed about the room, centered round the pelt of a huge, white bear.

The Commodore jumped to his feet, as if surprised the cub was in the room. "Ah, Mistress," he said, snuffing out his cigar. "Please, please, sit down."

She obeyed, warily watching his fretful pacing.

Dewey and the Bull stood towards the rear of the cavernous room. The Bull eyed the man-cub with contempt; Dewey gazed at her with genuine sympathy. Tiberius wasn't there. Othello knew that *Enterprise* had already left for Fort Isolaverde.

The trouble she gets into! complained the hiding cat. *Genetics! What a curious curse.*

"My dear," blurted the Commodore. His face was grave and somber, as if reporting the death of a beloved friend. "You must know that something serious has come to my attention."

The man-cub opened her mouth with badly-hidden shock. But before she could say anything, the Commodore continued.

"*Yorktown's* brought me word from Lady Uncial. She's ordered me to send you to University."

About time! thought the cat. He'd been waiting for this to happen.

"That's, uh…great," said the man-cub. "Isn't it?"

Othello smiled at her dog-like innocence. He knew that the slave had always wanted to go to University, the only "real" school in her entire world. Elena and the Twins would be going as well, as all the children of nobility were required to attend. But despite the princess's constant badgering, the Old Man refused to send her, saying it was too dangerous.

Yet the Lady Uncial, Chancellor of the Zoo, demands she go...

The cat, of course, was delighted. The Isle had become such a bore. Besides, this news – along with the arrival of Liam – meant that something was finally in motion. *I haven't seen him since he was a little boy, playing with his cousin in the glorious throne room...*

"That remains to be seen," grumbled the Commodore. "The Chancellor knows my thoughts on the matter, yet she sends me this order..."

"I told you, Father," groused the Bull. "Lady Oxymid..."

"Lady Oxymid, indeed! Since when does Uncial listen to that muddy old fool?"

"The Chancellor must have felt pressure from the other Taurans as well," said Dewey.

"I thought Gauntle would keep them in line for us. Any news from Clyme?"

"Not a single word," said the Bull.

"What good is it marrying my oldest granddaughter to a man twice her age if he's going to defy us like this?"

Indeed, thought Othello. It had been a clever ploy. Many years ago – when Catagen was still weak – he allied himself to the most powerful Earth lord with an arranged marriage. The goodwill that William's daughter engendered helped Catagen gain his Voting Chair. Yet now that the Commodore was a political rival, Lord Gauntle blocked everything he wanted, daughter or no.

"I told you this would happen," lectured the Bull. "That little stunt of yours in Capro Bay didn't impress anyone."

It certainly impressed the Gods, thought Othello. But the ignorant drones weren't to know that.

"Gentlemen, please," said Dewey, looking thoughtfully at the man-cub.

"Blimey," gasped the Old Man…as if he'd quite forgotten she was there. "My apologies, Mistress."

"Sir," asked the man-cub, "why don't you want me to go to University?"

Shut up, you imbecile! Don't change his mind!

The Commodore carefully considered his words. "Because, Mistress, I can't protect you in Greenstone the way I can here on the Isle…or at Sea."

"What could possibly happen?" she naively replied.

"There you are!" brayed the Bull. "The girl doesn't need our protection."

"You, Sir," warned the Commodore, "shall keep a civil tongue in your mouth."

"She has a point, Father," said Dewey. "Greenstone is neutral, a safe haven for all the nobility. No one would dare harm her there."

"Commodore," she said, "if this Chancellor, whatever that is, if she orders me to go, is there any way to refuse?"

"Out of the mouths of babes," said Dewey.

"Our only course is to obey," the Bull agreed.

Yet brazen imperiousness claimed the Commodore's face. "Aye…but we could defy her."

"And bring the entire House to ruin?" said the Bull. "Not exactly the scenario I had in mind."

"And what do you have in mind?" demanded the Commodore.

The Bull paced forward with a guttural growl. "I shall not stand by while you destroy my birthright for this...this..." He pointed at the man-cub.

"The Mistress," riled the Commodore, "is the *future* of House Catagen! Or hadn't you noticed?"

"The future has two courses, Father: fortune or ruin!"

"And you don't think I know the difference!"

The Bull huffed in answer, swelling his aggressive chest.

What an idiot! thought Othello.

Dewey placed himself between the two. "Father," he soothed, "if you feel that strongly about it, why don't you bring it up at the *Zoo*? Straightaway, when we first arrive. I'm sure you can canvas enough support to send her back, if you think it's necessary."

"Aye, I can," he shrugged, calmed by the younger son, "I can indeed. But I just don't like it, not one damn bit."

Othello studied the man-cub's patron, troubled by what he saw. The brazen mariner, so sure of himself and everything around him, seemed lonely and confused. A look of impotence stole his face.

A far cry from the bawdy Token who swore salty epitaphs in Capro Bay.

∞

The Twins could hardly contain their glee.

"You'll just love University!" said Lucy.

"Yeah," Casey said, "you won't believe the fun we'll have!"

"School is fun?" I asked, not daring to believe.

"Not school, silly," giggled Lucy. "The Games – the kids. The Uncial's are a bunch of snot-nosed brats, but you'll like Karl and Kaylie, and Joculo and Janice from House Joculo…"

"Then the there's House Duma. The new lord is only seventeen, can you believe it? His cousin, Corbel, is nice enough."

"So is Melvin, Mary's son."

"Don't go on about him. You just like him because he made the Team last year."

I felt bewildered by the blizzard of names. "So…I'll be in all of your classes, right?"

"Oh, no," said Lucy. "We're fifteen. You're sixteen."

"How old is Elena?"

"Seventeen," said Casey, "She'll be a sophomore."

I sighed with dismay. I wouldn't be in the Twins or Elena's classes. *As much as I want to go to University, I don't want to go alone!*

"Oh my Gods!" burst Casey. "I almost forgot about the Hunt!"

"My word!" clapped Lucy. "That's right!"

The Hunt! I whispered.

"Every year, we play the University Games."

"But every four years we play the Menagerie Games as well."

"I know that," I tersely replied. *I'm not that ignorant!*

209

Most folk in Kelly Tree didn't know much about University Games, as they were played by the nobility. But everyone knew about the Menagerie Games – and the magical Hunt.

Every four years, the best athletes from all over the world came to play in the Menagerie Games. It was an epic arena – sponsored by the very Gods themselves – in which a humble slave could leave as a living legend. Every child from every village dreamed of competing in the Games.

The event that started the Menagerie Games was the Hunt for the Golden Stag. Whoever killed the Stag won the unbelievable honor of wearing its hide in the opening ceremonies.

"It's quite smashing, really," said Lucy. "All the great Houses riding out into the woods, banners flying, dogs barking, horns blowing..."

"Zeliox won it last time," I stated. Though I knew nothing about the great Houses, I was an expert in sports trivia.

"Useless git," Casey said. "He's won the Wrestling five times in a row!"

"What's wrong with that?" I said. Zeliox was something of a hero of mine.

"He's a Tauran," giggled Lucy. "You silly goose! Honestly, the funny things you say."

I garlanded a timid smile. The idea of attending University was exciting and scary all at the same time. *What will it be like to be alone in class, surrounded by people who were richer, smarter, and more educated than me?*

π

"May I?" said the princess from the peasant's bedroom door. Her eyes were large and liquid – her nose, politely lowered.

"Sure," said the man-cub without bothering to look up.

The eldest daughter of Dewey floated in. Othello woke from his ceaseless slumber to study the new arrival. *An intriguing specimen. The epitome of what limited cunning and ruthlessness the two-legged species possesses.* Elena stood expectantly. *Ask her to sit down!* thought Othello.

But his pupil didn't offer.

"I wanted to thank you," Elena said humbly. "For what you did today."

"It was nothing," shrugged the man-cub, burying her face as she looked away.

Othello could tell she was still wary of the princess' porcelain face.

"No, it wasn't. You were really brave," said Elena.

"More like stupid. I can't believe the way I charged in like that."

"Did you see the look upon his face," Elena giggled, "just before you struck him?" Gracefully sitting beside the pauper, she engaged the man-cub with a captivating smile.

What's she playing at? thought the cat. *What does she want?*

There could be only one answer. *She's trying to needle something out of my pathetic pupil! Perhaps her birth from the Egg. Perhaps the origins of the prophecy!* Narrow-eyed and ready, he wiggled his whiskers, poised to pounce.

"How 'bout the way he landed in the Water?" laughed the peasant.

The princess gasped with happy alarm. "Oh, my Gods! And he just sat there!"

"Waiting for his cronies to arrive!"

To Othello's vast horror, the teenagers chatted for hours, abandoning Borelo for vapid, girly topics. And though he longed to escape from the adolescent tripe, duty dictated he monitor this very dangerous situation.

Elena was an excellent conversationalist, tittering at the man-cub's pathetic jokes and pampering her with her pleasant wit. Flattered by the princess' attention, the peasant basked in the warmth of unexpected praise. It wasn't until much later that Elena expertly steered the conversation to her secret interview with the Commodore.

"To be quite honest," she said with a wink, "I myself have never been inside Grandfather's inner chambers. Do tell, me Pallas. What was it like?"

So that's it, thought Othello. *She wants to know about Uncial's message.* A wave of calculating appreciation swept over the cat; both for the possibilities – and the perils – of the Catagen jewel.

Yesterday, he was sure his pupil would have told the princess absolutely nothing. But trapped in the enchantress' tempting web of charms, the man-cub revealed almost everything. She told her about the message from Lady Uncial, the Commodore's worries...even her fears about being in class by herself.

"Oh, bother," cooed Elena, "we'll just tell them you're seventeen and you can take classes with me."

"But...I already told him I was sixteen."

The princess patted the peasant's hands. "Not to worry, Pallas dear. Not to worry. I shall handle Grandfather."

And she did.

Chapter Fifteen

The Rape of Piraeus

Why dost thou gaze upon the Sky?
O that I were yon spangled sphere!
Then every star should be an eye,
To wander o'er thy beauties here.

Sir Thomas More
Lord Chancellor of England
circa 1530: Earth Standard

The little lad sat tending his sheep, strumming his harp as he sang along. His charges brayed their melodic lowing, keeping in time with his plaintive psalm.

His pack of friends surrounded him, wagging their tails with loyal glee. Golden, his favorite, gazed at him, lovingly nuzzling his master's knee.

The little lad sang of the heavens, the moons and the stars the Gods had ordained. He lauded the celestial beings, who lorded the Earth and governed the rain.

But mostly, he sang about the gray-eyed Goddess. Fair in beauty, gracious and kind, she'd stolen his youthful heart.

He worshipped her, he adored her, he loved her completely…in the sinless, selfless way only a young boy can. She was his night and his day, his past and his future, his waking moments and his every dream. He'd fight for her, die for her...even live his life for her. There was nothing he'd refuse her — not a request he wouldn't obey.

Yet he lived in crushing loneliness. Surrounded as he was by his loyal friends, his song was sad and forlorn. He was ravaged with yearning, fitful and cruel, for there was nothing to satisfy his deepest desire.

He was mortal. She was divine. The toils and struggles of his Earthly life...these were the lot of man. Yet he dreamed about her all the same, as only a young boy can.

Golden raised his inquisitive head. In unison, the rest of the pack did likewise. The retriever whined, rose to his feet, lifting his muzzle into the Air.

The little lad stood. A taint of smoke spoiled the breeze. A foul Wind was coming from the south.

Odd...it normally blows from the east.

That's when he saw it. A swift black column beyond the hilltop, marring the gentle sweep of the moor.

For a moment, he just stood there, curious at the spire. It thickened and climbed, ominous and mad.

Something horrible has happened! Gathering his staff and his four-legged friends, he ran to the growing danger.

He sprinted down the rolling hill, then crested the next top.

What he saw nearly Winded him.

Far below, Piraeus was burning...burning, burning with ghoulish red. The Wind in his face was ripe with screaming, the stench of burnt flesh, pungent with dread.

His face sank. His mouth drooped.

The fortress is fallen! Our people are dying!

Fear claimed his adolescent body. Quickening his breath and tingling his limbs, it almost stole his noble resolve.

But Golden growled. The pack hackled. They bared their teeth with thoughts of revenge. Their wolfish vengeance swallowed him whole, maddening him to fight...and to avenge.

He clenched his fist and ground his teeth. "Pirates!" he whispered. "They've sacked the village."

His friends barked their savage agreement.

But how did they orchestrate such a large attack? Pirates are cowards, preying on the weak. The fortress was well armed.

And where is the old Lord?

The questions were academic – the danger, real. He must hide his sheep as best he could, then run to Catagen City to spread the alarm.

That's when he saw them, topping the peak of one of the cresting hills: a wave of treacherous pirates.

The little lad blanched. *There must be six hundred! Why, with that many, they could sack Catagen City as well!*

Only...these aren't pirates! They're more like...more like an army! They wore pirate garb, yet they marched like a disciplined brigade. And there was something odd about the leader. He rode ahead of the morbid line, on what looked like a tiny pony.

The lad peered through his spyglass. *That can't be right.* There was only one horseman, and he was indeed riding a horse. But the man was so huge, the thoroughbred seemed to groan.

My Gods, thought the lad, *he must be eight feet tall!*

His dogs raised their hackles, eager to attack. But that would be suicide. He got out his silent whistle and blew it three times.

"Hide the sheep," he said to his friends.

They hardly needed telling. They knew what three whistles meant. Obediently, they turned the opposite direction and headed towards the flock.

The lad considered his options. *Is there any way I can slow them?* Instinctively, he knew there wasn't. The best thing he could do, the only thing he could do, was to warn his father in Catagen City.

If only I could send a message – tie something to Golden's collar – send him home. The dog could get there hours before he could. But there was no point in scripting a message, for no one in his world could read.

Guess I'll have to use my legs, he thought, discarding everything except his sling. He took one last look at the advancing army…then gazed into the defeated eyes of his older brother.

William!

Large and brawny, his sibling limped before the dread assassins, dragging behind him a thick sword.

Horror growing in his youthful heart, the lad took a tentative step forward. Blood flowed from William's head. He dropped his sword and fell on the heather.

The little lad nearly cried. There was no way to help him. The army was closing. They shouted and jeered.

William stumbled to his feet again, leaving his sword to the uncaring moor.

The giant laughed and spurred his horse, hastening to catch the cown prince.

The lad couldn't stand it. *I can't watch him die!* Without really deciding to – without thinking at all – he willed his legs to hurry him down the fateful Windswept side.

The army disappeared beneath the dip of the knoll. Hurrying forward – not daring to be too late – he vaulted over the next low rise.

The giant was on his brother. Hopeless, unarmed, William waited to die...

...when a streak of amber flew to the attack.

The labored horse panicked. The chestnut bullet howled a curse. Golden leapt upon the over-balanced giant, throwing him off the burdened horse.

"Golden!" he shrieked. "Get out of there!"

But his faithful companion would not obey. Instead, he rushed at the fallen giant.

William didn't lose a moment. Jolting himself forward, he mounted the frightened steed. Then he rode to his younger brother. "Dewey!" he shouted. "Get on!"

But the lad was frozen in awful anguish. With one brutal blow, the giant cleaved his gallant friend.

"No!" he cried with loving tears. "No!"

Then he charged.

William called from atop the horse. "Dewey! Stop! Don't be a fool!"

But the little lad would not heed him.

He rushed down another dip, racing towards the towering plume. Madness, crazed with fury, flung him towards his certain doom. He didn't have a sword, nor a bow...not an axe. All he had was a simple sling.

"Murderer!" he shouted as he mounted the rise.

The hellish giant laughed. "Killed your dog, did I?"

"No!" he shrieked. "You killed my friend!" Halting a moment to take his aim, he stormily loosed a single stone.

The missile sped towards the monster, striking his face at the bridge of his nose. The colossus swaggered, then crashed upon the heather.

Dewey rushed the abomination, fear and anger in raw supply. Using all the strength he could muster – heightened by his reckless rage – he grasped the giant's sword. Gory from the blood of his beloved dog, he lifted the weapon with both his hands.

The blood of Golden mingled with the pirate's, forever anointing the legendary blade. He knew a moment of proud satisfaction as the ugly head rolled away.

But the moment was fleeting. The army was coming. Nothing could stop their brutal advance.

Dewey wracked his mind, thinking. *What can I do to stop them?*

Desperate, he blew a short, silent whistle.

Dropping the gargantuan sword, he plunged his hands into the greasy hair. Strengthened by horror, girded by rage, he lifted the morass over his head. Blood spurted from the crimson gore, trickling hot down his frightened face. But he kept his prize high in the Air, shouting at the pirate race...

"Beware! Beware! I have felled this fey giant and summoned the Others! Hear how they come! Hear how they rumble! Hear how they rumble and roar!"

For a moment, nothing happened. The weight of the head was unbearable, the blood of the vanquished, thick upon his brow.

But then the hill started shaking, as if from an unseen stampede.

"They come!" he howled. "They come! Woe to those who defy

them! Come, and meet death! Or flee, and claim your prizes!"

The pirates stopped their greedy advance. They traded cowardly, treacherous looks.

The rumbling grew louder.

Dewey held his breath.

All at once, the pirates disintegrated under the weight of their avarice. The army fled down the rolling moor, disappearing beneath the withering hills.

Exhausted, the little lad collapsed.

Moments later he was surrounded by sheep, stamping and huffing and snorting in place. His woolly charges bleated their annoyance, at the senseless, pointless, roundabout chase.

But his canine saviors shared his sufferings, sniffing at the ruin of their fallen comrade. Some of them licked his amber face. Others whimpered their sadness.

Dewey crawled to his noble companion, crying over the golden remains.

π

The Atlantians giggled over the day's excitement. Though they rued the rape of Piraeus, they were delighted by the entertaining boy.

"Isn't it touching?" one of them said. "The way that two-legged animal fawns over that four-legged animal."

"Look at the way he's weeping," said another. "So silly. So

pathetic."

"That lad," said Triton. "What's his name?"

"Dewey," said Teresa. "The younger brother of William, each of them sons of Catagen II."

"That Dewey just saved House Catagen," said Triton. "Catagen City could never have repeled that army. If those pirates hadn't turned around..."

"Teresa," said Poseida, "be a good dear and look into these Catagens. I know they're a frightfully small House. But...there's something special about them; something...refreshing."

"Yes, mother," said Teresa. "I shall indeed."

Chapter Sixteen

Her Father's Daughter

"Everything is in place, my Lord God. The dolphin rider will walk straight into our trap."

"Excellent. But remember — there must be no mistakes this time. This Age of the Aquarius nonsense must end — here and now."

"Do not worry, my Lord God. Our spy has been most helpful."

The next two weeks were a Whirlwind of activity. Not only did the inhabitants of Castle Mare have to get ready for their voyage to Greenstone, they also had to transplant the entirety of House Catagen to the capital for the next three months.

Every fall, all the great Houses met in Greenstone to reconvene the *Zoo*, the governing body of our tiny world. There, the lords and ladies resolved disputes, collected taxes, and authorized civil projects. There were twenty-five members of the *Zoo*, though only nine could actually vote. House Catagen was a Voting Member, which made the Old Man a very powerful person indeed.

In theory, Greenstone was completely safe. It was forbidden for any House to attack another inside the city limits.

But the Commodore wasn't a very theoretical thinker. "Give me a sword in one hand and a bottle in the other, that's all the philosophy I need!"

This year, he had an additional problem...me. Oxymid and Rance were furious, as well as Mulciber, the son of the Goddess Vulcana. Throw in a miraculous rescue, a vague prophecy, and dogma from the depths of the mighty Sea...

...it was a very strange resume for a peasant from Kelly Tree.

But time passed quickly for me, as I wasn't concerned about security, great Houses, or parliamentary procedures. Almost immediately, Elena and I became fast friends.

The Twins were scandalized.

"How could you actually talk to her?" Lucy said with disgust.

"Have you completely lost your mind?" demanded Casey.

"She's really quite nice, once you get to know her."

"I don't want to get to know her," said Casey, revolted.

"She's an absolute horror," Lucy agreed.

But their nagging didn't keep us apart, for I found in Elena a quiet wisdom I learned to respect. Elena was a good listener – if she didn't feel threatened; and kind – as long as she was given her due. She was eccentric at times, but I decided allowances should be given to one so beautiful.

"It's a curse, really," she sullenly complained. "Honestly...what I wouldn't give to be normal."

It was strange, but I felt the exact same way. People in the streets stared at me. A mother asked me to bless her baby. The fairies in the tree were growing even louder, singing their songs about the magic of the Deep.

Our longing for anonymity formed a symbiotic bond, each extraordinary girl feeding on the insecurities of the other. For as much as I enjoyed the Twins, it was nice to have someone I could talk to about the fears that fame brought.

The problem with Elena was her constant preoccupation with politics. She waxed endlessly about the great Houses and their complicated feuds. "Of course, when Poseida and Terra married, Vulcana only allied herself with Zephyr as a way to balance the cosmos against the Water and the Earth."

"Yeah," I agreed, secretly startled.

"It is all so very fascinating the way Water and Earth form the tighter bond against the Fire and Air. Yet Water and Air can co-exist together as well. Just look at the cave behind the Waterfall."

"What about it?" I asked, hoping I didn't sound as stupid as I felt.

"The mist...the Water in the Air. It's what Grandfather hopes to accomplish with Lady Gemello with the utmost vigor."

"What does mist have to do with the Old Man?"

"Everything. Our strongest allies are, of course, Houses Uncial, Ionian, Cannes, Joculo...and, I suppose, I must include House Duma."

I perked up when I heard the name of Joculo, the Lord of Kelly Tree. "Why are they Catagen's closest friends?"

"Because they're Aquarians, silly."

"Aquarians?"

"Water Houses."

"Oh...yeah," I stammered, forcibly reminded of that horrible prophecy...

Born of the Sea, hatched from the Egg,
Child of Atlantis, God with us.
For she shall herald a glorious age,
and they shall call it – Aquarius.

Is that why people follow me in the streets? Do they think I'll bring power to Poseida and the Water Houses?

No! I vowed, digging my nails into the cushioned chair. *I won't do it! I refuse to obey that hateful queen.*

"But we need more allies than just the Aquarians. Dear me, yes. The Balance of Power dictates we ally ourselves with another element, either Earth or Air. For the Fire Houses are our mortal enemies, and always shall be. Especially House Excelsior."

"Why Excelsior?"

Venom reddened her ruby lips. "Because...after Grandfather destroyed the pirate fleet that murdered our great-grandfather, he learned that the pirates were financed by Lord Excelsior."

"Oh," I said, stunned that the Catagens had a long-standing vendetta against House Excelsior.

"That's why Grandfather forged an alliance with the most powerful Earth House by marrying his oldest granddaughter to Lord Gauntle."

"You have a sister who's married to Lord Gauntle?"

"Cousin. Captain William's daughter, Clyme."

"How old is she?"

"Oh, quite old," she said with a touch of pity, "thirty-six, in fact."

"Wow...that is old."

"Exceedingly. But now Grandfather desires to canvass support among the Geminis as well. For what we have witnessed is, indeed, the consequence of…"

Elena's voice droned on and on, but I was too fretful to listen. Instead, I thought about what Oliver had said.

"The Commodore doesn't have any friends…now that you've arrived."

What did it cost the Old Man to rescue me from Lady Oxymid? Was House Catagen truly alone?

"Like who?" I interrupted.

"Like House Gemello," she sighed.

I thought this through, surprising myself when I realized how this union might be accomplished. "But, you can't marry Borelo! He's nothing but a beast."

"He may be," she said dejectedly, "but he's also the most eligible bachelor for the most eligible daughter of House Catagen."

I huffed, understanding for the first time Elena's "infatuation" with the Gemelleon prince. *She doesn't like that stupid snot. She's pretending for the sake of her family!*

Loyalty. My father called it the most precious of emotions. *"Even the animals are loyal to their own kind,"* he'd said. *"You're not much of a man if you're no better than an animal."* Elena was loyal to the Commodore, and to House Catagen. It made me respect the beauty even more.

"Look. The Old Man isn't going to make you marry against your will."

"He won't *make* me…"

"Then that's that! And I don't want to hear any more about Prince Bore-us-loads."

I couldn't wait for University, for exciting possibilities presented themselves to the child of Lord Catagen that a slave could only dream about. *With a little luck and a lot of hard work, I might actually play in the University Games!* And who knew? I even tempted myself with every athlete's fantasy…to compete in the Menagerie Games!

But ever since Uncial's message arrived, Othello's lessons took on a new sense of urgency. The work was harder and the cat much sharper when I failed to meet his ever increasing standards. I didn't have anything to read of course, so he made me write instead.

This, I could not stand.

As Othello couldn't actually hold a pen, he had difficulty teaching me to write. "For the *r* we start with a single downward stroke. Then, at the top we produce a curl from the top towards the right, down to the middle, and…no, no, no!" I didn't have dyslexia, but Othello unfortunately did, so my *p*'s came out as *q*'s and my *b*'s looked like *d*'s.

I labored into the wee hours of the night, badgered by my merciless teacher. After teaching me his dyslexic alphabet, the cat made me write words.

Othello called this "Vocabulary." I called it torture.

But that wasn't the worst of it. After scribing my cryptic scrawl, he made me burn every bit of my work.

"Can't let those stupid drones see what you're up to," he said.

"What's a drone?" I yawned.

"Something you're not."

I frowned in answer.

"It's what makes you better than the animals. Well…some of them."

My midnight lessons lasted for hours, making me tired and irritable.

Elena noticed. "If you don't get more sleep, you'll get bags under your eyes."

I had just about had enough when Othello woke me the very next morn.

"I'm too tired," I drowsily complained, burying my head under my pillow.

"You need to work, not sleep. You sleep too much as it is."

"You're one to talk. It's all you ever do."

"I'm not going to tell you again," he said, unsheathing his razor claws.

"Alright, alright," I said, stumbling towards my desk. Wearily lighting a candle, I took out my parchment and quill.

"Ready?" said the cat.

I drearily nodded my head. "What time is it?"

"Two in the morning…perfect opportunity to resume your studies. Everything's quiet, no one to interrupt us."

But my patience had come to a bitter end. I was about to tell him off when he said…

"The naming of cats is a difficult matter"

"What?"

"Did I stutter?"

Finally! I thought. *The mongrel is telling me a story…one that doesn't involve those stupid Gods.* I scrawled across the parchment as quickly as I could. "Difficult, is that one or two *f*'s?"

"One, I think." He wasn't a good speller.

"It isn't just one of your holiday games"

"What's a holiday?"

"It's when someone takes a break from working."

"So…you're like on a permanent holiday, right?"

The cat continued as if he hadn't heard. *"You may think at first I'm as mad as a hatter"*

"Why would a hat be angry?"

"No, no," he explained, with far greater restraint than I would have expected. "It's an expression based on a character in a children's book. The Mad Hatter wasn't angry; he was crazy."

"What's a book?"

"Ah," he purred. "A book is a collection of thousands of words, bound together into hundreds of pages."

"Thousands?" I exclaimed, the delight of such a treasure dancing in my head. "What do books say?"

"They can say most anything, now can't they?"

"Wow!" The sleep that shrouded me a moment ago was magically erased. "Imagine the possibilities."

But then harsh reality sank in. *I've never seen a book, and probably never will.*

The cat, as usual, seemed to know what I was thinking. "The Gods have books, millions of them. More books than you could read in a lifetime."

My eyes grew as wide as saucers. *Millions!* I didn't know what a "million" was, just that it was a fantastically enormous number. *What a fabulous prize!*

Yet it was a treasure the Gods kept from us mortals. "Why don't the Gods allow us to read?"

"Why, indeed?" he retorted. Then he flourished...

"When I tell you a cat must have THREE DIFFERENT NAMES."

"Do you really?"

"Why yes, of course. On account we're superior to everyone else."

π

Othello continued the lesson for hours. Though it was nearly daybreak before she finished T. S. Elliot's poem, the man-cub begged for even more.

Her scrawl was barely legible. A first grader could have done better. Words were misspelled, and none of them were capitalized. But she was writing, as crude as it was. Perhaps one day – if she ever found a book – she could read it.

I know the poem will doom her, he thought. But it simply couldn't be helped.

π

Finally, after weeks of frantic preparation, House Catagen was ready to move to Greenstone. We girls would be sailing on the flagship *Yorktown*. *Hornet* would escort us to Fort Isolaverde before departing to investigate a new report of pirates.

"Where's Elena?" I asked as we strolled down the wharf.

"That obnoxious, pampered, landlubber?" said Casey.

"She's no sailor," said Lucy.

"Gets Sea-sick every time," said Casey.

Lucy laughed. "You won't see her until we pull into Fort Isolaverde."

I followed them across the narrow gangplank. Oliver stood at the top of the quarterdeck.

"Permission to come aboard, Sir!" shouted Casey.

"Permission granted," he grunted. But when he saw that I was with them, he straightened to attention, rendering a sharp salute.

"Blimey!" giggled Casey. "You've never saluted us before!"

"Honestly," said Lucy. "Isn't he adorable?"

Though his cheeks flushed red, he did not retort, nodding instead to a sailor. The mariner blew three sharp notes on a horn pipe. "Mistress of the Sea...arriving!" Oliver announced.

I hid my face in the palms of my hands, anxious to avoid his probing stare. The Twins added to my eternal embarrassment by singing a little chantey...

I love a maid 'cross the Water,
Aye, aye, roll and go!
For her I sail on the Water,
And save my money to be her beau!

"What's going on!" roared the Bull. "What nonsense is this?"

"Commodore's orders," said Oliver, saluting the captain as well. "The Mistress shall be hailed whenever she embarks, and saluted whenever she's on deck."

"Why?" he bellowed. "Because she's a God!" Swearing a string of epitaphs, he turned on me and snorted, "Get off my deck, God! Where you won't be a nuisance to my crew!"

I glared in answer, silent and cross.

"Fine," said Casey, pulling me by the hand.

"Didn't want to come on your wretched boat in the first place," Lucy fumed.

Together, we started down the narrow ladder.

The Bull rounded on Oliver. "You! Boy. Get below and man the bilge pump."

"Aye, aye, Captain," said Oliver, rendering another crisp salute. He whistled the chantey as he strolled away.

"And keep my ballast dry!" shouted the Bull.

"That man is such a boar," said Casey.

"Why should Oliver do such a menial chore?"

"Doesn't seem to mind, though, does he?" I said.

"Because he likes you!" savaged Casey.

"I've never seen him interested in a girl before," laughed Lucy.

"Enraptured by the enchanting, Mistress of the Sea!" crowed Casey.

They continued their playful jeering as we made our way to our magnificent quarters. But I ignored their banter to consider my thoughts. Like Oliver, I'd never been wooed by love before. Now I had to reconsider.

∞

I sat on the heel of the blowing bowsprit, thinking about the torrid Sea. House Catagen was a Water House. They called themselves Aquarians. They were loyal to Poseida and the Gods of the Sea.

But Poseida drowned my mother, *and that stupid prophecy makes me hate her even more. Besides...I'm not a child of Atlantis! It's all a horrible lie!*

Dolphins played in the billowing bow wave, flying Skyward as if dancing step in time. I jealously watched their mad capers, grudgingly welcoming the foamy brine. *At least we're going in the right direction. At least we're sailing towards Kelly Tree.*

Again, I thought about my beloved father. *How he must be missing me!* Shamed by my lack of resolve, I determined to find a way back home.

Soft eyes suddenly surprised me, completely delighting me with their strength and zest. Liam sat warm beside me; a hot tingling, oozing through my chest. Shocked, frightened, I hurriedly pulled away...and then immediately wished I hadn't.

"Hey, there Bright-Eyes. Thinking about your father?"

"Yeah," I said. "How'd you know?"

"Born to the Father on the River Triton. Motherless, yet Mother to us all."

"What are you talking about?"

"That's what we call you. She Dragon – Giant Killer – Dread Avenger. The Faultless Warrior who faults the tragedy of war."

"Who calls me that?"

Liam smiled, a coy grin that was laughing and knowing. "There's so much we know about you, Pallas, yet...so much more we've yet to learn. The important thing is...and the reason that I'm here...is to deliver a message."

"Did the Twins put you up to this?" I said, annoyed. The boy was obviously playing a trick on me.

"Please," he said, "hear me out. Born within your veins is the truth of the Polis; of man's equal and unalienable rights."

I looked at him with naked disbelief.

"There's a plan," he said devoutly. "A plan to seat you at the right hand of the Creator, to inherit the kingdom prepared for you amidst the cruel foundations of this troubled world. You need only reach out and seize it."

In arms rejoicing with Furies dire
wild the souls of mortals inspire.
Mother to all. Impetuous. Understood.
Rage to the Wicked. Wisdom to the Good.

He lowered his hand from his bursting chest, casting a heartfelt gaze at me. "I know you can't understand this, but...you are the harbinger of doom, Pallas. Your birthright is to loose the Great Catastrophe."

I gazed into his beautiful, delusional eyes. "Right."

He turned his face towards the brooding Sea. "Sorry. I've...said too much. You probably think I'm...insane. But I promise you this, Bright-Eyes; you shall destroy the Gods among us."

"Did Othello put you up to this?" I asked, irritated. *Just my luck! I finally meet the perfect guy...and he's a certifiable nut job.*

"Who's Othello?"

"No one," I mocked. "Just another ridiculous jerk."

Liam frowned. "I'm sorry. I've done this all wrong. I'm a soldier after all, not a..." he paused for a hesitant moment and then continued, "...only they didn't trust anyone else and..."

"Who's they?" I riled.

"No one," he said with a sudden smile. The effect was charming and surprisingly smooth.

Most girls would have fallen for the splendor in his eyes. *Only I've never been that naïve...* "What do you want...really?"

"Honestly?" he whispered with tender affection. "I want to see you smile."

∞

It was a wet, wintry night. The toddler lay safe in her father's arms, giggling at his funny faces. Her mother sang a sad and lilting lullaby, a song she hadn't heard before.

But her singing was cut short by a brutal blow to the door. Merciless soldiers, cold and cruel, roughly seized her father. The toddler cried – torn from his embrace – as they dragged him out into the freezing rain...

"Father!"

The man-cub woke to her own startled scream. Othello was patient and waiting. Her heart beat murderously against her teenage chest, thumping so loudly he could hear it across the room.

The Twins were on the bridge with Oliver, keeping him company during his midnight watch. Thus, his prey was all alone.

"When are you going to tell me that secret of yours?" he whispered.

"I...don't know what you're talking about."

The predator paced into the sordid moonlight, swaying his tail like a menacing cobra. "You need to work on that nasty little habit of yours. Your bottom lip twitches when you tell a lie."

The man-cub covered her mouth with her hands. "How do you *know* that?"

"Years of practice. But it isn't very difficult with humans. It's that guilty conscience of yours. Your species is far too benevolent for your own good."

"I'll try to remember that," she snapped.

"So," he cooed, "can we talk?"

"No."

"No?" *My, my; that isn't going to do at all!* It was two in the morning, his favorite time of day, and he was in the mood for hunting. *Or perhaps a game of cat and mouse?*

For a sanguine moment, he enjoyed a luxurious stretch, his satin-white fur rippling with delight.

Then he began.

"Your mother wasn't born in Kelly Tree, was she?"

"What do you know about my mother?"

"In fact, you don't know where she was born, do you?"

"No," she whispered, as if troubled by this admission.

And now that secret haunts you. You wrestle with it every night. And while you grapple with your doubt, I'll use your pain to get what I need.

"How did your mother and father meet?"

"I don't know. She came to Kelly Tree a few years before I was born...on a ship, I guess."

"Which ship? What was its name?"

"I...I don't know. Why do you care?"

The cat didn't answer. He'd been preparing this inquisition for months, planning what he would say and how he would say it to reveal her most precious secrets. "Do you remember her at all?"

"Just glimpses, really."

"Tell me."

"Well, I remember the three of us hiking through the woods on a moonlit night. I was riding on my daddy's shoulders."

"How very quaint."

"There was this clearing on top of a knoll where we gazed at the stars. Father called it his 'little planetarium,' though he wouldn't tell me why."

"Did he?"

"He liked to point out the stars; tell me their names. Even after Mother...you, know." She sighed a melancholy frown. "Even after she died, Father would take me there and show me the constellations. Orion the Hunter, Taurus the Bull, Ursa the Bear. He said they weren't quite right, they'd…moved somehow. But I didn't care. I was happy to be star gazing like…like my father and mother used to…before she…before she…"

"Is your father old?"

"Yeah."

"And he's an only child."

She gazed at the ceiling and nodded.

"You don't have any other family, not a single cousin, aunt, or uncle. Do you?"

"How do you *know* that?"

The heart knows its own bitterness, he thought, enjoying her growing discomfort. *And your heart, young man-cub, is as easy to read as a book.* Besides, he'd been working out this puzzle for half a year. *Only a few more pieces left to place.*

He sardonically rolled his eyes. "Please. With all that howling you do in your sleep? It's a wonder I don't know everything about your paltry life…what precious little there is to know."

"Whatever."

Othello smiled. Pleased with the information he'd already gathered, *I must know the secret that haunts you.*

"The Gods can be very vengeful. Did you know that?"

"Duh," came her surly reply. "Mulciber wants to kill me, though you refuse to tell me why."

"Maybe it's because of your father. Maybe he did something to offend the Prince of Fire."

"That is such a lie! He's just a slave. He has nothing to do with that wretched God."

"I think I know more about that wretched God than you do!" he hissed, suddenly staccato and rude. Gone were his patient platitudes, replaced by merciless indictment. *Just a little closer…then I'll pounce.*

"Come off it. You know I don't believe in that God stuff."

"Don't believe! My, but that's rich. Don't believe in pixies if you like…or leprechauns, perhaps. But you cannot deny the Pentathanon Five."

"Sure I can. I've never seen a God, or met any who has. How do I know they even exist?"

"Your friends saw Triton rising out of the Sea…"

"They *think* they did. But isn't it more likely they were fooled somehow? I mean…just 'cause they saw some guy riding a dolphin, that doesn't make him a God."

How delightfully cynical, he admired. *How wonderfully keen. Really, she's far too intelligent to be anything except…* "I've seen a God," he said. "*I* was the pet of Mulciber's daughter."

"Another one of your stories."

He raised his albino brow, delighted by her stubbornness. "Do you believe in the raft, the compass…the flashing light?"

"Of course I do. They're real. I can touch them…hold them in my hand."

"Mulciber is real," he sniggered. "I've seen him burn a man alive, just by pointing his finger."

"You have?" she said with a hint of horror.

"He's quite ambitious. Forming an alliance against the Water. Hoping to unite Fire, Earth, and Air to become the dominate deity."

"Not my problem."

"Did you ever consider why Mulciber wants to kill you? Why the dolphins saved your life?"

"How would I know? You won't tell me!"

"Why did Triton tell the Commodore to rescue you?"

She worried her brow in answer, trapped by the inescapable conclusion.

"The prophecy, the Egg, the shark, the God…"

"Shut up!"

"It all began with *you*. Surely you must see."

"Shut up! I've got nothing to do with any of it!"

"Oh," he purred, mad and vile. "But you're wrong. *Everything* begins *and* ends with you. You're the fount of the great catastrophe…a reckless tempest that will destroy the world!"

"Shut up!" she screamed. "Shut up! Or I'll…I'll hurt you, I swear I will."

He reveled in a maniacal laugh. "Are we forgetting our little lesson?"

"No," she whispered, hiding her face.

"You must trust me," he snarled. "If I'm to help you, I must know everything – *everything* – about you *and* your parents! Now…if you think your secret is more valuable than your father's life, by all means keep it. But don't come crying to me when your father is dead and the rest of your smelly village is reduced to a pile of ashes because you…wouldn't…tell me."

Thus swung the pendulum of the teen's emotions: love to anger to rancid guilt. The poor man-cub was utterly defeated, a shadow of the dignity she once possessed. Not realizing what she was doing, she gushed out the secret she swore she'd never tell.

"One night, when I was three, soldiers came to our house and took my father. They said he'd been caught...stealing," she smothered the word, "a golden cup from Lord Joculo. The trial was quick and private. My father was sentenced to hang."

"But they didn't hang him..."

"No. Lord Joculo released him a few days later. Said there'd been a terrible mistake. I mean...they found the golden cup and everything," she said, contorting her mouth into a pathetic frown. "Only most people don't believe that! Most people think he was only released to take care of his baby daughter."

"Why would they think that?"

"Come on," she sniped. "Everyone knows how wonderful Lord Joculo is. Even my father says it. Most people think..." and here she spoke in a timid whisper, "...most people think my father was a thief."

The cat proceeded cautiously, knowing that humans were prone to hysterics. It was a weakness he used to great advantage. *Still, I hardly want to sit here and listen to her wail...* "Why couldn't your mother take care of you?"

It was a long time before she answered. "Because...she was...she was gone."

"Where?"

"The night my father was jailed, she left me with a neighbor."

"Why?"

Her eyes were filled with remorse. "How should I know? The neighbor told me...she told me...she was crying." The pitiful man-cub cried as well, brutally reliving that odious night.

Again, Othello hesitated. *There's something she hasn't told me, something I need to know.* "Did she say...*where*...she was going?"

The cub's voice wheezed and twanged, spiraling high with unsettling intensity. "The old woman heard her say something...something like, 'Lily was right; this is what I get for helping them.' Then she ran to the shore...and she never came back. She never came back...to get me."

Uh! gasped Othello. Rare compassion filled his face; emerald eyes, large and lilted. He drooped his tail with shocking grief; abusive whiskers, soft and wilted.

Chiding himself for his amateurish display, he buried his sympathy within his carnivorous heart. Grateful that her sodden eyes were huddled in her arms, he slinked away, mumbling something about being sorry...

...leaving the man-cub to the comfort of her tears.

Chapter Seventeen

Fort Isolaverde

HOUSE EXCELSIOR – Excelsior was the most powerful Fire House. It held the offices of Lord Defender of the Titan and Voting Member of the Zoo. Located in Turner Hill, the largest city in the world, it dominated the entire northern half of the mainland. Easily the wealthiest of the great Houses, it was continually locked in a bitter power struggle against House Uncial to become Chancellor of the Zoo.

...it was ironic that it was House Catagen, not House Uncial, that was embroiled in constant conflict with House Excelsior. For the Uncialian ladies wisely let the Catagens do the fighting, while House Uncial enjoyed the fruits of their labors...

"Rise and Fall of the Pentathanon Gods"

Herodotus III

Fort Isolaverde was nestled southwest of the mainland. Because of its central location in the southerly half of the "S" shaped archipelago, it was a convenient place for ships to bring on fresh provisions. Since House Catagen owned half the warships in the world, the Commodore visited Isolaverde more than any man alive. His late wife often complained he spent more time there than he did at home...a charge he never successfully denied.

Not to say it was a safe place, for it was nothing of the sort. I didn't know anything about the lords and ladies from my "education" in Kelly Tree, but I'd heard plenty of stories about Isolaverde. The island was a haven for the great Houses because of its neutrality. But that same neutrality also made it a sanctuary for pirates and thieves.

I couldn't wait to explore its winding streets, famous for their hard-to-find merchandise and notorious wares. And of course I felt perfectly safe, surrounded by sailors sworn to protect me.

Cindy would be so jealous!

So I was quite dismayed when I heard I wouldn't see the town at all. Though *Yorktown* would stop for the night to purchase a few necessities, the Old Man wasn't letting any of his princesses ashore.

"There, there, lassies; let an old dog lie," he said. "The streets of the town are much too dangerous."

"I quite agree," said Hebe. "The village is full of fantastic anomalies and wild curiosities of the most bizarre natures. You're far too innocent to roam such streets."

The Twins pleaded liked lost puppies. Their shameless display made their grandfather very uncomfortable. But he was resolute. "I said no, and I mean it," he growled as he fled the wardroom. Hebe followed timidly after.

Casey furrowed her conniving brow. "We're going."

"But you heard him," I said.

"We've been there a hundred times," said Lucy. "It's not that dangerous."

"And it's so much fun!" said Casey.

"The pubs are out of this world."

"Full of guys. Cute guys."

"You wouldn't *believe* how cute some of them are!"

243

I *could* believe it. I'd never liked the schoolboys back in Kelly Tree. But these sailors were quite different. Rugged, strong and lean, they always treated me with diligent respect...as per the Commodore's orders. Though I was disappointed I hadn't seen the handsome young sailor I danced with long ago...

I quickly warmed up to their complicated scheme. The plan was full of what I called "lies" and the princesses called "disinformation." Our masterminding complete, the Twins left to "borrow" some things we'd need. Tired from my midnight confessions, I took a nap.

"You're *not* leaving this ship," ordered the cat.

"Why not?" I griped, still stinging from last night's lamentations.

"Because...a God wants you dead."

"That's what you always say. Can't you come up with something more original?"

"I forbid it," he declared, turning his hindquarters towards me in a rude sort of way.

It's almost like he's taunting me, daring me to disobey. But I'll get him...pay him back for what he did last night.

And though I promised I'd stay...

...I'd already decided to go.

∞

The town was small but lively, full of dingy vessels and motley wharfs. The fort sat high upon a granite cliff, looking down upon the village like a stern schoolmarm.

We waited until it was dark. Engaging Ensign George in a convoluted lie, we scurried aboard a gig.

"Where first?" I asked as we reached the smelly quay.

"The Red Lion!" Casey mischievously replied.

"The notorious!" Lucy giggled, bustling up the crowded street.

Wide-eyed with giddiness, I spied a sign which looked like a lion, whatever color it might have been.

Men grunted as we entered the pub. Layers of smoke blanketed the room, though it couldn't hide the reek of spilt beer and illicit *ambrosia*. A toothless band was huddled in a corner, playing a ballad about a maiden and her long lost sailor. There were very few women, all of them waiting tables. We were greeted with cat-calls as drunks waved tankards high into the Air. I was starting to think this was a bad idea when I suddenly locked eyes with my handsome young sailor. He looked at me with surprise, as if I were the last person he expected to see.

"DG!" I said to myself.

The sailor rose from his table, walking towards me with a "cat-who-ate-the-canary" grin.

Watch that scene!

Then he said hello.

My entire existence shrank to his handsome, hardy face. Forgetting about my misgivings (and the sniggering Twins), I basked in the rapture of his rugged smile. Soon I was dancing without a care in the world, the band playing a jig about Davy Jones' locker.

But my piece of heaven didn't last very long. Unexpectedly, a stranger tried to cut in. I noticed a crimson garment hidden under his jacket, when...

Wham!

It happened so fast, I didn't know who threw the first punch. My sailor decked the man, spilling him over a sodden table. Immediately, several locals pounced upon my sailor. Catagen sailors rose with a cheer, eager to do battle.

I backed away in fright. *I've never seen so much fighting in my entire life!* Lucy grabbed my hand as Casey broke a bottle over a scruffy head. I was nearly pelted with a flying mug when a redhead caught it in mid-Air. Another man, this one blond, grabbed me by the arm.

"What the devil are ye doing here?" hissed O'Brien, punching a local before dragging me towards the door. The blond on my left was Rees.

"I don't know!" I sobbed. "We just wanted to have some fun."

"Criminy!" Rees swore. "Of all the cockamamie…" He slugged a man who was blocking the door. The ruffian toppled to the ground as O'Brien pulled us through.

The last thing I remembered was the sharp, blinding pain. Then, nothing.

∞

I woke to a chorus of crickets, chirping happily in the forest night. How much time had passed, I could not guess. I tried to reach my wounded head, but I was bound at the wrists. Then I heard something that made my blood freeze…

"That's right. Mulciber Himself is coming to get her."

Too shocked to breathe, too frightened to move, I closed frightened my eyes. *Oh, my Gods! Where am I?*

"Mulciber!" said another voice. "The Volcano God! What a coup for House Excelsior."

"And Prince Alexander," said another. "He'll show those Water scum who's really in charge."

I stifled a manic scream, yearning to thrash against my bonds. Yet I willed myself not to panic. *If they see that I'm awake, I'll never escape!*

I opened my eyes to a narrow squint. Scarlet robes gathered around a roaring Fire. *Fire Jesters!* I whispered with silent dread. *Disciples of Vulcana!* To my right, several horses were tied to a tree.

I searched for a moment of hope. *How stupid can they be? Starting a Fire when they know they're being followed.*

But what if no one was looking for me? *Does anyone know I'm alone and captive; waiting, helpless, for a ruthless God?*

Terror rose within my chest, threatening my power to reason. *What if Rees and O'Brien are dead? What about the Twins?*

Think! I demanded. *Think!*

The words of my father tried to comfort me, willing my mind to calmly obey. *"Humans,"* he said, *"real humans think. It's the only thing that makes us better than the animals."*

Yet I *felt* like an animal: a desperate, cornered beast.

"I couldn't believe it was so easy," said one of the men. "The tramp walked right into our trap."

"I was a little worried when none of the dainties came ashore with the others."

"Not me, not at all. Our spy said she'd come."

My heart stopped a single heinous beat. *Spy?*

"It's too bad we couldn't get all three."

"We got the one He wanted, the one with the gray eyes."

Othello! I gasped. *He's always talking about my gray eyes. He's been a spy for them all this time!*

I was now absolutely terrified, far more than I'd been at Capro Bay. The wild carriage ride, the dolphin's rescue...they all seemed like a thrilling adventure. I'd been surrounded by strong, brave men; all determined to save me.

Now I'm alone, surrounded by enemies!

I wrestled with my bonds, but they were simply too tight. My legs were bound as well, though I could reach them if I dared. Careful to check that they weren't watching, I slowly crouched.

That's when I saw it – a smooth, black box. Constructed of polished steel, it was sitting on a stump between the men and the horses. I looked even closer, almost laughing for joy. On the box were hundreds of strange markings. Only they weren't strange to me. *They're letters...letters of the alphabet!*

"So...how is Mulciber going to find us?"

"He's a God, you idiot. Besides, we have the magic summoning box."

"Summoning box?"

"That's right. It's full of flares that will call Him with bolts of Fire."

"What's a flare?"

"How should I know? All I know is we use the box to summon the God. Only we have to wait for Prince Alexander. He wants to be here when Mulciber claims her."

"Hey, Verne! Put some more wood on the Fire. I'm freezing."

I was freezing as well, but I welcomed the cold as my captors huddled round the glow. Struggling with the ropes at my feet, I studied the box more closely.

To my dismay, I only recognized a few of the words. I thought I was quite clever, having copied *Growltiger's Last Stand* a few nights before. Now I realized how limited my vocabulary really was.

The light from the Fire grew stronger, dancing like a jinni upon the magic box. I knew the word "WARNING," as I'd seen it placarded on the flare gun. It was inscribed inside a red arrow that pointed towards the bottom. "FIRE" was another one I recognized, but I didn't know what "SIMULTANEOUSLY" or "JETTISON" meant. There was a larger arrow pointing to the top of the box with words like "EXTREME CAUTION" and "FIRING END." These were words I'd seen on the barrel of the gun.

Whatever comes out of the box, it must come out the top.

Think, Pallas, think! If I didn't do something soon, it would be too late. *Alexander — whoever he is — could arrive any minute. Then they'd summon Mulciber.*

As if to confirm my worst fears, I heard the sound of hooves. I hoped it was a rescue party. But by their welcoming voices, I knew it was not.

"I need a knife!" I prayed aloud, frantic with desperate longing.

Yet suddenly, I *had* a knife. Magically descending from the ink black Sky came a strange, gray bird. Two round eyes flickered and stared as ceaseless, wings swirled and crooned.

Whooooooo.

What on Earth!

But the owl-like creature wasn't from Terra, the Earth God, nor any of his ruddy kin. Instead, hovering right in front of my nose, the silver blade he was carrying was shaped like a dolphin.

Poseida!

My eyes were wide with wonder. My heart was full of grace. I seized the knife with blessed relief.

The riders arrived. The horses snorted. Their warm greetings chilled my bones.

Should I run for it? I thought as I cut my bonds.

No. They'd catch me on those horses.

An arrogant voice, young and shrill, rose above the crackling embers. "Is she here? Do you have her?" The prince, it seemed, was a boy my age riding tall upon a huge black gelding. Two dangerous men, clothed in black, rode close behind. They had stares of death about them.

It's now or never!

I sprang to my feet and raced towards the box. The top was filled with dozens of round openings. I dumped it on its side, pointing what I hoped was the business end at the men. Then, I traced the red arrow that read "WARNING" to the bottom. There, I saw a tiny brass handle. I turned the handle to the left and...

Nothing.

That's when they saw me. Cursing, they sprinted towards me.

"Seize her!" shouted the prince from atop his rearing horse.

I looked at the handle, said a prayer, and turned right.

Nothing.

I could see more words written around the handle, but didn't have time to read them. Panicking, I nearly made a run for it when I glimpsed the word "OUT."

I pulled.

The box fired its pyrotechnic arsenal, shrieking with fantastic, frenzied violence. Furious colors of red, green, and blue blinded my eyes with their sacred brightness. Staccato explosions punctuated the Air; whistling flares erupted the night. The Flaming volleys turned the men into cowards. The black gelding threw his master.

For none dare brave the fury of the box.

I sprinted to the panicked horses. Terrorized, they wrestled against their leather reins. With one swift blow, I cut the reigns of five of the animals with my divine dagger. The sacred gift, forged by the Gods, sliced through the leather like butter.

The horses bolted away without a second glance. I hurried to what looked to be the fastest – a tall paint. I sliced her reins and leapt on her back.

The beast ran like a demon possessed. I didn't really care where she was running, *as long as she's running away!*

The red, green, and blue emblazoned the trees in a carnival of colors that morphed into a hot, angry amber.

One of the riders was following.

The trees got thicker. The horseman was gaining. *What am I going to do?* In a moment, he would catch me. I ducked beneath a low-hanging limb. I looked behind to see him brandish a sword. I looked forward and saw another low branch. Before I could reconsider, I yanked viciously on my horse's mane. The frightened paint reared its head, nearly throwing me. The lone pursuer was on us. He slashed his savage sword…

I ducked, pinning my body against the sweaty back. I heard an empty swish as the assassin swept mercifully passed.

The rider looked back, gnashing his teeth.

THUNK!!!

A sickening thud; a grunt of pain. I ducked again as we passed the branch.

The black assassin writhed on the ground.

My paint galloped on. I didn't stop her. The trees started thinning. I prayed I'd find a clearing that would lead me to the fort.

The clearing I found. Stars gleamed brightly over a beautiful knoll. And just over the knoll was…

Nothing!

Again, I tugged on the horse's mane, willing her to a desperate stop. I couldn't have hoped to halt her a minute ago. But the paint was tired now – startled by what she saw. I slid out of the saddle and onto the ground. The paint reared back with fright. I looked down and saw…

Nothing.

We were standing at the edge of a high jagged cliff, hearing – but not seeing – the Sea below.

What am I going to do? I was on a narrow precipice…my only escape, back towards my enemies. I imagined hearing voices…

Do something! Rummaging through the saddle bags, I hoped to find…

Yes! There it was – a long rope. I pulled it out, along with a sword.

"Sorry, old gal," I muttered, slapping the horse with the flat of the blade. The poor thing nearly jumped out of her skin, bolting back the way we came.

I tied the rope to the sword, plunging it deep into the ground. Then I grabbed the rope and said another prayer, amazed at how spiritual I'd suddenly become. Swallowing my fear, I scrambled down the cliff.

I went about ten feet down when I found a tiny cliff-side cave. I crawled inside, hoping something large and furry didn't already live there. Instead, I found what I was looking for – a dog-sized boulder. After tying the rope around the boulder, I pushed it over the edge with rubbery legs. The sword flew wild into the gloomy darkness.

I collapsed with a sigh of desperate relief, the raucous Sea thrashing the rocks below me.

I heard hooves approach and men giving orders. Several horses galloped away, but two of the riders stayed. One of them held a torch. Its solitary light danced against the inky blackness.

"Curse that brat!" riled a young man's voice. "She'll pay for this, I swear."

I gasped. *It's that Excelsior prince, the one they called Alexander. He's only a few feet above me!*

"No need to swear to me," rasped an older voice. "Best do that to the Volcano God."

"Shut up!" said the prince, more fear than menace in his voice. "I should never have trusted those stupid Jesters."

"You should have let Devon and me take care of it."

"I know," he spat. "I know, I know!"

"This is an evil night, my Prince. I've never disappointed a God before."

"He'll...understand?" It was a question, not a statement. "Why we didn't get her?"

"We're about to find out."

A thin long shadow stabbed through the light. The man was obviously pointing at something. I looked to the spangled heavens and saw a tiny, red-hot glow. Horror claimed me as the inferno grew, blossoming into red and yellow and orange. The glistening light spawned three chariots, emblazoned with daring, dazzling Flames...

I nearly fainted. Hurling towards me with a mind-numbing shriek, the chariots' speed was unbelievable. They were destined to splay themselves on the cliff when they suddenly halted, mere feet away.

There he hovered, unsuspended, far above the crashing waves...

...the Lord God Mulciber, Prince of the Eternal Flame.

Two cars flanked the leader. Their sly drivers wore black leather, glistening in the ghoulish light.

The furious Flames tormented me. My cave was now an oven. Cowering with fright, gripping the knife, I cramped myself into the stolen shadows. *It's stupid to hide,* I told myself, certain the God would reach out and snatch me. *Still...I have to try.*

Yet the God did not address me. Nor did he look at me in any way. Instead, he spoke to the Excelsior prince. "So, Alexander," he said in a magnificent voice. "Where is she?"

"My Lord God Mulciber," pleaded the boy. "Oh most powerful Lord of the Heavens..."

"Do not bore me," said the God, sounding very bored indeed, "with your pathetic pandering. Where...is...the girl?"

"The girl, my Lord God?"

"Do you have her or not?" said the God, clearly not bored anymore. "You Fired the sacred summoning box. I have come. Where is she?"

"In...in the wood, my Lord God."

"Bring her to me. My patience wears thin."

There was a horrible pause. I gasped as I saw the reflection of the God on the polished hood of one of the cars. He was tall and handsome, with striking dark brows and long blond hair. A pretty boy, I might have called him, except for his dangerous, ugly sneer.

"I...I...I can't, my Lord God. She cast an evil spell upon me, and...and escaped."

"A spell?" said the God. "What sort of spell?"

"A Fire spell," he said with a bit more composure. "Shot it right at me."

"A Fire spell?" he repeated. "How inexplicably...fascinating." Then he pointed a solitary finger, emitting a red, luminescent ray.

An agonizing shriek echoed through the cave...

The drivers chuckled. The God grinned. The ray vanished. The scream whimpered.

"She's a Water Witch!" roared the God. "A Water Witch does not cast spells of Fire!"

"Please, my Lord God," begged the boy, "We captured her, I swear we did. But the Jesters let her escape. Please! Let me find her."

"Fool!" howled the divine creature, veins popping out of his hallowed neck. "Do you hear the slimy waves below? Do you think I shall wait, in the odious realm of Water?"

Sweat poured like a fountain down my trembling brow; the heat becoming unbearable. I gripped the sacred knife so hard, the silver seemed to ooze from my fingers. *Why doesn't he see me? Isn't he a God?*

"Please, my Lord God. Please wait!"

But the God did not wait. Instead, he turned to the driver on his left. "I must have her. Run a sensor scan."

"Already done, my Lord God. Her code does not register on the GPS display."

"Did you try the mother's?"

"Yes, my Lord God. Nothing."

"Damn that woman," he whispered, blanching his beautiful face. "I might have known. I wanted her alive, but...it's better that she's dead than with that Water scum. Burn down the forest."

"Your kin won't be happy. The *Forms* do not allow."

"I don't care about the *Forms!*" bellowed the omnipotent creature. "We must end this prophecy...here...and...now!"

"Yes, my Lord God." Banking his car into a gentle turn, he quickly jetted away. The killing heat slowly ebbed, much to my relief.

"Please, my Lord God. Please!" beseeched the boy. "I am the heir of House Excelsior. We are Your most faithful supporters."

"Another word from you, dog, and I shall rid the world of your wretched hide. It is because of your father's *faithful* service that I do not slay you, as I should. But you, my friend," he paused a moment, letting his bitter words sink in, "you shall be an old man before I forgive this night."

The prince broke into morbid mewl, sobbing uncontrollably.

"Take the fool and his companion back to Turner Hill. Deposit them in front of his father."

"Yes, my Lord God," said the remaining driver.

To my horror, Mulciber lowered his chariot to the level of my eyes. I'd never seen anything so wonderful – so awful – as that gorgeous, malignant face.

He's toying with me! In a moment, I'll feel his evil ray! Cornered, petrified, I breathed my very last breath...

But instead of claiming his helpless prize, he turned to face the crashing waves. Raising his arms to the ceaseless stars, he shouted at the Milky Way. "I shall have her!" he theatrically proclaimed. "In ashes...or...on a plate! I shall destroy this Age of Aquarius, and replace it with an age of my own!"

He took a moment to spit at the brine before quickly flying away. A moment later I heard the simpering prince crawl into the remaining chariot. Then, it too was gone.

Water Witch? I gasped. *Is that what he called me?*

But before I could dwell on his hateful homily, I collapsed upon the rocky floor.

Chapter Eighteen

Deliverance

*When I think back on it now, I'm simply amazed at how
totally oblivious the shallow-brained creature truly was.
Uncouth, uneducated; without the barest awareness of the world
around her: the man-cub crept into my raft totally unprepared
for the challenges that lay before her. It was only my careful
planning and superior intellect that allowed her to survive...*

"Memoirs of a Saint, the Cat who saved the Dawning"

Othello

I woke to a stab of pain, involuntarily withdrawing my hand. An albatross, perched upon the ledge of the cave, gave me a curious stare.

"Go away," I muttered.

The huge bird pecked again, as if deciding whether I was to be counted amongst the living or the dead.

"Get!" I said, shooing the bird with a flip of my hand.

He gave me a quizzical look before indignantly fluttering away.

I was alone again.

But...where am I?

Squinting at the sunshine, I felt around the cave. Horrible scenes raced though my head…

The knife.

The box.

The prince.

The God.

I shuddered uncontrollably, realizing how lucky I was…just to be alive.

Gingerly, I crawled to the entrance of the cave. I nearly threw up. Hundreds of feet below me, waves dashed upon the rocks with the jagged ferocity of the mighty Sea. Behind me was a wall of stone. It was only ten feet to the top, *but it may as well be sixty*. I had no chance to climb that wall.

But…how did I get here?

Then I remembered.

The horse. The sword. The rope. The boulder. *It seemed like a good idea at the time*. My trick saved my life, of that I was sure. But I was fresh out of swords, ropes, or ideas.

But I'm alive!

A dozen men were trying to kill me. The God stood mere feet away. Yet here I remained, healthy and whole, breathing the sweetness of the salty Breeze. A moment of triumph coursed through my veins as I gloried in the enormity of my impossible escape.

I looked towards the solemn Sea, relishing the beauty of the bright summer day. Powder-blue Sky and indigo Ocean spanned as far as the eye could tell. Sharp Wind howled in my ears, whispering life into my waking soul.

I'm alive!

I trembled anew, placing a hand upon my heart. Against all odds, I'd escaped the fabled fury of Mulciber. Humble pride filled my soul, as I suddenly realized...

...I outwitted a God!

Yet...how could that be? How could a mortal fool an omnipotent being?

I looked again at the torrential Sea. Whitecaps marched indomitably onwards, hurling themselves against the rocky cliff. I marveled at the ferociousness of the obedient waves, determined to crumble this hallowed cave.

Do they mock me? I thought. *Are they angry at my lie...pretending to be the Mistress of the Sea?* Or did they rage in glory, celebrating my heroic victory?

Somehow, I knew. The Tempest was calling me...like the delicate tide of the gentle Eastern Sea. The rhythm was different, the drumbeat of the Ocean pounding Her thunderous din. Yet it was the same melody I'd heard upon the sugar-white sand. The Sea was calling me.

I know it!

I hugged myself, tears streaming down my dirty cheeks. A blissful frown garnished my face, making me proud and strong and weak.

What sorcery hid me from that hideous God? Who endowed me with such powerful magic?

I picked up the knife from the floor of the cave, staring solemnly at the sacred gift.

There could be only one answer. Both loving and hating the Water Goddess, I prayed to holy Poseida, Queen of the Unquenchable Sea...

"Thank you!" I whispered to the dashing waves. I'd always hated her for drowning my mother, "but...you saved me. I see that now.

260

And for that, I shall always be grateful." And though I'd lived on the Ocean my entire life, I never felt closer to the Water than I did that very moment.

But something distracted from my holy reverie. As much as the knife had helped me, it wasn't nearly as useful as Othello's gift.

There's no way I could've escaped those men, if I hadn't been able to read!

And so I wondered…was the sacred largess of the heavenly Gods equal to the teachings of a simple cat?

Or did he try to kill me? Was he the treacherous spy?

Before I could answer my confusing thoughts, I heard a quiet, rolling thunder. I cowered at the sound of rumbling of hooves, remembering the chariots and their Fiery wonder.

More Disciples of Fire!

Someone dismounted from a horse. I scuttled back into my hole.

Please, oh, please…don't be wearing red!

"See anything?"

"Blymie, Sir. Don't make me look down that cliff. What if they threw'd her down, and me seeing her in the rocks and all."

"Nonsense, man," said the second voice. "They'd have burned her or stolen her, that's all. No Watery graves from that lot."

"But maybe they burned her, then threw'd her down. It'd be just like 'em. Fer a joke, perhaps."

Heavy boots advanced to the edge of the cliff. My heart climbed into my throat as I squeezed inside my tiny sanctuary.

"Nothing," said the voice, deadened with a sigh. "Let's go. I'm afraid we'll never find our fair lassie." The footsteps walked away to the sound of stretching leather.

I wanted to scream. *He sounded just like Lieutenant O'Brien!* But the terror of that horrible night muted me to silence.

"Aye, Mr. O'Brien, tis an awful shame. I've never seen the Old Man look so sad."

My heart skipped a beat. *Mr. O'Brien! The Old Man!*

I opened my mouth but couldn't find my voice. I screamed...

"Wait!"

But the pounding of the waves reverberated through the cave, punishing the jagged rocks below.

They didn't hear me!

I sprang from my hiding place...out onto the ledge as far as I dare...

"WAIT!"

But they did hear me! Peering above me was a mop of crimson, and a grin the size of a giant whale.

"I don't believe it!" said Mr. O'Brien. He wiped his face with both his hands, as if to erase some heavy burden. "I simply don't believe it! She's here, Charlie! She's here!"

"Holy Poseida!" swore the sailor, joining the lieutenant on the perilous ledge.

Long, weighty moments passed. The mariners gazed with wonder, marveling at the miracle of this teenage girl.

"Please, Mr. O'Brien. Could you, uh...please get me up?"

"Right!" he said, as if awakened from a dream. "Right you are, my Mistress. Charlie, lend a hand!"

The sailor was way ahead of him. Tying a rope to the horse's saddle, he handed the opposite end to O'Brien who secured it around his waist.

"We'll get you out, Mistress," he said as he gingerly descended the cliff. Then he surrounded me with strong arms.

"All right, Charlie! Easy does it." The horse pulled the two of us to the top of the cliff.

Safe upon the precipice, the lieutenant released his sacred prize. Again, there was a long moment of strangled silence, both men too reverent to utter a single word. Instead, they stared at me as if I were wearing a halo.

Finally, Mr. O'Brien broke the stillness – with a veneration quite unexpected from the rosy-cheeked man. "It's…it's like ye're back from the dead," he trembled. "Ye don't know…ye don't know what this will mean to the Old Man."

A wave of bliss overwhelmed me. I tried to restrain my rapture, but it was simply too much…the fear I felt the night before released upon a sudden rush of tears. Unbidden, I flung my arms upon the lieutenant and cried.

"There, now, lassie," he said, gently patting my back. "It's all right."

But I cried all the same, the hellish terror of the beautiful God branded upon my soul. I remembered the panic of the tiny oven – the sword that swiped above my ear – the violent explosion of the evil flares. I witnessed the malice of the hateful God – heard his shrill vendetta.

Finally, after a very long while, I let go of the loyal lieutenant.

O'Brien looked mournful and sad, crumpling his hat in his hand. "Mistress, forgive me. I should have died before…before…."

I put my hand upon my chest, stifling a new torrent of emotions. *I refuse to cry again!* Instead, I gathered my embattled resolve. "Please, Mr. O'Brien. *I* should be the one apologizing."

263

He gazed into my eyes of gray, as if searching for a source of divinity. "No, no, my Mistress. If anything had happened..."

"I'm fine!"

The noble mariner swallowed a sob, looking more tragic than ever.

"Look, you just saved my life."

"It was my duty to protect ye," he said to the ground. "My duty to the Old Man. I'd sooner die than fail him...or you."

Loyalty: it was my first real taste of it. Renewing my spirit like a fresh morning Breeze, I basked in the faithfulness of his noble love.

"Then let's not keep him waiting."

"Right," he said, his cheeks ablaze – as if waking from an embarrassed gloom. "Right! Charlie, sound the horn!"

The sailor blew a cheery call as the lieutenant helped me onto his horse.

We rode together through the tortured wood, surveying the disaster of last night's adventure. The charred remains of the denuded trees looked like a sad, gargantuan skeleton. We came upon the stump where the box had lain, but the engine of destruction was gone. A radial pattern, black with malice, fanned out to defeated trees.

Mulciber told them to burn down the forest. But surprisingly, only the trees near the box were destroyed. *What happened? Who saved the woods?*

The horses splashed through a puddle of Water. I heard the babbling of a brook, swollen after a hard summer rain.

Odd, there wasn't a cloud in the Sky...

"It rained last night?"

"Aye, Mistress. Right out of the blue, it was. Sometime 'round three in the morning."

How extraordinary, I thought. "After Mulciber told his thugs to burn down the forest…"

"Mulciber?" gasped the lieutenant. "Ye…ye spoke to the Lord God Mulciber?"

Charlie gawked with horror. "He…he…told some'en to burn them trees?"

"Yeah," I said, realizing how incredible that was.

"Last night," whispered O'Brien, "we saw Fiery chariots flying amongst the stars…"

"And the sudden shower that followed…" said Charlie.

"The…the Lord God Mulciber?" stammered O'Brien.

"How did ye?" Charlie asked.

I held my foolish tongue. *I've said too much already!*

"Best," quavered the lieutenant, "best ye wait till ye see the Old Man."

"Yeah," I said, "I think you're right."

Charlie sounded the horn again, more out of nervousness than anything else. A moment later, O'Brien's parrot landed upon his outstretched arm.

"Aye, Polly. There's a good lass. Go find the Old Man. Tell 'im we found our Mistress!"

"Squawk! Found the Mistress! Found the Mistress!" With that she was off, rising with a stroke of her colorful wings.

"Can she…talk?" I asked, intrigued.

"Of course not," he chuckled. "Ye tease me, my Mistress."

"Of course not," I agreed. But then I thought of Othello.

Has he been a trusted friend…or a filthy, traitorous spy?

We passed a host of searching sailors as we drew closer to the lonely fortress. They cheered when they saw us, followed as we passed, the caravan gathering into a happy parade. Horses cantered proudly, sailors laughed and sang. Merry horns punctuated my soul with happy pangs.

"Huzzah!" they shouted as we broke into a clearing, bathed in the sunlight of the bright summer morn. Before me stood the castle of Fort Isolaverde. My heart leapt when I saw the Old Man, riding tall upon a white palomino.

"HUZZAH!" they roared in a gallant cheer. The Commodore, his face as stoic as a stone, galloped towards me in proud career.

"HUUZZZAAHH!" they shouted, tossing their hats into the Air. The parade was now a pageant, the voices growing stronger and stronger, louder and louder until…

The Old Man reached me, his rugged eyes glistening in the new-born sun. A frown was carved upon his heavy face, a ferocious scowl of love and loss.

Then, Lord Catagen, Commodore of the Three, dismounted his dappled steed and stood reverently below the reckless slave. Amongst the din of the jubilant crowd, he looked into my eyes, and whispered, "Come, my Mistress."

I obediently slid off my horse. But he surprised me by catching me before I reached the ground, cradling me in his steely arms.

Then Lord Catagen, Commodore of the Three, Voting Member of the *Zoo*, carried me to the castle.

The parade turned to silence, homage conquering the lusty throng. Seeing their Old Man so prostrate touched a tender chord. Unbidden, a sailor knelt to his knees. Another knelt…and then another. Daring swashbucklers sank to the ground, their hardy faces softened by grace. Even the birds stopped their singing. The only sound that dare vex the silence was the crunching gravel of the Commodore's pace.

I gazed upon the sailors, humbled by their adoration. I felt like a princess…and then like a child. I looked up at the man who was carrying me, then quickly glanced away. I refused to start crying again.

The Old Man's mouth was an upside-down smile, his face twitching with barely-contained emotion. But his eyes were steady, steely, resolute…

He'd been given a second chance.

Yet something spoiled that wonderful moment, a disaster that made me blanch with fright. All at once, like the surprising wetness of a sudden rain, I saw something in the sailor's eyes – something I hoped I'd never see…

…belief in that odious prophecy.

> *Born of the Sea, hatched from the Egg,*
> *Child of Atlantis, God with us.*
> *For she shall herald a glorious Age,*
> *and they shall call it – Aquarius.*

Their Mistress *had* been born of the Sea, commanding dolphins upon her Golden Egg. Triton foretold her miraculous birth; the Fairy Tree lauded her many praises. She'd summoned the power of the Aquarian Gods, proving her worth over the Volcano God. How many miracles must there be, how many proofs must be given, before they gloried in the wonder…right before their eyes?

The fragrance of the fallen rain mingled with the sweet bouquet of pine. Like a broken bottle of cheap perfume, the heady aroma permeated the Air, goading the mariners into a zeal quite unlike anything their world had ever seen.

My emotions ripe with magic, my heart so full I thought I might swoon, I prayed the words I vowed I'd never say…

Am I really the dawning of the Age of Aquarius?

To be continued in "Whom the Gods Destroy"

Appendix

AEOLIA: Home of the Air Gods.

ARCHIPELAGO: Fourteen islands, arranged along an "S" shaped pattern, which make up the known world.

ARGO: Warship commissioned to House Tel (Air).

ARIEN IV: Fire Lady.

ATLANTIS: Home of the Water Gods.

BISMARCK: Warship commissioned to House Rance (Earth).

BULL, THE: *see William Catagen.*

CANNES III: Water Lord.

CAPRO BAY: Capital of House Oxymid. The city where Pallas made her appearance upon the Golden Egg.

CATAGEN I: Water Lord. Massacred during the Rape of Piraeus.

CATAGEN II: Water Voting Member. Won Voting Chair from House Duma. Commodore of the Three.

CATAGEN, CASEY: Twin daughter of Dewey.

CATAGEN, DEWEY: Captain of *Hornet.* Second son of Catagen II. Father of Elena, Casey, and Lucy.

CATAGEN, ELENA: Daughter of Dewey. Kidnapped by Excelsior II.

CATAGEN, LUCY: Twin daughter of Dewey.

CATAGEN, TIBERIUS: Captain of *Enterprise.* Third son of Catagen II.

CATAGEN, WILLIAM: (The Bull) Captain of *Yorktown.* Eldest son of Catagen II.

CINDY: Childhood friend of Pallas.

CIRCUS: Last and most popular event of the Games. The winner has the honor of driving the Golden Chariot during the post-Games parade.

CORPS, THE: Army sworn to protect the *Zoo.*

CORSAIR III: Fire Lord. Warden of the Southern Sea *(Yamato).*

DEME: Queen of the House of Wonders.

DEMES: Healers. Followers of Deme.

DJINCAR III: Air Lord.

DUSAN I: A Water Lord. Lost his Voting Chair to Catagen II.

DUSAN II (DUMA IV): Warden of the Northern Sea *(Hood).*

ENTERPRISE: Warship commissioned to House Catagen. One of the Three. Captained by William Catagen.

EREBUS: Home of the Earth Gods.

EXCELSIOR II: Fire Voting Member. Lord Defender of the Titan. Grandfather of Alexander. Made Turner Hill the wealthiest city in the world. Responsible for the Rape of Piraeus.

EXCELSIOR III: Fire Voting Member. Lord Defender of the Titan. Father of Alexander.

EXCELSIOR, ALEXANDER: Son of Excelsior II.

FLETCHER: An officer aboard *Yorktown*.

GAMES, MENAGERIE: Played once every four years by any drone. Includes 10 events.

GAMES, UNIVERSITY: Played once a year by the children of the nobility. Includes 10 events.

GANYME III: Air Lady.

GANYMII: Capital of House Ganyme. Smaller of the twin cities.

GAUNTLE III: Earth Voting Member. Lord Master of the Pass.

GAUNTLE, CLYME: Wife of Gauntle III. Daughter of William Catagen.

GEMELLO III: Air Voting Member. Lord Defender of the Twins. Mother of Borelo.

GEMELLO, BORELO: Teenage son of Gemello III.

GEMINUS: Capital of House Gemello. Larger of the twin cities.

GERARD VII: Father of Pallas.

GOLDEN EGG: Raft on which Pallas, pushed by a pod of dolphins, first appeared in Capro Bay as the Mistress of the Sea. Historians mark the event as the advent of the Great Catastrophe.

GREENSTONE: Capital of the nobility. Seat of University and the *Zoo*.

HEALERS (DEMES): Followers of Deme.

HOOD: Warship commissioned to House Duma (Water).

HOUSE OF WONDERS: School of the Healers on the island of Solüt.

HORNET: Warship commissioned to House Catagen. One of the Three. Captained by Dewey Catagen.

HYPERIUS III: Fire Lord.

ISOLAVERDE: A tiny island situated in the southern loop of the "S" shaped archipelago. The site where Pallas first escaped Mulciber II.

JESTERS: Clerics of the Gods

JINGO III: Earth Voting Member. Marshal of the Corps.

JOCULO III: Water Lord.

KELLY TREE: Capital of House Joculo. Birthplace of Pallas.

LIBERION III: Air Lady.

MARSHAL: Commander of the Corps.
MED III: Water Lady.
MENAGERIE: *see Games*
MISER II: Air Voting Member. Chief Justice of the *Zoo*.
MULCIBER: Fire God.

OTHELLO: Cat who mentored Pallas.
OXYMID III: Earth Lady.

PALLAS: Harbinger of the Great Catastrophe. Mistress of the Sea.
PENTATHANONS: The Five major Gods. Poseida (Water), Vulcana
    (Fire), Terra (Earth), and Zephyr (Air) brought together by Deme
    (Life). Water and Fire are opposites, as well as Earth and Air.
POSEIDA: Queen of the Sea.

QUID IV: Fire Voting Member. Treasurer of the *Zoo*

RANCE II: Earth Lord. Warden of the Western Sea *(Bismarck)*.
RHODES: Water Goddess. Daughter of Poseida.

SALAMADRO III: Fire Lord.

TEL III: Air Lord. Warden of the Eastern Sea *(Argo)*.
TERRA: King of the Earth.
THREE, THE: The fleet of warships commissioned to the Commodore.
    Yorktown, Hornet, and *Enterprise.*
TRITON: Water God. Son of Poseida.
TURNER HILL: Capital of House Excelsior. Largest city in the world.
TZU: Deme Voting Member. Master of the Lone One.

UNCIAL: Water Lady. Founder of the first Great House. First
    Chancellor of the *Zoo*.
UNIVERSITY: School of the nobility. Located in Greenstone.

VIRGON III: Earth Lady.
VOLCANO: Home of the Fire Gods.
VULCANA: Queen of Fire.

WARDEN OF THE EASTERN SEA: (Lord Tel) Owner of the *Argo*.

WARDEN OF THE SOUTHERN SEA: (Lord Corsair) Owner of the *Yamato*.

WARDEN OF THE NORTHERN SEA: (Lord Duma) Owner of the *Hood*.

WARDEN OF THE WESTERN SEA: (Lord Rance) Owner of the *Bismarck*.

YAMATO: Warship commissioned to House Corsair (Fire).

YORKTOWN: Warship commissioned to House Catagen. Flagship of the Three. Captained by William Catagen.

ZELIOX III: Earth Lord. Lost Earth Voting Chair to House Jingo.

ZEPHYR: King of the Air.

ZOO: The parliamentary chamber that governs the world. Holiest spot on the planet.

ABOUT THE AUTHOR

D.C. Belton works internationally and is an elected Georgia State Representative from Buckhead, Georgia. When a constituent's son accidentally killed himself texting-while-driving, Belton spearheaded the successful passage of two safety laws to prevent future tragedies. Belton has a passion for literacy and female empowerment.

Learn more about Pallas at dcbelton.com.

Quantity discounts are available on bulk purchases of this book for educational purposes. Please contact Flying Lion Press, P.O. Box 36, Buckhead, Georgia, 30625.

59151885R00170

Made in the USA
Charleston, SC
29 July 2016